A GRAND OL' MURDER

A Grand Ol' Murder

A Doyle Malloy Mystery

Amy & Kelly —
Thanks for your support!

Brian Landon

NORTH STAR PRESS OF ST. CLOUD, INC.
St. Cloud, Minnesota

Title logo: Jesse Landon

Cover art: Jeffrey Holmes

Copyright © 2009 Brian Landon

ISBN: 0-87839-327-7
ISBN-13: 978-0-87839-327-5

First Edition, September 1, 2009

Printed in the United States of America

Published by
North Star Press of St. Cloud, Inc.
P.O. Box 451
St. Cloud, Minnesota 56302

northstarpress.com

Prologue

The Gala on Grand Avenue

O n the night of her death, Marta Ramirez was cleaning vomit off a very expensive Italian carpet, wondering how an actress with so much potential could get stuck with such a crappy job.

She wasn't a famous actress by any means. Not like her boss's friends who walked cautiously around her as she scrubbed the floor, chit-chatting about their various projects and awards. Her employer, Timothy Chapman, had even more friends now that he had been voted "Man of the Year" by the American Guild of Magazine Editors. Having been in over a hundred films in forty years, Chapman garnered an almost mythic presence in Hollywood.

In Saint Paul, where Timothy Chapman lived and occasionally worked, he wasn't just a Hollywood legend, he was also a philanthropist, a local business supporter, a good neighbor, and a friend to many. More than that, he was a Minnesotan who had made it.

On the other end of the spectrum, Marta's most high-profile gig was portraying "Mexican Restaurant Worker #2" in the film *Jingle All the Way* starring Arnold Schwarzenegger. When she told her parents back home in Colombia that she had gotten an acting job, they were thrilled. When her father, a fervent Colombian patriot, discovered that his daughter would be portraying a Mexican, he became furious. He refused to speak to her ever again, and the last thing he said to her was, "*¿Por qué numero dos?*"

Having learned enough English in school, she was able to get by working as a waitress in a small café off Lyndale Avenue. The flexible schedule allowed her to audition for roles in local commercials, TV spots, and on rare occasions, films. Regardless, her lack of experience—and, some might even say, talent—this resulted in few opportunities beyond playing an extra in low-budget fare.

The day she got the call to be in *Jingle All the Way*, she was working in the café, pouring coffee into local beatniks' ceramic coffee mugs. With the phone cradled again her face, she screamed out in joy and pain, realizing too late that she was pouring hot coffee directly onto her hand rather than in the mug. If one were to pause *Jingle All the Way* during the fifty-two seconds Marta is on camera, one can see the burns her excitement had caused.

Chapman was cast to play a supporting role in the film. When Marta heard that Chapman was to appear, she didn't really believe it. Why would such a prestigious actor stoop so low as to work in a silly Schwarzenegger vehicle? The idea of her sharing any amount of screen time with a legend was far too much to comprehend. She was completely taken aback when he approached her on her one day of shooting.

"I just want you to know, madam, that you are doing a wonderful job of portraying a Mexican girl, despite the fact that you are clearly Colombian."

"How did you know?" she asked, not knowing how to respond to such a prestigious actor.

"Your accent—it's a dead giveaway. I've studied accents for years, though I've rarely used them in film. I always end up playing an American guy. Apparently they can't see me as Hispanic."

Marta didn't know how to respond to this either. "I like your movies," she said.

"Thank you, dear. That's very kind of you."

"That Tarantino movie? You were very good," Marta said.

"Thank you, again."

"The alien movie was okay."

"Yes, well—"

"That one movie with Jack Nicholson, I didn't like so much. But it wasn't you. You were still good."

Chapman nodded.

At that moment, Arnold Schwarzenegger had walked by and barked to Marta, "Hey, little lady person. Ahh you my new ahhsistant? Ahh need some coconut bahtah for my pectoral muscles. Dis is an urgent situation. Hurry as fast as you can. Go now!"

"Man," said his co-star Sinbad as he passed by on his way to the snack table. "You don't even show off you pecs in this movie. What the heck you need coconut butter for?"

"Ahh feel naked without it," explained Arnold. "Ahh been wearing it for thirty years."

Marta and Chapman shared a moment of uncomfortable silence.

After Marta returned with a bottle of coconut butter and subsequently finished her one day of acting on the film, Chapman offered her the somewhat less glorified role of maid in his home. He said that it would give her the freedom to make it to auditions while still earning a modest living. It was the best paying job she ever had.

As the water in Marta's bucket turned from clear to tan to a sickly beige, she pondered how many other actresses had to put up with such demeaning work before making their first big break. She didn't know, and she realized that she also didn't really care. Marta was ready and willing to scrub all the nasty carpets in Minnesota—the entire Midwest, for that matter—if it made her a star. Maybe she'd even venture to Los Angeles someday. The long struggle would make the reward all that much sweeter.

But still, there wasn't any pleasure in cleaning such a mess. Marta was less mad at the situation than she was at the cause—specifically Chad Wilkinson, the current boyfriend of Chapman's only daughter, Kimberly. For the life of her, Marta could not figure out what Kimberly saw in Chad. Kimberly was in every respect the typical college girl—fashionable, studious, sociable—except for the very large bankroll under her name, which she never discussed, apparently out of modesty. Chad, on the other hand, always came to the house smelling of booze and pot. Dreadlocks hung over his eyes, and he was usually attired in tattered shirts and jeans with long, metal chains stretching around his waist. Marta stayed as far from him as possible.

The only thing Kimberly and Chad seemed to have in common was their social and charitable activism, which was what brought Chad to the Chapman home to vomit all over the fine carpeting. Kimberly was throwing a fundraising party for an organization called Pause for Paws, which her father supported financially, as he was a staunch feline fan and usually gave generously to several pet-oriented charities.

But when Chad arrived earlier in the evening, it was clear he was not of the right mental state to be socializing and requesting donations from Chapman's wealthy peers and colleagues. Marta saw that his eyes were bloodshot, and he was off balance.

"Whoa, there's a lot of freakin' people here," Chad said, stumbling along the main entrance to Chapman's multi-million-dollar home. "Dude, is that Bruce Willis over there?" he mumbled to no one in particular.

Timothy Chapman must have heard the drunken babble and left a conversation mid-sentence to approach Chad.

"Yippy kai-yay—am I right?" Chad hiccupped, as he slapped Chapman on the shoulder.

Chad pointed at a painting on the wall adjacent to the staircase. The painting featured Marilyn Monroe in a classic pose.

"Whoa, nice painting," he said, squinting in the direction of Monroe's image. He was now holding on to Chapman's shoulder.

"Man, it always sucks when an actress dies," said Chad.

Chapman, dressed in a black Armani tuxedo, leaned away from Chad and feigned a smile. "That's an astute observation, young man," he said with sarcasm, though the youth didn't seem to notice. "I especially like your attire. Tell me, son, is that shirt Versace?"

"No," Chad answered, his eyebrows lowering in confusion. "I bought it at a concert."

"A concert," Chapman repeated enthusiastically. "Funny, that's where I do most of my shopping. In fact, I almost wore a giant foam hand with '#1' printed on the side. But then I realized, I would have looked a bit out of place."

The young man's face slowly sunk as he realized he was being mocked.

"Why are you here?" Chapman said, suddenly becoming very serious. His eyes were fixed on Chad's.

"I'm helping with the fund raiser," Chad responded. Marta could see his breathing was growing heavy. His forehead was glistening with sweat. "And I'm dating your daughter."

"That's very amusing, son, but I assure you, you're not. Kimberly isn't currently dating, and if she were dating, it would be someone who owns at least one necktie."

Small drops of sweat settled on Chad's pale brow. He was very still. From what Marta could tell, Chad had stopped listening to Chapman's lecture on proper dress and concentrated on keeping the contents of his stomach from traveling upward.

"They don't sell neckties at concerts, do they, Tad?"

Chad probably would have corrected his name if it weren't for the torrent of vomit that spewed from his mouth, splattering on Chapman's black Armani suit and landing on the white carpet.

The hum of chattering died as the guests watched with amusement and fascination.

Remaining as composed as possible under the circumstances, Chapman removed a handkerchief from his pocket and proceeded to remove as much vomit from his expensive tuxedo as possible.

"Marta," he called. "Marta, please come here and escort Mr. Wilkinson to a taxi cab. I think he was on his way to a Nine Inch Nails concert and ended up here by accident . . . once again." His guests chuckled and returned to their conversations as if there had been no interruption.

Marta had been in the process of hanging up Tim Burton's coat in the guest closet when Chapman called her over, but she'd heard the exchange between Chapman and Chad. This wasn't the first time Chapman had thrown Chad out, ignoring the pleas from Kimberly.

"Dad, just let him be. He'll be fine," she said, having just realized Chad arrived. Then she saw the vomit on the floor and on her father's tux. "Never mind. Chad, maybe you should leave."

Marta saw Kimberly look apologetically at her father.

"I'll let him out," said Kimberly, pulling Chad's arm towards the door.

"I'm not going," Chad slurred.

"Come," said Kimberly, yanking him forward.

Chapman shook his head. "Marta, will you take care of that, then?" he said, pointing at the mess on the carpet. "I'm sorry," he then whispered.

"It's okay," Marta said. She considered asking for a bonus, but Chapman was already heading upstairs towards the master bedroom, followed closely by Darren, his butler.

As Marta continued to scrub the floor, rinse, then scrub again, she kept an eye on the hallway on the opposite end of the living quarters. Prior to the start of the fund-raiser gala, Chapman had specifically asked her to monitor the hallway and keep people away from it, if possible. The only rooms connected to the hallway were two guest bedrooms, each with its own private bathroom, and an office where Chapman conducted most of his business.

The office also contained his secret safe.

Marta supposed no one else knew about the safe except herself, his butler, Darren, his daughter, and possibly his lawyer. She doubted anyone else at the party knew about it, but Chapman obviously wanted to keep people from snooping around just the same.

Marta was busy scrubbing and swearing to herself when a brief glance to her side ripped Marta away from her thoughts. She thought she saw—no, she most definitely saw a figure slink into the office.

She dropped the sponge into the rank water bucket and sprung to her feet, excusing herself as she walked by Chapman's guests. She nearly tripped over Paul Reuben's white platform shoes. As Marta approached the office, she wondered how Chapman had accumulated such strange friends.

The sound of clanking and crashing metal slowed her steps. While the party was a steady clamor several yards away, in the hallway it seemed that the only sounds were those emanating from the office, Marta's delicate footsteps, and her nervous breathing. It sounded like whoever was in the office was using a crowbar, or maybe a hammer— she couldn't tell which. Whatever it was, it was doing some serious damage.

Then the banging paused, and she heard a low voice. She couldn't make out what it was saying, but it definitely sounded male. *Is he on a phone?* She wanted to get a closer listen, so she inched her way across the floor. As she leaned towards the door, the floor beneath her squeaked, sending a bolt of fear straight up her spine. The voice stopped.

Not a good sign, she thought.

She considered running back down the hall into the party and telling Chapman or his daughter, or calling the police. But if she did that, the culprits would have an opportunity to escape or blend into the soiree and, thus, go completely unpunished. If Chapman put so much faith in her, the least she could do would be to find out who the bad guys were.

The metal-on-metal sound started again.

Good, Marta thought. *They didn't notice me. Or if they did, they didn't think anything of it.*

The door was open a tiny crack, but not wide enough to see into. Marta gently put her hand against the door and pushed it very, very slowly. The first thing she saw was an open window. Then, she saw a sledgehammer striking the steel safe in the wall. Sparks flew, but the safe remained closed.

He's not having much luck, she thought—when suddenly the door flew open and a hand grabbed Marta's shirt and yanked her into the room. Stars burst in front of her eyes as she heard a loud crack that sounded awfully close to her ear and then she felt wetness like someone had cracked an egg on her head . . . but why would anyone do that? and then she realized what happened but was surprised that she really didn't care so much. As her right cheek hit the floor, she thought it funny that those shoes looked so familiar but even that didn't matter, not really. . . .

If Marta had known she was going to die that night, she would have requested an execution more dramatic than a bop on the head. Something more befitting a real actress.

Funny thing was, as consciousness slipped steadily away from her, she could most definitely make out distinct sounds of applause.

And as the last of her life's blood drained out of her, faintly but surely, she smiled.

1

I T WAS A TYPICAL SUMMER DAY in Minneapolis. That is to say, it was over ninety degrees. The humid air was filled with clash of construction and car horns, and flashing squad cars raced up and down Hennepin Avenue attempting to pull over daytime drunk drivers and cars inexplicably driving in the bus lane. Plain-clothes officers dotted the sidewalks, attempting to purchase narcotics from known dealers and solicit sex from underage prostitutes. Shots were fired a few minutes earlier, probably from a down-on-his-luck criminal making a last ditch effort to escape certain incarceration.

Meanwhile, Detective Doyle Malloy, specialist in high-profile and celebrity cases in Minnesota, sat comfortably in a poofy leather chair in the Rabbit Hole, his favorite java joint. He sipped a vanilla latte made by Shay O'Connor, the girl who ran the place. Doyle had actually dated her in high school before she turned into a lesbian. Sadly, she was not the only girl he "turned." He had an unusual way with women.

Being as the Rabbit Hole was a fairly upscale establishment, Shay tended to pick up pieces of information from her customers relating to Doyle's cases.

Shay walked over to Doyle and added some whipped cream to the top of his drink, just the way he liked it.

"Timothy Chapman's house was broken into last night," she whispered in his ear.

"*The* Timothy Chapman?" Doyle whispered back. "The most famous actor in the world?"

"And a Saint Paul resident. Yes, that Timothy Chapman," said Shay with a smile.

"How'd you find out?" asked Doyle.

Shay shrugged. "Some kid with a bunch of metal in his face. Sounds like he overheard it somewhere."

"I can't believe I haven't been called in for this yet," said Doyle.

"Do you usually take cases in Saint Paul? I thought you usually stuck to our lovely city of Minneapolis," quipped Shay.

Knowing that shew as teasing him, Doyle still squared his shoulders and said, "I go wherever I'm needed. I've done cases in Duluth, Bemidji, Park Rapids, Rochester, you name it. If it's in Minnesota, and someone of high status is involved, usually I'm there."

Shay nodded. "Well, enjoy the latte," she said.

Then Doyle heard a familiar voice.

"Well, if it isn't Detective Doyle Malloy," the sweet, yet sultry voice said.

"Officer Amanda Hutchins," said Doyle, swiveling in his chair to see his curvy, yet classy co-worker from headquarters.

Shay winked at her as she returned back to the coffee bar.

"How've you been, Doyle?" asked Amanda.

"Same old," he said.

"Sticking to the celebrity beat?" she asked.

"So far."

Doyle liked Amanda. Quite a bit, actually. She had a slender, albeit muscular body, which was usually adorned by her blue uniform. Amanda kept her dark-brown hair in a ponytail, although Doyle had a few opportunities to see her hair down when they'd gone on friendly dates. She was attractive, intelligent, and was young enough where she hadn't been scarred and calloused by years of work in law enforcement.

But, thus far, he'd turned down her advances. No need to steer another woman away from heterosexuality.

"Do you really get many celebrity cases in Minnesota?" she asked.

"You'd be surprised," he responded. "More and more movies are being filmed here. Our state gives huge tax incentives and grants to film-makers. I stay pretty busy."

"If you're so busy, why do you spend so much time in a coffee shop?"

Doyle wasn't sure how to respond at first. Despite how he talked, he didn't have a strong reputation for being a hard, diligent worker. In fact, he was a little lazy at times.

"I do my best thinking here," he said. "Besides, Shay lets me know the word on the street." He gestured his head in Shay's direction.

"She's cute," said Amanda.

Doyle rolled his eyes. *There goes another one*, he thought.

Just then, his cell began to ring. It was his boss, Chief Burnside.

"Doyle here," he said.

"Doyle, where are you?" Chief Burnside screamed. "It's ten in the morning."

"Sorry, chief. I was just grabbing some coffee," explained Doyle.

"Get your ass in here. This is urgent!"

"I'll be right in," said Doyle. He snapped his cell phone shut.

"That didn't sound too pleasant," said Amanda. "I could hear him crystal clear from here."

"He likes to make sure he's audible," said Doyle. "He's also kind of an ass."

Amanda nodded. "Well, have fun at work. I have to go in soon myself. I'm working the second shift tonight."

"Are you working the streets?"

She shook her head. "Naw, I just got the front desk. I swear, they don't want me out there because of, well . . ."

"The attractiveness?" said Doyle helpfully.

"That's what I was fishing for," said Amanda, glowing. "But, yes, I'll be chained to the reception desk all night. Lucky me."

"Have fun. It was good seeing you again."

"Hey, if you have some free time tonight, why don't you give me a call? I'll probably be bored. Not much has been happening lately. Or maybe this weekend . . . ?"

"Sure, maybe," said Doyle. He doubted he'd call. It just wasn't in him.

"Okay," she said, possibly picking up on what was going through Doyle's head. "See ya."

Doyle drove to work fast, far exceeding the speed limit. He was usually late to work, but then again, usually it didn't matter. Either Doyle was in trouble, or a big case had just developed. Doyle wondered if maybe it was the Timothy Chapman case.

When Doyle finally walked into his office, he was greeted by his favoritest person in the whole wide world.

"Good morning, you lazy bastard," shouted his boss, Oliver Burnside. "I'm glad to see you're helping out your team. Christ, Officer Wendell was nearly shot, and you're sipping a latte like you're on vacation."

"Do they know who shot at him?" Doyle inquired.

"Probably some god-dang cokehead who didn't want to go to prison," grumbled Chief Burnside.

"Was it a famous cokehead?"

Burnside's nostrils flared a bit. "No, it wasn't."

"Is there an investigation in place? Are you sure this cokehead actually fired the gun, or did he sort of lob the bullet towards Officer

Wendell? I mean, that'd make a difference, don't you think? Did Wendell have to amble sideways or was the guy just a really bad shot?"

Burnside turned three shades of red and began to flicker the annoyance like a cuttlefish. "Listen, smart-ass. Your colleague could have been killed, and you're cracking jokes like—"

"Listen, listen," interrupted Doyle. "I mean no disrespect to Officer Wendell. But if there's no investigation, and it's not a high-profile case, what do you expect me to 'detect'? You know, being as I'm a 'detective' and all?"

"Just make sure you're doing your job," said Oliver Burnside. "And I don't like walking in here and seeing this mess."

Burnside was pointing out the VHS videos that covered Doyle's desk. Doyle realized he had left the television on in the corner of his office, with a video still paused.

Burnside followed Doyle's eyes. "What the hell have you been watching?"

"*Speed 2*," responded Doyle.

Burnside crossed his arms and approached Doyle.

"Can you give me one good reason why you're watching *Speed 2* during work hours?"

"It was actually *after-hours* last night," Doyle responded curtly. "And it's part of my current investigation."

"What investigation? You mean the Keanu Reeves dog-napping?"

"Exactly," said Doyle.

Burnside flickered through several more shades, but they were actually headed toward normal rather than that degree of pissed-off where Doyle knew to vacate. "So what happened, specifically?" he asked. "What have you uncovered, Sherlock?"

"Okay," began Doyle. "Keanu's up in Park Rapids filming a scene for *The Day the Earth Stood Still*, minding his own business, when his lab Stallyn gets nabbed from his trailer."

Burnside nodded. "Yeah, Doyle—I already know that part. The dog was stolen from northern Minnesota. Local investigators hired you because you're the most experienced with celebrity cases. I know all that. I also know it's been three months and you've gotten absolutely nowhere—because, despite your experience with Hollywood types, or in some cases Minnesota-types-who-think-they're-Hollywood types, you have very little in the way of detective skills. Or logic. Or street smarts."

"Are you trying to butter me up?" asked Doyle with a sideways smile.

"Let me guess what's going on here," continued Burnside, his color rising again. "You're digging through films looking for clues, is that right?"

Doyle nodded. "That's the gist of it."

"Now, I may not be nearly as into movie gossip and trivia as you are," Burnside said with complete condescension and distaste, "but I know for a fact that Keanu Reeves isn't even in *Speed 2*."

"Yeah, but haven't you ever wondered why?" asked Doyle rhetorically.

Burnside stared at Doyle with utter abhorrence. The flickering red edged deeper.

"I'm kidding, Chief. Mellow out for a second. It's true: Keanu Reeves in not in this movie. But his *dog* is."

Now Burnside eyed Detective Malloy with interest. "Really?" he asked.

Doyle rewound the video and hit play. "After the high-speed boat chase, Sandra Bullock ends up on the beach where several extras are portraying your average beach-going crowd. These extras include Keanu Reeves' lab, Stallyn, Sandra Bullock's golden retriever, Ginger, and their mutual trainer, Dimitri Prutkov."

"So you think the trainer is the dog-napper?" Burnside asked doubtfully.

"Well, it's a strong possibility. I mean, the trainer would know a lot about the dog no one else would know. Not to mention Dimitri spent a good deal of time with Keanu, meaning he had inside access. He could have swiped the key to the trailer while no one was looking."

"But let me ask you—what possible good came out of watching this movie? You already knew Pritchov or whatever-his-name was, the dog trainer, beforehand, right? So what clues did you gather from this?" Burnside sounded like he knew he had the upper hand on this.

"Well, I guess visually seeing the relationship between trainer and dog . . . especially on camera, well I suppose it—"

"And what evidence do you have? How about physical clues? Do you have anything beyond conjecture?"

"See, that's not easy to answer—I mean, define 'clues.'"

"Malloy, you're a shoddy detective. We keep you working on celebrity cases because you seem to know more than anyone about the goings-on in Hollywood, despite us being hundreds of miles away. Lord knows we need that real bad right now, especially with all these Coen fellas coming into our state to film movies that make us look like idiots. But let's face it, Malloy. You couldn't solve a mystery even if the bad guy confessed. You're off this case, effective immediately."

"C'mon, Chief. Don't do this to me. I was doing some good work here," Doyle said defensively.

Burnside laughed.

"I swear," Doyle added. "I'll find the dog-napper by the end of the week. Just don't pull me off."

"Don't get your panties in a twist, Malloy. I'm taking you off the case because I'm giving you a bigger one."

Doyle searched Burnside's face for the punchline. "Didn't you just say I was a shoddy detective?"

"Yes, I did, and it's absolutely true. But this case needs immediate attention. There was a robbery at Timothy Chapman's home off

Grand Avenue. Apparently his personal safe was broken into, and everything's missing."

"I knew it!" said Doyle, realizing shortly afterwards that he should have kept his trap shut.

"What?" said Burnside. "You knew it? How did you know about this? It wasn't in the news, was it? God, if those TMZ bastards have caught wind of this . . ."

"No, no, nothing like that," said Doyle. "I just have an inside source that picked up on it. That's all. It's still on the down-low."

"Good, good," said Burnside. "Just be careful—you're dealing with possibly the most famous actor in the world here. Thank God you're used to working celebrity cases."

"I am—but not necessarily of this stature. I've seen his house before. It's ginormous! My God—he must be a go-zillionaire."

"Something like that," said Burnside. "Which means a whole lot of paparazzi if this thing gets out. For Chrissakes, don't let this leak to the media, okay? We don't need that kind of pressure on our department."

"Don't worry. As far as I know, the media haven't heard a thing. And TMZ hasn't come to Minnesota yet," said Doyle.

"Let's keep it that way," said Burnside.

"Okay. Chief, I can do this," Doyle said, growing increasingly excited.

"Other than the sensitivity of the situation, it shouldn't be that difficult," continued Burnside. "It's not a bloody scene by any means, so you should be able to handle it. Apparently the maid's missing, and she was one of the few people who knew of the safe. Not to mention she was quite poor and could have used the money. Some of the details are still a bit fuzzy. But you're going to clear that up. Talk to everyone, find out where she is, find out if there were any accomplices. Like I mentioned before, this could make it to the tabloids quickly. So get as much work done as fast as you can, before everything we do is scrutinized, and all your mistakes get blasted all across the TV news programs."

Doyle quickly stood and put on his sports coat.

"Don't worry, Chief. I'll make you proud."

"And for the love of God, clean yourself up a bit. You look like you haven't shaved in a week. Frankly, you don't smell all that grand either. You're representing this department, Malloy. Start acting like it."

"I promise to look sexy and do a good job."

"You better," said Burnside. "Because if you fuck this up, you're out. Understood?"

"I love it when you get angry, Chief. You get so . . . red."

"Get out of here!"

Doyle did as he was told.

Burnside hollered after him. "And don't come back until you have this case wrapped up in a pretty little package. Any loose strings, and I'll strangle you with 'em!" Burnside had a few more colorful remarks to add, but Doyle was already gone.

2

IT WAS EARLY AFTERNOON WHEN DOYLE pulled the unmarked squad car onto the stone driveway that wound uphill towards Mr. Chapman's estate. His mansion was at the more peaceful end of Grand Avenue, away from the kitschy shops and eateries that lined the road where the first cable cars ran a century prior.

Doyle's mother used to take him shopping on Grand when he was young. Everything on Grand had been ridiculously expensive, even back in those days. Though the Malloys didn't have much income, certainly not as much as the well-dressed business folk and old-money families that regularly patronized the local businesses, his mother believed that even being on the street around these fashionable people, going into those shops, eating at those restaurants, elevated them to a higher social plane.

It was at one of the swanky clothing boutiques where Elizabeth Malloy met the man who would eventually become her second husband. He was the president of a small, albeit successful local bank, and had the means to make her a social butterfly rather than a hard-working urban wife of a cop. It was only a matter of time before the right form of persuasion came along to lead Elizabeth Malloy to a better life than what Senior Detective Harry Malloy could provide.

On the bright side, Doyle and his father became much closer as a result. Both harbored a resentment towards Grand Avenue and the well-to-do folks who, as far as they were concerned, destroyed families and stole away wives and mothers. They both had to admit, though, that the ice cream at the Grand Ol' Creamery was pretty damned good.

Doyle parked amongst a fair flock of squad cars and stepped out shaking his head. He'd driven his unmarked vehicle. Celebrities preferred unmarked because it didn't draw the kind of attention that would inevitably lead to local headlines.

On the other hand, if Doyle was certain the celebrity was guilty of whatever crime had been committed, he drove the flashiest squad possible, just to scare the bejesus out of the perp. But somehow, he couldn't picture Timothy Chapman stealing from his own safe. Especially if it was uninsured. What possible benefit could there have been? Then again, the maid had all the reasons in the world to steal. After all, she was a maid. If Doyle was in a position of servitude, he'd be stealing left and right. Which explained Chief Burnside's empty pencil holder and Doyle's excessively full one. Doyle grinned.

From the outside, the mansion was almost modest in appearance. While most of the homes Doyle visited consisted of sharp edges and blacks and whites, this place somehow reminded Doyle of his childhood home in Roseville. Just ten times bigger. The brick outer walls, the dark wooden trim, the fancy bushes lining the sides of the home all made it seem so . . . homey. From what Doyle could tell, Timothy Chapman was probably the most down-to-earth actor in the world, and he hadn't even met the guy yet.

Too bad the maid had to rip him off, he thought.

Doyle felt his anticipation growing as he approached the door. He was going to meet Timothy friggin' Chapman! He wondered if it would be terribly unprofessional to ask for an autograph during a formal police interview. Or what about a Polaroid snapshot? Would that be out of the question? Could he get the maid to shoot it so he could stand with his arm around Chapman's shoulder like they were buddies? No, the maid was gone. Wait, surely Chapman had more than one maid.

There was, of course, the possibility that he could accidentally insult the actor before the interview even began. If he was too quick to ask for something, like any typical fan, he may lose any respect he had from Mr. Chapman, and he might not get his critical questions answered.

Patience, grasshopper. Doyle, you've been through all this before, he told himself. *Remember when you interviewed Judd Nelson about the theft of his Dodge Neon? Just pretend you don't give a damn that he's a celebrity. He's just like anyone else.*

When Doyle pushed the button on the side of the door, he could hear the reverberating dong that followed. He was half-expecting Lurch to stick his head out and say, "You raaaaaaang?" Instead a quaint little fellow with a puff of blond hair and what Doyle suspected was a put-on British accent asked, "Hello, sir. How may I assist you?"

"Is this the residence of Timothy Chapman?"

"Who, if I may inquire, is asking?"

"Detective Doyle Malloy, Minneapolis Police. I'm a specialist in high-profile cases, on loan to St. Paul. I understand there's been a robbery."

"Oh, yes, sir. Mr. Chapman's safe. I will escort you."

The butler led him slowly into the foyer, which was much more extravagant than the outside of the house. On his left, he looked into what might be the living room, though it was as large as a ballroom, at least compared to the small, musty room where Doyle once sat in his little-boy pajamas watching cheesy detective shows like *Dragnet* and *Get Smart*.

"Do you really think Marta stole from Master Chapman?" asked the butler sheepishly. He looked worried and upset.

"I have to be honest, I didn't know her," responded Doyle. "Let me ask you a question. What's your name?"

"B-Brookes, sir," said the butler, with a slight stutter. "Darren Brookes."

Doyle meticulously took out his notebook and poised a pen.

"Would you spell that for me, please?"

"B-B-B, r, o. . . " The butler leaned toward him, watching him write his name on the pad. The process seemed painful for him, as if being in an officer's notebook was physically hurtful.

"Is that with three 'B's?" asked Doyle. "I'm just kidding. Clearly you're nervous. Right?"

"A bit, sir. I'm not used to this," said Brookes.

"Don't worry, Brookes, you're doing just fine," said Doyle.

"You may call me Darren, if you wish, sir."

"Very good, Mr. Brookes. Now, do you think Marta stole from your employer?"

"I-I-I don't know," said Brookes. "I mean, she was really nice, and she didn't seem like the type that would steal. Especially from someone who was so kind to her."

They walked down the hallway—a really long, wide hallway—towards the room where the alleged robbery took place. Doyle could hear photographs being taken.

Doyle put an arm in front of Brookes and stopped him before they reached the room. "What do you know about Marta?" he demanded, staring Brookes in the eyes.

Brookes backed away, fluttering easily under the pressure. "Not much . . . I mean, I know she's an actress. A good one too, based on how Master Chapman speaks of her. Though she never got any roles, from what I understand."

"So you're saying she never got any roles, then?"

"Yeah . . . I mean, yes. Does that really matter?"

"Do you think it matters?"

"Well, I . . . don't really know?"

"What are you hiding, Brookes?" Doyle grabbed the butler by his starched white collar. Brookes squeaked.

Though Doyle hadn't expected any new information, the scared butler said, "I . . . I saw her in a commercial once." He squeaked again. "It was a coffee commercial with that guy from Colombia. I think he had a donkey with him."

Doyle pushed his finger into Brookes' chest, threateningly. "And what did you think of it?"

Brookes' fluffy blond hair was beginning to clump with sweat. "Okay . . . okay . . . I thought it was poorly acted. When she drank the coffee, I got the distinct impression that she didn't like it at all. I mean, what kind of actress can't pull that off?"

Doyle pulled back from Mr. Brookes. He studied the jittery butler. "Good," said Doyle. "Good. Always be honest with me, you got that?"

"Sure thing," said Brookes, straightening his bowtie. "Can we . . . I mean . . . you don't need me anymore now, do you? I think I need to lie down . . ."

"Just show me the crime scene, please."

"It's right in there," said Brookes, pointing towards the office.

Doyle nodded and entered.

Aside from the metal safe that was hanging open within a wall on the far side of the room, the office appeared pretty normal. Except, that is, for the numerous paintings that lined the walls, each of which featured kittens in playful poses. *That's a little off-putting*, Doyle thought.

The office was pretty well filled with cops. Then, among the sea of blue-uniformed bodies, Doyle spotted a familiar face.

"Hanratty? Jesus, Hanratty, what the heck are you doing here? I didn't see your squad out front."

"Hi, Doyle," said a pencil-thin officer. His uniform draped loosely over his bony frame. "They won't let me drive a squad anymore, what with the DUI's. Apparently they frown on that at headquarters," he said, which, of course really didn't answer the question of how he had arrived.

"Still on the bottle?"

Hanratty bobbed his head over his prominent Adam's apple. "I do AA weekly, of course, but doesn't seem to be taking yet. Jack helps me drown the pain of photographing grisly crime scene after grisly crime scene. Heck, I have a bottle waiting for me when I'm done with this one."

Doyle did a double-take. "But this isn't a murder. There's no body It's . . . it's . . . just a robbery. What's so grisly about that?"

"Robbery . . . it's so senseless."

Doyle thought Hanratty had been misnamed. Eeyore sure would have fit him. Hanratty resumed taking snapshots of the open safe. The metal surrounding the lock was smashed and twisted from repeated blows.

Doyle began his investigation. He looked into the safe, he crawled along the floor, he rummaged through the desk, he studied the window and the outside surroundings, and looked up and down the street.

"Hey, Hanratty, is that your bike down by the sidewalk?"

"Yeah, and I'd like to point out it's really hard to carry all this photo stuff on a bike. I fall over all the time."

"Maybe that's due to the drinking."

Hanratty shook his head. "I only drink *after* work. Or when it's a particularly stressful day."

Doyle grinned but not so Hanratty could see. He looked around the room. In *CSI*, this was usually the moment when William Peterson finds a strand of hair or a fingernail clipping. The lab has a go at it, and the bit of evidence points to one and only one perpetrator.

Doyle got on his hands and knees and combed the carpeting, searching for that single clue that would crack open the case.

"What are you doing, Doyle?" asked Hanratty. "The safe's over there."

"Looking for *the* clue," said Doyle. "You know, something that points conclusively to the robber."

"What kind of clue?" asked Hanratty, curious.

"You know—the *big* clue. A strand of hair or something," said Doyle, concentrating hard enough that he wasn't checking what he said.

Hanratty chuckled. "Hair? What the hell are you gonna do with that? There's probably tons of hair down there. You've probably shed a couple yourself since you've been in here."

"Okay," said Doyle. "What about a fingernail?"

"You think the robber clipped his nails before he robbed the safe? That doesn't make any sense."

"What am I looking for?" he asked, trying his best to mask his frustration. "I mean, what do you make of all this?"

"I'm not the detective," replied Hanratty. "I'm just the bike cop who takes lousy photos."

"I know, I know . . . but you've taken lots of photos. You're familiar with crimes scenes. Right? Does anything about this room seem peculiar to you?"

Hanratty's brows crossed, and he was thin enough that one eyebrow came dangerously close to folding over the other. He was silent, almost thoughtful in a dour sort of way, and he looked about the room.

Doyle waited. For a long time. Had Eeyore fallen asleep?

"Hanratty?"

This skinny detective jumped. He met Doyle's eyes, looking a bit amazed. "Wow, have you ever fallen asleep with your eyes open? Freaks me out every time," he said.

Doyle was indeed familiar with Hanratty's "spells." He chose not to go there. "The room, Hanratty . . . does anything look odd about the room?"

"Well, now that you mention it, the walls are sort of a beige color. I'd definitely expect white walls from such an affluent celebrity."

Doyle sighed. "Sure, but that doesn't really—"

"That rug over there is a little crooked." He was pointing to the Persian rug near the door.

Doyle and Hanratty looked at each other, then back at the rug.

Batty, dour Hanratty was right. "Let's check it out," said Doyle.

Doyle took one end, and Hanratty the other. They lifted the rug, exposing a giant red stain underneath. Had the stain been much bigger, the rug couldn't have possibly hidden all the blood. And in the realization that it was blood, everything about the crime scene . . . and the crime shifted.

"My God . . ." whispered Hanratty. "I need a drink . . ."

Meanwhile, Doyle was forming conclusions in his head.

"So," said Doyle. "Either . . . missing Marta hurt herself real bad while stealing from the safe or . . ."

Hanratty snickered at this idea.

"Or," Doyle continued, "she killed someone before getting away with the loot. Probably somebody who caught her at the heist."

Hanratty nodded. Apparently Doyle's latter conclusion sounded reasonable enough.

Doyle took his cell phone from his pocket and speed-dialed.

"Chief—this is Doyle. I got big news. This isn't just a robbery—I think there's been a murder. Prime suspect: Marta Ramirez."

"IS THAT SO!" Chief Burnside yelled through the phone. "And just what makes you think that?"

Damn, thought Doyle. *He must be racing through more than the average range of colors. I sure hate to miss a good light show.* "There's a whole lot of blood here, Chief. I think Marta might have caught someone watching her commit the crime. Then she bumped him off. It makes total sense."

"I see," responded Burnside. "Was this before or after she bashed her own head in and jumped into Lake Calhoun?"

Doyle didn't respond. Obviously, the rest of the world hadn't gone into a stand-still while he was seaching the office.

"She's dead, Doyle. Some jogger spotted her body not twenty minutes ago. We've just confirmed that it's Marta Ramirez."

"But why would—"

"That's for you to figure out, Doyle. And I hope you realize this case is far more sensitive now that a murder is involved. We need to be very tight-lipped about this. Absolutely no speaking with the press, no outside resources, everything strictly by the book. Got it? Now, figure out who robbed Timothy Chapman's safe, and most importantly, find out who killed Marta Ramirez."

Doyle heard a click and knew the conversation was over.

"Wanna go get a little pick-me-up?" Hanratty asked.

"Love to, Hanratty. Trust me, I'd really love to. But I can't." Doyle realized he was about to say something he'd never said before:

"I've got work to do."

ALTHOUGH DOYLE SUDDENLY FOUND HIMSELF in the middle of a homicide investigation, he figured he must have at least a few minutes to stop at home for lunch. Besides, he was hungry, and he didn't have enough money on him to buy any food.

Doyle took a right on Snelling Avenue and pulled into the Retirement Village apartment building where he lived. Doyle was the only thirty-something in a complex full of silver and occasionally blue-haired octogenarians. The Retirement Village was far cheaper than other buildings in the Roseville area, and fortunately for Doyle, they had been desperate for tenants.

At his apartment door, he was greeted by the last person in the world he wanted to see that day . . . or any day, for that matter.

"Good afternoon, Mr. Malloy," said the man in the white suit, standing directly in front of Doyle's door. Doyle couldn't remember his name, but he's seen that white suit several times now. He was sick of it.

"You're blocking my entrance," said Doyle. "I believe that's illegal."

"You believe?" said the man, smirking. "Well, you're the cop, so I guess you should know, right? But regardless, I am not blocking your entrance. I've merely chosen an ideal location from which to demand payment on the large amount of money you owe Gaff and Gafferty Collections."

"Is there really a Gaff and a Gafferty? Seems kind of unfortunate name, doesn't it?" asked Doyle.

"Yes, it is quite the coincidence. Where's the money, Mr. Malloy?"

"You sound threatening," said Doyle. "And you're harassing me. That's *definitely* illegal."

"Although it's quite subjective," said the man. "Most courts would likely side with the company that's owed a great deal of money as opposed to the bum who's unwilling to pay it."

"I've been making payments," said Doyle.

"You've made two payments this year," said the man.

"Yeah, so?" said Doyle.

"They're monthly payments. It's September."

"So, I've been a bit behind," said Doyle. "I'll catch up. Just stop coming to my apartment. I don't like it."

"Very well, Mr. Malloy. Failure to make at least the minimum payments will result in a court summons. You've had your fair warning. Have a nice day."

The man in the white suit stepped away from Doyle's door and exited the complex.

Doyle entered his apartment in a very foul mood.

However, once he was inside, he found himself slightly more at ease. His apartment, albeit quite small, was filled with the things he loved. Classic movie posters, some of which were autographed by celebrities he had helped in his years of police service, adorned the walls. Three priceless light-saber replicas were enclosed in plastic protective cases, which hung on the wall. Action figures from his childhood occupied small shelves placed decoratively around the apartment. Doyle also had a very expensive entertainment system which he had purchased the year before, though he couldn't really afford it.

In fact, much of what Doyle owned he couldn't really afford. While some of the cases Doyle took on were rather high-profile, his income was not. And frankly, he never got the hang of the whole "budgeting" thing. Doyle's dad had been in charge of many of Doyle's finances before he passed away, even though they had lived separately and Doyle was a grown man. But after his dad died—well, things just rather fell apart.

Doyle quickly made himself a sandwich, gobbled it down, and left his apartment just as fast as he arrived.

After all—he had a murder to solve.

Doyle pulled into the morgue just as the sun was beginning to set. Though it was late, Doyle was certain that his good friend Dr. Sylvester would be hard at work. Dr. Sylvester always wore his white lab coat over a sweater, blue jeans, and white Nike high-tops. He also wore an oversized pair of glasses. Doyle thought this made him look like a bald Elton John.

"Well, if it isn't Officer Doyle Malloy himself. I haven't seen you in ages. Still working the high-profile gigs?"

"Sure am. And if I do really well tonight, I might still have this job tomorrow. Now, I need to see the body."

"Which body, Doyle? We have lots of bodies here. Every size, weight, gender, race . . ."

"Marta Ramirez. She should have arrived a few minutes ago."

"Doyle, I've only received one elderly gentlemen a few hours ago, and he certainly doesn't look like any Marta."

Doyle looked around the room.

"But I just received word that her body was found. Where is it? I need to look at it . . . and get clues . . . and such. Why are you smiling?"

"When the last time you worked a murder case, Doyle?"

"Well, it's been a while. I mean, there were a couple cases a few years ago where I had to see a body, but that was more of a training thing, but still I . . . wait a minute, how about you just tell me where the body is. Let's start there."

"The body, Doyle, is most likely at the nearest hospital where a medical examiner would autopsy it and pronounce the time and cause of death. Once that's all done with, I go pick up the body in my morgue-mobile, slap some make-up on it, and put it on display for the viewing."

"That was. . . morbid, Dr. Sylvester. God. Hospital—right. I remember that now. Thanks. I guess I'll see you if I have any more questions."

"You really need to stop calling me doctor, Doyle. I'm not a doctor. I don't have a doctorate. Stop calling me doctor."

"But the lab coat . . . the glasses—"

"You should probably get to that body, Doyle."

"Right." Doyle turned to leave.

"Wait, Doyle," Sylvester said.

"Yeah?"

"Are you really in that tough of a spot? I mean, with your job?"

Doyle thought for a moment. "Yeah, I think I am. I'm used to Burnside making threats, but this time I think he's serious. If I screw up this case, it could cause a lot of damage to the department, and it'd certainly end my career. Frankly, I can't let that happen. Just between you and me—I'm not in the best financial situation. When I got home today, there was a collection agent waiting for me."

"You're kidding me," said Sylvester. "At your apartment? Is that legal?"

"I'm pretty sure it isn't," said Doyle. "But I'm not positive. It's not really my area of expertise."

"I probably would have punched the guy," said Sylvester.

"I was tempted," said Doyle. "I really was."

"Well, I think I may be able to help you," Sylvester said. "Not with punching collection agents, mind you, but something else altogether." He removed a pen and a small notepad from his lab coat pocket. "This guy's done a lot of work for me in the past. Trust me, he's brilliant."

"Is this a shrink, Dr. Sylvester? Honestly, emotionally I'm quite stable. It's just that—"

"He's not a shrink. But if you need any help, just ask him. Okay?"

"Sure. Thanks."

"Just tell him Sylvester sent you. Like I said, he's done a lot of work for me, so, if anything, he should be able to cut you a deal."

"I'd have to pay him?" asked Doyle. "Doc, I'm not sure I can give anyone money for anything. Seriously, I'm broke."

"Just talk to him. Work something out. Don't worry about it," Sylvester said.

Doyle nodded. "All right. I appreciate the help."

"Now get going. Dead bodies don't stay pretty for very long," Sylvester said with a chuckle.

Doyle turned his head before walking out the door. "You find them *pretty?*"

Sylvester thought about it for a moment.

"No."

DOYLE PULLED INTO THE GAS STATION directly in between the morgue and the hospital. While he was normally expeditious when it came to detective work, and he knew that Chief Burnside would frown upon any wasted time during an investigation, Doyle figured the body wasn't getting any colder.

Speaking of cold, thought Doyle, *I could really go for a Mountain Dew*. Approaching the soda aisle, Doyle noticed a tan, bleach-blonde woman in a sundress giving him the look. The look Doyle assumed meant, "Hey, big fella. Could you help me with these milk jugs?"

"Good afternoon, ma'am," said Doyle, even though he wasn't looking for love at the moment, nor did he generally have the confidence with which to speak to ridiculously attractive women. The trouble, really, was that Doyle didn't consider himself handsome, although many of the female variety seemed to be of that very opinion. In many ways, Doyle still saw himself as the frail, zit-faced boy of his youth, even though his appearance had improved considerably since then. With brown hair and broad shoulders, Doyle had grown into the spitting image of his father, a legend amongst Minneapolis law enforcement.

As Sundress Woman paid for her milk and left, Doyle wondered bemusedly if all the other officers thought his name and appearance had kept him in his current cushy position. Doyle had no problem taking advantage of nepotism, but he'd like to think he had substantial detection abilities that others did not possess and that most people were underestimating him. Regardless, Doyle knew his potentially undeserved success was a sore spot with many of the other officers, particularly the ones who had worked for years on the street risking their lives. Although Doyle wasn't on the street, he consistently felt on the edge, as though the rug could be pulled out from beneath him at any moment. When that happened, he knew he'd lose the celebrity cases and end up working the street himself.

Or worse, thought Doyle, *some dead-end job like that woman behind the counter.* Doyle realized he had been staring, deep in thought. The old check-out clerk scowled at him. Doyle quickly turned to the tiny stationary aisle and grabbed a six-inch vertical-flip Mead notebook, his reason for stopping in the first place. He almost always had one with him, but he must have forgotten his today. He thought it would look horribly amateurish for a detective to show up without a way to take notes, and his other pad was down to the last page.

The next aisle contained snack foods. "Ahh, Pringles," said Doyle out loud, without realizing it.

The old clerk looked at him apprehensively.

"They're good," Doyle stated matter-of-factly to her. She nodded out of courtesy, but Doyle had the sneaking suspicious she thought he was crazy.

"Caught ya staring there," the old woman said. "See something ya fancy?"

"Only your precious smile, m'lady," said Doyle with a tip of his head. He always felt far more confident with women to whom he felt no attraction whatsoever.

"Well, isn't that sweet," she said. "That'll be two dollars and thirty-four cents."

Doyle opened his wallet, and cringed. He only had two dollars.

"Oh, geez . . ." Doyle began to say.

"We accept all major credit cards," the clerk said, eyeing up the plastic in Doyle's wallet.

The truth was, Doyle had all the major credit cards. They just happened all to be totally maxed out.

"Umm . . . no, that's okay . . ." said Doyle, fumbling around in his pockets for change.

The clerk, sounding like a mother teaching her child about responsibility, asked, "Which one of these items would you like to put back? The notebook or the soda?"

"Neither . . . oh, here we go," Doyle said, spotting the "leave a penny take a penny" jar. He lifted it and emptied the contents into the clerk's awaiting hands. Her look of disgust made Doyle feel two feet tall. For a moment anyway.

"Keep the change," said Doyle. He grabbed his items and left. Behind him, he could hear the clerk's voice trailing off as the door closed. Something about being seven cents short. Doyle whistled to himself as he drove away.

Moments later, Doyle parked in the hospital parking lot. Several other squads were in the lot as well. Doyle wondered how many officers Burnside had assigned to the case. Inside the building, Doyle asked the blonde receptionist with the Coke bottle glasses where he could find Marta Ramirez.

"Who?" asked the receptionist.

"Marta Ramirez. Arrived this morning. Medium height. Black hair. Won't be doing much slow dancing any more."

"Was this an injury?" asked the receptionist, looking confused.

"No, she's a stiff."

"Paralysis?"

"No, she's dead."

The woman's eyes went wide behind her glasses. "Oh, I see," said the receptionist, her tone starting surprised and ending reproachful. "You could have just said that, sir. She was a real person. I don't see any reason to make light of that."

Doyle felt a pang of guilt, which always seemed to happen after his mouth took control of his brain. One should never let a tongue feel like it had the bit. "Sorry . . . sorry. I just need to know where she is."

"I mean, what if her relatives were in this room and heard you say that! Imagine how horrible that'd be."

Doyle felt his face grow hot. Damn that unfettered tongue. "I'm sorry, ma'am. Truly. I guess I didn't think of that. But I'm already running late. Is there any chance you could just tell me . . ."

"And what if she were here right now? What if her soul heard you talk about her like that? Why, you could be torturing her. Imagine, dying in a hospital then hearing someone talk about you like you're nothing. Well I think that's just horr—"

There was also a problem in letting someone else's tongue get the upper hand. "Ma'am, please. This is a serious investigation. I need to know exactly where she is, right away."

". . . And what if she really liked slow dancing! That would have been an awfully cruel joke. You should really think before you . . ."

"DOYLE!" Chief Burnside's voice echoed through the hospital lobby, reverberating off the walls. "What are you doing out there? We have an investigation to run."

"Sorry, Chief. But this woman's being obstinate. Might even say she was hampering our investigation. Maybe we should arrest her."

"Just get over here. We'll deal with that later."

Before he joined Chief Burnside, Doyle mouthed the words, "Just kidding" to the receptionist, whose mouth hung open. She didn't seem amused.

Doyle followed his boss into the room where Marta Ramirez was being thoroughly inspected by a medical examiner.

"So, where have you been?" demanded Chief Burnside.

Doyle thought about his pit stop for a bite of lunch and then at the gas station, and what had turned out to be the unnecessary stop at the morgue.

"I was . . . securing things."

Burnside eyed him suspiciously.

"For the investigation," added Doyle.

"And?"

"At this point, everything seems to be pretty secure. I suggest we proceed with the investigation, if you don't mind me saying so, sir."

"Whatever you wish, Detective Malloy. After all, this is your investigation." Burnside folded his arms across his chest and stared at Doyle. "Well?"

"Well what, sir?"

"Today would be a good day to start. This is Dr. Thompson. I bet he'd be a darned good person to ask questions."

"Thank you, sir. Might I add I love your sense of humor. You're a regular Bob Saget."

"Wise ass. I'll be outside. I want to talk to you when you're done here, okay?"

"Sure thing, Burnsie."

His eyes narrowed, and his color rose. In a tone of death, he said, "If you call me that again, I'll kick your teeth in."

Doyle licked his teeth and frowned. Chief Burnside left the room.

"You're new, I take it?" asked Dr. Thompson. Unlike Dr. Sylvester at the morgue, Dr. Thompson was dressed very professionally. Doyle could see the knot of a tie above the pressed, white examiner's coat.

"Why would you say that?" asked Doyle.

"For the other officer to talk to you like that, you have to be pretty new. Or does he speak to all of his subordinates like that?" Dr. Thompson was using one instrument that looked like a blade and another one that looked like a pair of tongs. He was removing bits from the top of Marta Ramirez's head. What was left of it, anyway. *Bet that's what killed her.*

"No, only to me, though I'm not that new. But we have a long history. He knew my dad because they were on the force together, and then when my dad passed on . . . oh MY GOD!"

A torrent of blood splattered against Dr. Thompson's pristine white coat after he removed what looked like a small stone from Marta's scalp. It pooled on the gurney and even dripped over the side. Doyle stepped back.

"Sorry . . . Detective Malloy, was it? I hope you're not too squeamish around blood. Because this one's a doozy."

"Why . . . why would it do that?"

"Well," said Dr. Thompson thoughtfully. "It looks like she'd been bleeding for a while. When she was dumped in the lake, whatever her head was resting against stuck to her and formed a sort of a thick clot holding the remaining blood inside. I removed some of this debris, and it all came loose."

"But doesn't her heart have to be beating for it to do that?"

"Not necessarily. Depending on how she was positioned when she died—I imagine in this case it was upside-down—then that could cause all the blood in her to settle within the head. If there was any sort of built-up air pressure in there, it could cause it to move out quickly, as you've just seen."

Doyle took out his new notebook and started making notes. He tried to stay focused on that so he wouldn't have to look up and see the gory examiner.

"Umm, Dr. Thompson, do you think you could determine the instrument used in the murder?"

"Lucky for you, that's easy."

"It is?"

"Definitely. If you look right here, Detective, you'll see . . ."

"I'll take your word for it," Doyle said, swallowing hard. "Just tell me, what do you see?"

Dr. Thompson looked at Doyle reproachfully. "You don't work too many murder cases, do you, Detective Malloy?"

"Sure I do. But they don't all involve blood."

"What kind of murders don't involve blood?"

"Oh, you know. Stranglings. Drownings. Electrocutions. Uhh . . . freezings."

"You get a lot of murders in the form of freezings?"

"Absolutely. Ice fishing holes. One little push, the deed is done. Anyway, you were saying about the instrument used."

"Right. It appears a large portion of the skull went inward, which is an indication of a blunt instrument being used. However, this one particular part of the skull shows indication of being pulled outward, which would suggest the murder weapon could be one of two instruments."

"Oh, let me take a shot at this one," said Doyle. "A hammer because of the back side, which could pull as well as smash in. Or a crowbar, which could also pull when it comes up, even if it's unintentional."

"Very good, Detective," said Dr. Thompson, impressed. "Due to the size of the damaged area, and the shape of the area that's been pulled up, I'd say a crowbar is much more likely. Besides, a hammer would have gone in deeper. A crowbar will smash the top of the skull and do some damage to the top portion of the brain, but a hammer can go all the way through and turn the brain to jelly if the perpetrator puts some muscle to it. If you take a look at Ms. Ramirez's brain, you'll see that only the top . . ."

Doyle could actually feel the blood draining from his face.

"Are you feeling okay, Detective? If you want to leave, that's okay. I can give you more information later. Perhaps over the phone."

"That might be a good idea. Let me give you my card."

Dr. Thompson studied Doyle's business card. "That's an awfully impressive card for a public detective."

Doyle would have snickered another time. Right then he was struggling to hold down his stomach. "I mostly use them for winning free lunches." The thought of food made Doyle cringe. "I should go."

D OYLE WAS AMBUSHED BY HIS BOSS on the way out of the examination room.

"Listen, Doyle. I want to talk to you about something," Burnside said. He adjusted his tie and exhaled.

Away from the blood, Doyle began to recover quickly. A few deep breaths helped. "Should I be worried?" he asked. He could tell that, whatever Burnside was about to say, it probably wasn't pleasant. He looked like he was about to vomit but was trying his best to keep it in. Doyle had a mutual feeling.

"No . . . well, okay, yes. You probably should be worried."

That sent a tiny spurt of adrenaline into his system. "I know what you're going to say, Chief. If I screw up, I'm canned. I understand that."

"It's not just that, Doyle. I know I've been hard on you lately, and for good reason. You . . . you have the potential to be a good detective. You really do. But in this situation—"

"Whoa, whoa, wait a minute. Who are you? What happened to the Chief? You gave me a bona fide compliment? Imposter!"

A nurse walking down the hall stopped in her tracks. "Is every-thing okay?" she asked. She seemed worried.

"Sorry, miss. This asshole doesn't know how to keep quiet," said Burnside.

"You're back! There's my big Burnsie-Wurnsie." Doyle gave him a slap on the shoulders. The nurse rolled her eyes and continued on her way.

"Fine, Doyle. I'll be blunt. I want to keep you on this case. Like I said, you have a lot of potential. You seem to be good at reading people, even if your logic stinks. But sometimes instincts can be more important than logic. Your father had incredible instincts, and I can see the same in you."

Doyle lowered his head. "Thank you, sir."

"But you're still a young detective, and I think it might be too early for you to have this important of a case."

"Listen, Chief. I know I can do this. I want to prove to you I can. But I have to stay on the case for that to happen."

"That's the dilemma, Doyle. Superintendent McDonald is riding my ass like a steel bull, and if I leave you on this, any small misstep could cost both of us our careers. I could retire, but it's awfully early for you to be out of work. I'm just not sure this is right for either of us. Do you understand what I'm trying to say here, Doyle?"

"I do, sir. And I realize how important this case is. I know I can do it. If that means you have to scrutinize every move I make, so be it. But just don't pull me off the case. Then I wouldn't even have a chance."

Burnside nodded. "I'm glad to hear you're actually taking this seriously." He paused for a moment. "Well, as seriously as you have the ability to take it, anyway. That's good, Doyle. It shows growth."

"Say," said Doyle, as delicately and smoothly as possible. "Any possibility that if I successfully complete this case . . . there might be a little extra cash in it for me?" Doyle waited anxiously for Burnside's reaction.

Burnside huffed like a bull about to charge before saying, "You're pushing it, Doyle. You barely earn the money you already receive—don't expect extra money for actually doing your job for once. Is that perfect-ly clear?"

"Crystal," Doyle said, deflated like a balloon with an air leak.

Burnside looked at Doyle long and hard. "I want to give you this chance, Doyle. And you're right, I'm going to be riding you throughout this case. It'll be hard. Maybe if you do well here and in future cases, we can discuss a bump in salary. But the most crucial thing is—if at any point you don't think you can do it, I need you to tell me. Immediately."

"Yes, sir."

"I have detectives Jacobson and McNulty at Mr. Chapman's residence as we speak, as well as Detective Rabinowitz at the lake where the body was found. They've been ordered to retrieve as much information as possible from these sites and report to you in the morning. Do any further investigating necessary based on the findings and give me a full report tomorrow evening. Understood?"

"Yes, sir. Thank you, sir." Doyle shook hands with his boss.

"Don't fuck up."

"I'll do my best, sir."

"I was afraid you were going to say that."

5

THE MARTINIAPOLIS TAVERN WAS especially full that night. The usual drunks lined the bar stools, the few semi-attractive women who dared be seen in such an establishment played pool, and a couple families, likely with alcoholic fathers, ate deep-fried chicken strips and cheesesticks from little red-checkered baskets lined with waxed paper.

Doyle managed to find an unoccupied barstool next to his favorite drunk.

"Hey, Doyle."

"Hey, Hanratty. It's a surprise seeing you here."

"You're a funny man, Doyle."

The bartender, a scruffy middle-aged fellow, cleaned a glass with a rag as he approached Doyle. "Usual, buddy?"

Doyle nodded.

"Are you still on the Chapman case?" asked Hanratty.

Doyle turned to his friend. He'd been close to Hanratty since they both entered the police force. While Doyle was bumped up to higher-profile, often easier, cases because of his father's legacy in the department, Hanratty continued the day-to-day street beat, eventually taking photography courses and becoming the only full-time photographer employed by Minneapolis Law Enforcement. Other cops took photos when necessary, but Hanratty was the only one they didn't trust to have a gun.

"What, you don't think I can handle it?" asked Doyle.

"I didn't say that." Hanratty took a swig of his whiskey. "Though I guess I did *imply* it. Insinuated, even."

"I love your confidence, old friend."

"C'mon, Doyle. You're about as good being a detective as I am being sober." Hanratty emptied the contents of his glass and signaled the bartender.

"Maybe you're right. But that doesn't mean I can't get better."

The bartender placed another whiskey in front of Hanratty and a blueberry daiquiri in front of Doyle. Doyle stared at the drink. As the bartender started walking away, Doyle said, "Ah-ah-ah," said Doyle. "Not so fast."

The scruffy bartender turned back and shook his head. He reached under the bar and pulled out a small paper umbrella with a floral design. He popped it open dramatically and snugged it into Doyle's drink.

Doyle smiled. "Good man. You just got yourself an extra dollar."

"Joy," muttered the bartender.

"Which reminds me, do you mind getting this for me, buddy?" Doyle asked.

Hanratty groaned. "Dammit, Doyle—when are you gonna start paying for your own drinks? I'm nearly broke paying for my own."

"I've gotten a little . . . behind lately. I can catch up, but it might take me awhile."

Hanratty nodded. "Do you think if you solve this case, you might get a nice bonus?"

Doyle pondered the question. Burnside hadn't made that prospect too hopeful, but, then, it might just be that he didn't want Doyle focusing on the wrong prize.

"I guess it's possible." *It'd sure help get me out of debt*, Doyle thought.

"Do you really think you can solve this case?" asked Hanratty seriously.

"Don't know yet," said Doyle. "I know I have to try. What would it say about me if I stepped down, or even worse, got thrown off? Everyone would know I'm not a real detective. I'm just a guy who puts the bad guys in the squad car and smiles for the camera. I look confident and say, 'justice is served, ladies and gentlemen' and Minnesota continues to believe they have a competent and effective police force. I don't want that to be just an image. It should be the truth."

"That's deep," stated Hanratty.

Doyle sipped his daiquiri.

"I'm a detective. I've solved cases. They haven't always been complicated. Most criminals want to get caught. It's just part of human nature. Sometimes, I've gotten lucky."

"How so?" asked Hanratty.

"Well, one time this kid, couldn't have been any older than twenty, broke into Josh Hartnett's home and stole everything he could carry out. And he was smart about it, too. He got in and out completely undetected. He'd done his research and knew Josh's acting schedule, so he knew when he could get in without much trouble. He knew security systems and how to get around them. As far as criminals go, he was one of the brighter ones."

"How did you catch him?"

"I went to the nearest pawn shop. He was there."

"He doesn't sound all that smart."

Doyle took another drink. "He was smart. He just wanted to get caught. They all do at some level."

"That may be so, Doyle. But you can't always expect that. Things may not always be so simple."

"Exactly my point," said Doyle. "I've never dealt with a murder before. I don't know how murderers think. All I know is that I need to make damn sure I find the perp. The right one. Or else I'm fucked. This one is for all the marbles."

Doyle took another sip.

"So, you haven't had much experience in murder investigations," said Hanratty. "Can you talk to some other guys on the force who have?"

"It's too late for that," responded Doyle rather sadly. "I have to give Burnside a report tomorrow. I don't have time to interview my fellow officers about Investigating Murders 101. Besides, if word gets around that I'm not confident in what I'm doing, I'll be even more of a laughing stock, and maybe get thrown off the case."

Doyle emptied his daiquiri and said, "I should be fine. I've seen enough cop shows."

Hanratty snorted. "It's really sad that television has provided the majority of your detective training."

"Hey, those shows have good writers," said Doyle. "I'll assume they've put in a lot of time studying police investigations. Hence, my nightly hour-long dramas provide a condensed version of everything I need to know."

"You know, Doyle, you could spend some time studying police investigations. I mean, really studying, like out of books."

"I read John Sandford novels," said Doyle.

"I give up," said Hanratty. He stared at his glass of whiskey for a long moment, then said, "I want to tell you something, Doyle. This is important. This is about life."

"Okay," said Doyle.

Hanratty pointed at his glass. "An optimist would look at this glass and say, 'This glass is half full.' A pessimist would look at this glass and say, 'This glass is half full . . . and I probably have rectal cancer.'"

Doyle and Hanratty laughed good and hard. Hanratty slapped Doyle on the back.

"But seriously, Doyle. You're sure you don't have any other options? You're just going to walk in tomorrow and solve that murder? Just like that?"

Doyle thought for a moment.

"Yup."

Hanratty waved over the bartender, who brought the tab. "Well good luck to you, my friend. I hope your detective work ends up being as exemplary as your false confidence."

Doyle stood up and took out his keys. A small scrap of paper fell out of his pocket. He bent over to pick it up.

"What's that?" asked Hanratty.

"Another option," said Doyle. He laughed and returned Hanratty's slap on the back. "You're a lifesaver."

"Glad to be of assistance."

Doyle turned to leave.

"Hey, Doyle," Hanratty said, grabbing Doyle's shirt.

"Yeah?"

"I know I'm not in the best mental state right now, but if you need any help, you just let me know, okay?"

"You got it, buddy," said Doyle. "Really, I appreciate it."

With the slip of paper in hand, Doyle walked out of the Martiniapolis and drove to the address Dr. Sylvester had given him.

Be an optimist, Doyle thought to himself.

6

THE SMALL, BRICK BUILDING off Central Avenue in North Minneapolis had been at some point a dentist office. At least, this was what Doyle deduced from the "Reginald Jackson, D.D.S." plaque affixed to the wall. The plaque had been covered in black spray paint that continued onto the tan door, where the words "Bite Me" were displayed in street-born graffiti artist perfection. An eight-by-ten sheet of paper with the name "Wright" spelled out in black marker was attached to the door with scotch tape. *Professional. Real class.*

Doyle again compared the address on the building with the address given to him by Dr. Sylvester, just to make sure. Why he was being sent to a dentist, he had no idea. As far as Doyle could tell, his teeth were flawless.

It was past eight o'clock, and being as there were no lights on within the brick building, at least none that Doyle could see through the two tiny bar-covered windows, he assumed there was nobody there. But Doyle hadn't driven out to a dangerous neighborhood after dark for nothing. He knocked three times.

A light came on, glowing faintly on the other side of a window. Doyle thought he heard footsteps approach the door. Then, nothing. Doyle knocked again.

"Who's there?" called a man's voice from behind the door. The tone was deep and a little cautious, with a touch of an accent. Doyle couldn't tell what nationality it was, but it sounded European at any rate. Where had Dr. Sylvester sent him?

"My name is Det . . . Doyle Malloy." Doyle though maybe saying he was a detective might not be the right idea. Best to keep that information private until he knew who he was dealing with. "Dr. Sylvester said I should speak with you."

"I'm afraid I'm not acquainted with any doctors," said the man behind the door. "At least not with the surname 'Sylvester.'"

"Oh, well you see, he's not really a doctor," responded Doyle. "He's just works at a morgue. But he has the white coat thing going, so I call him doctor."

"You don't mean Ronald Sylvester? The pervert?"

Doyle sniffed. "I can't say I was aware of *that* particular bit of information, but thanks for sharing. Wait a minute, you don't mean in the morgue . . . ?" That image was decidedly disturbing.

"Oh, no, nothing of that sort. You see I . . . here, wait a moment, please."

Doyle heard a bolt unlock and a chain rattle. The door opened, revealing a somewhat unkempt man in a t-shirt and sweatpants. He had short, black, frazzled hair and seemingly oversized facial features—a big, round chin, big ears, and a large nose, all of which was offset by a pair of tiny eyeglasses. He was several days unshaven and squinted as though he was woken up from a deep sleep. He offered his hand to Doyle.

"My name is Wright, William Wright. I'm a private detective."

"And a professional one at that, I see." Doyle shook his hand. While the man looked rather unhygienic at the moment, Doyle did notice something about him. Maybe it was the tiny eyeglasses or simply the sharp look in his dark eyes, this detective Wright seemed to convey a great deal of intelligence.

"It's after business hours, and business has been poor lately, so I apologize for my appearance."

"You're English," said Doyle matter-of-factly.

"Maybe you should be the detective."

"I am."

William paused. He looked at Doyle apprehensively. "Then . . . why are you here?"

"I'm not really sure," Doyle lied. "I guess I could use some . . . assistance, perhaps. Do you live here?"

"Are you a government official? If you are, I assure you I maintain a separate residence. Occasionally I find the need to nap here, you see. And I'm also *not* a dentist. I loath it when people inquire whether or not I practice dentistry. This office was cheap, albeit run-down. I have yet to get a new plaque out front, but regardless . . ."

"I really don't care, Mr. Wright. I was just hoping you might be able to assist me with a case. It's big."

"How big?"

"Do you know . . ." Doyle added a dramatic pause for effect, "Timothy Chapman?"

"I'm afraid not," replied William, his expression not wavering a bit. "Does he know Ronald Sylvester?"

Doyle slapped his forehead. "How do you *not* know Timothy Chapman? He's one of the most famous actors in the world!"

"Apparently not the entire world," replied William. "Besides, I generally do not give much attention to media. I tend to stay . . . busy."

"Yes, I see that. Taking a nap at eight o'clock. You must have worn yourself out today."

"You're quite a sarcastic man, aren't you, Mr. Malloy?"

"I don't mean to squabble, Mr. Wright, but I do want to know if you can help me."

"Please, call me William."

"How about Will, or perhaps Bill?"

"You can call me William."

"Okay."

"What sort of case are we speaking of, Mr. Malloy? Robbery? Extortion? Embezzlement?"

In a deep, melodramatic voice, Doyle growled, "Murder."

"This Timothy Chickman was murdered?"

"His name is Timothy Chapman, and, no, he wasn't murdered. But a murder did take place on his property. The victim's name is Marta Ramirez. She was an actress, but she was also working as a maid for Chapman. At this point, the evidence suggests someone, possibly more than one person, broke in through the window of Chapman's study and smashed their way into his safe. Marta came in, probably caught them in the act, and they bashed her head in with a crowbar, took the body out through the window, drove up to Lake Calhoun where they dumped her off."

William was nodding thoughtfully. "Any suspects?"

"There was a party going on at the time. Which means lots of people were there and a lot of noise to cover the breaking glass and smashing of the safe. It could have been anyone."

"What time did the murder take place?"

"Late last night, close to midnight," said Doyle.

"What has been done so far in the investigation?"

"Well, I went to Mr. Chapman's home to investigate what was only a robbery at first. At that point, we didn't know about the murder. I combed the study for clues."

"And what did you find?" asked William.

"A broken, empty safe and a rug concealing a whole lot of blood."

"Anything else? Hairs, fingerprints, a bloody crowbar perhaps?"

"The lab is researching the fingerprints we lifted. At this point there have only been prints for Timothy Chapman and the victim herself."

"What happened next?" asked William.

Doyle gave that a moment's thought. "I got a call from my boss. He told me Marta's body was found on the shore."

"Then what did you do?"

"I went to the morgue," said Doyle.

William knitted his brows. "Why did you go to the morgue? She wouldn't have been . . ."

"I realize that. I had to speak with Dr. Sylvester . . . about something."

William looked tired and impatient. "And then?"

"I went to the gas station for a notebook and some Mountain Dew. From there I went . . ."

"You're not a terribly good detective, are you Mr. Malloy?"

Doyle sighed. "Please, call me Doyle. And you might be right, but that doesn't mean I can't become a good one. This is my first real murder case. It's fair to say I could use some help. But what I don't need is constant criticism, so if you please . . ."

"Very well, Mr. Malloy . . . Doyle. Where did you go after the gas station?" asked William.

"The hospital. Her body was there. That's where the doctor, a *real* doctor, that is, explained the cause of death, which, in this case, was a crowbar blow to the head."

"And then?"

"That pretty much brings us up to speed," said Doyle.

"What time were you at the hospital?"

"Around 6:00."

"What have you done the past couple hours?" asked William.

Doyle shifted uncomfortably. "I was at the bar."

William arched an eyebrow. "We have a lot of work to do, indeed."

"Will you help me, William?"

"I'm not free, you know."

Doyle glanced around at the dentist office. "No, I suppose this fine up-scale detective office, especially in such a well-to-do neighborhood must cost you a pretty penny."

"This is a temporary residence, Mr. Malloy. Aside from the work I've done for Ron Sylvester, I've only been in the states a short while. Things aren't quite as lucrative here as they were back home."

"Then why are you here?" Doyle asked.

"Women," responded William.

Doyle nodded. "Yeah, we do have some hotties here."

"Only one in particular interests me—but that's neither here nor there, and I'd rather not discuss that situation this moment. Now, about the compensation . . ."

Doyle, considering his ridiculous amount of debt, decided to roll with things for a while, see how they turn out. "I'm willing to pay whatever your normal rates are."

William nodded, and just for a fleeting moment, Doyle saw a hint of avarice in his eyes. Times had been hard for the man. "Excellent, I'm glad to hear that. I require five hundred dollars up front, then fifty dollars an hour for each hour worked. Does that sound reasonable?"

Doyle knew the money was a problem, but he also knew he could be awfully clever. Doyle looked William up and down, from unkempt beard to sweatpants, then looked over William's shoulder at the untidy dentist office, supposedly where William was sleeping.

"I tell you what, Mr. Wright. I will pay you your hourly wage, plus five hundred cash, when and if you achieve results. I'm not throwing down five benjamins if you're nothing but a vagabond taking up residence in a dentist office. Does that sound reasonable?"

"Very good. Give me five minutes."

Doyle wondered if William Wright was as desperate for money as he was himself.

"Five minutes for what?" Doyle asked.

"To get dressed. We have work to do," said William enthusiastically.

"But it's nighttime."

"That didn't stop you from coming here. And that won't stop us from doing our work."

"But what if I want to sleep tonight?"

"You're a detective, Doyle. It's time you get used to not sleeping."

With that, Detective William Wright walked past the small reception area through the door where Doyle imagined dentists formally performed root canals and other painful operations.

This isn't going to be so painless, either, thought Doyle.

DOYLE WAS DRIVING HIS UNMARKED SQUAD with William in his passenger seat when Doyle's cell phone began to vibrate.

"Hello?"

"Hey, Doyle," said the voice on the phone.

"Oh, Amanda—how are you?" He realized he hadn't spoken with her since his last trip to the Rabbit Hole.

"I'm good," responded Amanda. "What are you doing tonight?"

"Apparently I'm working," said Doyle, glancing at William.

"Funny. Seriously, what are your plans?"

"No, really—I'm working tonight. I just got assigned to a really high-profile case," responded Doyle.

"No way! Get out of here!" said Amanda.

"Seriously. Are you familiar with Timothy Chapman?"

"Are you kidding me? Of course, I'm familiar with him. He's been in a ton of movies."

"Well, his place on Grand Avenue was broken into recently, and shortly after his maid was killed. I'm responsible for the investigation," said Doyle, with an air of pride.

"Really?" she asked. "You?"

"Don't act so surprised," said Doyle, deflated. "I've had big cases before."

"Oh, I know you have, Doyle, but nothing that's required you to work past 6:00 p.m. I'm impressed you're actually doing that."

"Gee, thanks," said Doyle. She was really starting to make him feel lousy.

"I don't mean it to sound bad," said Amanda. "It's just—I'm glad you're working hard, that's all. You're trying to better yourself."

"I've been doing okay," said Doyle.

"You have," agreed Amanda, "but let's be honest. Since your dad died, you've been pretty reclusive. You've been in your own little Doyle world. But now, taking on a big case, working hard and late hours, it's really a good sign . . ."

"Listen, Amanda—this isn't a good time. I really should . . ."

"No, it's okay—don't let me bother you. I was just going to ask if you wanted to do something after I get off work. You know, a movie or something. But don't worry about it. Just let me know when you have some time, okay?"

"Okay," said Doyle.

"Hey, do you need any help? I could really use some time away from the desk. I mean, if you needed me, I'm sure my boss wouldn't mind me tagging along with you."

Doyle looked over at William. "I'm afraid I already have a partner on this one."

"You do?"

William nodded.

"That's rather unusual, isn't it?" she asked.

"Well, this is a rather unusual case," stated Doyle.

"Okay," she said.

Doyle felt a pang of guilt. He knew he'd disappointed Amanda many times before, and he figured she must be rather used to it now. But still, he wondered if he was causing more harm than he thought. She really did deserve better.

"Next case, I promise I'll have you join me," added Doyle.

"You promise?" she asked.

"Absolutely." Doyle felt confident he could find a way to make that work, even if she played only a small role in helping him out.

"Oh, what's the count at?"

Doyle thought for a moment. What was she talking about? Then he knew, and smiled. "Sixty-three."

"You've swiped sixty-three pencils from Burnside this month? Hmm . . . that's roughly two a day. Not bad, but you'll have to step it up if you want to reach 100 before the month's out."

"Your five dollars will be mine—have no doubt about it." said Doyle. Despite his awkward feelings the past few moments, Amanda had managed to make him smile.

"Call me soon, okay?" said Amanda.

"I will. Promise."

"Bye, Doyle."

Doyle flipped his phone shut.

"Who was that?" asked William

"Some chick who's sweet on me," said Doyle.

"Of course," said William as he rolled his eyes.

Doyle parked his squad on the street near Timothy Chapman's driveway. The outside lights were on, as Doyle assumed they always were for security reasons, but no lights shone inside. This led Doyle to believe that either Mr. Chapman was not home or he was asleep.

"You know, Doyle, you could have parked a wee bit closer to the curb. You're nearly half a meter away."

"If I knew you were going to criticize me the entire way, I should have had you drive," Doyle said with a sigh.

"Ah, yes. But then, you're not paying me to be a chauffer, are you?"

"Jesus, you're worse than Simon Cowell."

"Please," responded William Wright with a playful smile. "He has nothing on me."

Doyle turned off the headlights and inspected his face in the rearview. His eyes were bloodshot. He just wasn't used to staying up this late, especially for the sake of work.

"Wait, Doyle. Before we go in, I need to know a little more about this actor," said William.

"I still can't believe you don't know who Timothy Chapman is," said Doyle. "He's more famous than Hugh Grant and Clive Owen combined."

"Oh, I highly doubt that. You must be exaggerating a bit."

"Well, let's see here," Doyle said, pulling out his notebook and flipping it open. "He's roughly sixty-five years old and has appeared in over 100 films."

"Did you say 100 films?" said William, seemingly impressed.

"He claims to have never turned down a part."

"I'd say he's probably telling the truth," said William.

"He's won nearly twenty awards for his acting and almost twice as many nominations total," said Doyle.

"Hollywood hands out awards like candy," replied William with a derisive sniff. "I could have an Oscar for all you know."

"He's appeared in some of the most critically acclaimed motion pictures of all time."

"Name some," said William.

"*Pulp Fiction*," said Doyle.

"Never saw it," responded William. "But didn't it have that *Staying Alive* chap in it?"

"You're familiar with John Travolta but not Timothy Chapman? How is that possible?" asked Doyle

"Please, everyone knows John Travolta," said William.

"Did you see the second Batman flick?" asked Doyle.

"I don't think so. Why? Was John Travolta in it?"

"No, Timothy Chapman! Forget Travolta already."

"Well, no, I didn't see it. I loathe superhero movies, at any rate," said William.

"Oh, Chapman works with Tim Burton a lot," said Doyle.

"Is he related to Richard Burton? I know him," said William.

"No, he's not. But trust me, Chapman is very well known, and he has the reputation of being quite an eccentric character," said Doyle.

"How so?" said William.

"Well, for example," said Doyle, "rumor has it that on the set of each movie, he likes to pick a day and tell everyone that it's his birthday. By the end of the day, his trailer is loaded with cakes, presents, and other goodies. Of course he films two to three films each year and does this for each film."

"That's actually rather brilliant," said William. "I mean, he can get away with it. So why not?"

"True," said Doyle. "He's also a feline enthusiast. He's written a number of articles on the matter, and has appeared in numerous Animal Planet specials and documentaries."

"He's a homosexual?" asked William.

"No, no—well, I guess I don't know about that, but I'm pretty sure he's not. He just really likes cats," said Doyle. "Oh, and he does have a daughter. That kinda nixes the whole gay thing."

"That doesn't mean anything," said William. "George Michael has a daughter."

"No, he doesn't," said Doyle.

"No, wait, that was George Harrison. Never mind," said William.

"I'm quite sure Chapman is straight. Like I said, he's just a bit eccentric."

"Is he married?"

"No, though he was. He's been divorced for the past seven years," said Doyle.

"Do you think he's an honest person?" asked William. "Do you think we'll have any trouble with him?"

Doyle thought for a moment. "As far as I know, he'll be on the level. But still, he has his eccentricities. I have no idea how trustworthy he is. I don't know him that well."

"Well, I guess we'll find out soon enough. Is that his house?" William pointed to the giant mansion in front of them, the same one Doyle had been in earlier that day.

"That's the one," said Doyle. "But what exactly are we doing here, William? It's late. What if Timothy Chapman is trying to sleep and he doesn't want us here?"

"If he wants the crime solved, he'll be happy to oblige us in any way possible. And if he doesn't want the crime solved, he'll put on the *façade* of being happy to oblige us. Either way, we should be welcomed with open arms and allowed to investigate."

"Okay, but you get to explain that to him if he turns out to be mister cranky pants."

William stared at Doyle.

"I'm just saying, is all. Let's go."

Doyle and William walked purposefully up the curving stone driveway. Although the lights were off inside the house, Doyle swore he saw movement behind a first-floor window.

There's a reason why Doyle never worked at night. It gave him the willies. He didn't trust shadows, and he was highly suspect of people who routinely spent time awake into the wee hours of the night.

William approached the door and knocked on it determinedly with one fist. Shortly after, the drapes behind the little window adjacent to the door spread open, exposing the face of Darren Brookes. He smiled uncomfortably when he saw Doyle and looked apprehensively at

William. The drapes closed again, and Doyle could hear fidgeting behind the door.

"Who might that be?" asked William. "Is that Timothy Chapman? Rather pale sort of fellow."

"That's the butler. Darren Brookes. Don't worry, he's a wuss."

"Right," said William, as the door opened, exposing the butler in his usual tux. *Perhaps he slept in it.*

"Detective Malloy, a pleasure to see you again," said Brookes. "And you are?"

"I'm Detective William Wright. I'm assisting Detective Malloy on the case involving the death of Marta Ramirez."

"Oh, I see. I appreciate you coming, but you see, tonight is really not a good night. Master begins shooting a new film tomorrow, and his rest is of the utmost importance."

"Which movie?" asked Doyle, excitedly.

"That's really of no importance," said William. "Please ignore my colleague. Sometimes his curiosity gets the best of him. But may I speak plainly, Mister eh—"

"Brookes, Darren Brookes, sir."

"Yes, Mr. Brookes. While I do appreciate your master's dedication to his craft, I assure you that our investigation here is just as important, if not more so, than his beauty sleep. The information we gather tonight may not wait until tomorrow, and it would be an utter shame to lose vital clues to apprehending the culprit of this ghastly deed. Mr. Brookes, you do understand the gravity of this situation, do you not?"

"Oh, yes sir. I didn't mean to imply—"

"And I'm certain your master would agree that, when a crime as scandalous as murder takes place on his premises, it's in his best interest to allow an investigation to resume as thoroughly and discreetly as possible. Wouldn't you agree to that, Mr. Books?"

"Brookes."

"Yes, Brookes, of course."

"Mr. Wright, I understand that you . . ."

"That's Detective Wright. I am a detective. You understand that, don't you Mr. Brookes?"

"Yes, I understand that, but . . ."

Suddenly, in the distance behind Brookes, a light appeared. A tiny, flickering flame. It grew brighter as it, or whoever was carrying it, came closer to the doorway.

"Darren," a voice said. "Are these boys giving you a hard time?"

In the doorway behind Darren Brookes stood Timothy Chapman. He was covered head-to-toe in pajamas, from his stocking feet to the little night cap on his head. He was holding a tiny candle on a flat dish. Doyle thought he looked like Ebenezer Scrooge.

"Master, these are the detectives working on Marta's case. Detective William Wright and Det—"

Doyle grabbed Timothy Chapman's free hand. "The name's Doyle. Doyle Malloy. It's a pleasure to meet you, Mr. Chapman. I'm a huge fan. I've seen all your movies and all of your SNL appearances. This is really terrific. I thought . . . Ow!"

William removed his foot from Doyle's shin and offered his hand to Timothy Chapman.

"Hello, sir. I apologize for my colleague's behavior, and I must also apologize as I'm unfamiliar with your work."

Brookes guffawed and turned away.

"I'm sorry, too, Mr. Chapman," said Doyle, still speaking a bit too fast. "I really don't mean to come off like an obsessed fan or anything, although I guess I'm somewhat borderline. This is just a special honor, getting an opportunity to track down the criminals who robbed you and murdered your maid."

"Again, I apologize for my colleague's antics," said William. "Regardless, Doyle and I are investigating the murder of Marta Ramirez, a murder that took place on this premises little more than twenty-four hours past, is that correct?"

"Yes, I understand this to be true. Murder—it's crazy. One minute someone's walking around, being a maid. The next, they're not walking around much at all because they're dead. It's crazy," said Chapman.

William and Doyle nodded in unison, William somewhat thoughtfully, and Doyle pretty much like a bobble-head dog.

Doyle was absolutely thrilled that Chapman spoke just like he did in the movies: as if punctuation didn't exist. It was as though Chapman owned his own language, and he'd pause his sentences where he damn well pleased.

"Where are my manners? Please, come inside. Investigate all you want. Darren, please bring these men some tea."

"Master, are you sure this is what you want?"

"Absolutely. And do me a favor, leave a message with Tim Burton's assistant that I'll be late to the shoot. Murder is afoot! Murder most foul! Would either of you care for lemon cheesecake? I have far too much left over from the other night. It would be a favor."

"No, but thank you," replied William. "Now if you don't mind . . ."

"I'd love a slice," blurted Doyle.

William stared at Doyle, giving him a look just short of a sad shake of the head.

Doyle shrugged.

"Excellent, a man who isn't afraid to say what he wants. I like that in a man. You said your name was Doyle?"

"Yes, sir."

"Wonderful name. Has anyone ever called you 'doily' by accident? I can imagine that would be embarrassing."

That sobered Doyle a bit. "Actually, that's never happened."

"But you'd agree it would be amusing if it had?"

"That goes without saying."

"You're damn right. Please, both of you follow me." Chapman turned around and began walking down the hall.

"What are you doing?" whispered William into Doyle's ear.

"Building a rapport with Mr. Chapman," Doyle whispered back. "Trust me, I work with celebrities all the time. You have to be sociable to get what you want."

"And in this instance you want cheesecake?"

"I'm merely accepting his gracious offer. I'm being friendly. You should try it sometime."

William sneered.

"Darren!" yelled Chapman. "Turn on all the lights! And don't forget to bring the tea and cheesecake."

Chapman led them into a dark room. Doyle could just make out a large couch in the thin candle light.

"Please, sit," said Chapman. The lights came on suddenly, illuminating a large, rather elegant living area.

It seemed to Doyle that everything in the room was grandiose and fluffy, from the couch to which he was shown, to the drapes, to the carpet beneath his feet. Larger than life, like the homeowner himself, but also quite comfortable if in a sufficating kind of way.

Chapman blew out the candle.

"Please, make yourselves at home. Tell me, is there any way at all I can assist you in this investigation?"

"Would you be willing to answer some questions?" asked William. "Perhaps give us a rundown of last night, as you remember it? Would you be willing to do this?"

"Absolutely," replied Chapman. "Ah, here comes Darren."

Darren Brookes set down a silver tray with a teapot, mugs, milk and sugar in their respective serving dishes, and a generous slice of lemon cheesecake for Doyle.

"If there isn't anything else, Master, may I retire?" Brookes stood with his hands folded in front of him. To Doyle, he looked like an obedient lapdog.

"I should be able to handle it from here, Darren, thank you. You must arise early tomorrow. I'll stay up awhile longer with my good friends William and Doily."

"Doyle," corrected Doyle apprehensively.

"I know, son," Chapman said with a smile. "I just thought Doily would be much funnier. As it turns out, it wasn't as funny as I thought it would be, but it was at least worth a try."

"I can't argue that," responded Doyle.

Darren Brookes was turning back around and heading towards the staircase when William called, "Mr. Brookes, why is it you have to awaken early tomorrow?" William had a notebook and pen in hand, ready to take notes.

"That's rather personal, Mr. Wright. I'd rather not say," said Brookes.

"You can tell him, Darren," said Chapman. "He's a detective. He probably already knows where you're going tomorrow by the way you have your shirt tucked, or how your hair is combed. These men—they're good! I can tell."

Brookes sighed. "I have an appointment with a doctor. I'd rather not go into it further than that. Okay?"

William jotted down a note. "Thank you, Mr. Brookes. Your cooperation is most appreciated."

"The professionalism! It's wonderful!" praised Chapman.

"Good night, Master," Brookes nodded toward his boss. "Gentlemen." Brookes turned away and disappeared up the flight of stairs.

"Though it may seem like a cliché," Chapman said, "good help is hard to find. Darren has done a wonderful job for me the past few years."

"Do you trust him?" asked William.

"Absolutely. He's given me nothing but the most loyal service. I've had butlers and maids in the past who have not been trustworthy, and I always found out immediately. But Darren has never given me any reason to suspect anything but loyalty."

"Where was he last night? Specifically, when the murder took place?"

Chapman seemed somewhat hurt by the question. "He was with me, nearly all night long. Or he was nearby, assisting my guests with drinks, and keeping the other workers busy."

"Was he ever out of your sight?"

"Perhaps now and then. Only for the briefest moments, I assure you. Darren isn't seriously a suspect in this case, is he?"

"Technically, Mr. Chapman, everyone that attended your gathering is a suspect until we get some further information."

"I see. Several policemen were here today investigating. I told them as much as I knew. Did they come up with anything?"

Doyle piped in. "That was my team of investigators. We only have preliminary findings at this point. We'll be compiling the facts and sifting through the physical evidence intensely over the next twenty-four hours. Until we have a solid lead, we have to be very skeptical of everyone involved."

"I understand," Chapman responded. "If your team already investigated and gathered the evidence, may I ask why you're here now?"

"They may have gathered plenty of evidence," said William. "But we're here to gather what fell through the cracks. We'll find out who attempted to steal from your safe, and most importantly, who killed Marta. But to do so, we must be as thorough as possible. Is that fair?"

"Absolutely," said Chapman. "Of course. I'll help in any way possible. You do realize that tea will not stay hot forever. You really should consider drinking it."

Doyle took a sip. "Wow, that's good!"

Chapman smiled. "I know, son. I know."

"Mr. Chapman," continued William. "Would you be willing to go over your story again with us? I know you relayed what you remembered to our investigative team earlier, but simply to make sure nothing is missed, would you mind?"

"Of course I will, detective. But on one condition."

"And that would be . . . ?" asked William, intrigued.

"You try a bite of that cheesecake. I'm telling you, it's fantastic! The cheesecake—it's incredible!"

"I'd be happy to," replied William, as he picked up a tiny silver fork off the tray.

"Wonderful," said Chapman. "Now, where would you like me to start?"

"The day of the crime, before the party started," said William.

Doyle wiped his mouth with a napkin and took out his notebook and pen.

"Take us through everything you did that day," added William, politely taking a bite of cheesecake. "From the time you woke up until the time you went to sleep."

8

"I REMEMBER WAKING UP FEELING very refreshed," Chapman began. "It was about six o'clock in the morning, which is when I usually wake up. I put on a robe and slippers, then I walked downstairs and through the kitchen. Marta was making a breakfast. She was a darned good cook. I understand she worked in a café not long before she began working for me.

"I took a step outside through the backdoor. I remember it was very hot, unusually hot for that early in the morning. And humid, which made it feel all the more uncomfortable. Usually I like to spend more time in my backyard, looking at the birds and trying to imitate their calls. It's a bit of a hobby of mine. But that morning I came in quickly and spoke with Marta while she cooked my omelet.

"She was excited about the audition I secured for her. It was just a very small part in the film I'll be in. Tim Burton's making a live-action version of *Puff the Magic Dragon*. Marta would have been playing a large metal robot named Rusty. It wasn't in the original script, but Tim thought it would be interesting to write in. Marta wouldn't have been seen at all, but she would have gotten her name in the credits. I think she would have liked that.

"After I had my breakfast, Marta cleaned up, and I began preparing for my day. Darren selected a suit for me to wear. After taking a brief shower and putting my face on, I directed Darren and Marta as to how I wanted them to ready the house for my gala."

7

"I apologize for interrupting," said William Wright. "But I don't believe we've yet established what sort of a gala this was. Was it some sort of birthday event?"

"Cats," responded Chapman with a satisfied smile.

"The musical, or . . ." inquired Doyle.

"Felines. House cats, to be more specific. I don't much care for those Siegfried and Roy type shenanigans. No one should ever own a pet that can eat them."

"Do you own any cats?" asked William.

"Yes, I have an orange tabby named Buloxi. He was given to me by Matthew Broderick in the early nineties. Great cat, but not a friend of strangers. Mostly keeps to himself."

"Any others?"

"I used to have many, but when Suzanne and I divorced a decade ago, she took most of the cats with her."

"That's sad," stated Doyle.

"Not that sad," responded Chapman. "She takes the cats, I keep the mansion. And I'll tell you one thing: I can always buy more cats." He bellowed with laughter.

Doyle and William looked at each other inquisitively.

"But seriously, I really do miss those cats," said Chapman, looking down at his folded hands.

"It seems I've taken you on a tangent, Mr. Chapman. Let's get back to the morning of the gala. You said you were directing Darren and Marta to prepare for the event. What specifically did you have them do?"

"Only little things. Supervising. For an event like this, I hired both a decorating company and a catering company, of course, to assist with the event. Darren and Marta were to remain close at hand to deal with any of the little matters that inevitably arise."

"What sort of matters were you expecting?" inquired William.

"Nothing in particular, but things always come up. For example, my darling daughter, Kimberly, and her supposed boyfriend, who had drunk far too much that night, vomited all over my new carpet. For such matters, it's wonderful to have someone like Marta close at hand."

"I couldn't help but notice you used the word 'supposed.' I take it that you're not terribly enamored with your daughter's boyfriend?" asked William.

"Chad," Chapman emphasized, "is *not* her boyfriend. He's some college fling that's probably over by this point. At least, one can hope."

"This cheesecake is astounding!" exclaimed Doyle.

Chapman and William looked at Doyle with curiosity.

"Off-topic. Right," said Doyle. "Mr. Chapman, this 'Chad' fellow. Is there any reason in particular that you don't like him, other than the fact that he's dating your daughter?"

"His jeans."

"Is he carrying some sort of terminal illness?" Doyle asked. "Were his parents circus freaks?"

"No, not his genes. His jeans. You know, denim. Blue."

"I'm not following you, sir," responded Doyle.

"Chad always wears these designer jeans—very tight fitting, an intricate faded pattern, and always a small tear around the buttocks region. A guy who wears jeans like that, he's not wearing them to impress himself. And he's certainly not trying to impress any girl's parents, I'll tell you that much."

"Still, the point is, you don't like that he's dating your daughter, is that right?" asked William.

"And his hair!" said Chapman with a sour look on his face.

"Let's move back, just a minute, if you don't mind," said William. "At what time did the gala begin?"

"I guess it would have been about 7:30."

"Did anything significant happen between the time you got dressed and the time the party began?"

"Well, Kimberly came over, which always makes my day. She's going to school at the University of Minnesota. I would have preferred a private college, any school she wanted, but she insisted on going to a public university. She said she just wanted to feel 'normal.' I guess I can't blame her—her childhood was far from normal."

"But at least she's close by, right? You can see her all the time," said Doyle.

"Very true, young man. Very true. I don't know if anything can make me smile quite so much as seeing my little baby girl."

"What did you do once she arrived?" asked William.

"We put up some banners that she had made along with her sorority sisters. Kimberly is very active in Pause for Paws, and she's the one who got me active in the organization a few years ago."

"What exactly is the purpose of the organization?" inquired William.

"Pause for Paws began with ads at the beginning of VHS video tapes. They would show various pets that were available from local shelters, and the idea was for viewers to 'pause' the tape and make a donation by calling the number on the screen. Hence, Pause for Paws. To be honest, I didn't much care for the whole video/phone call thing. But I do love a good pun."

"Who doesn't," agreed Doyle.

"Was the gala supporting this specific organization?" asked William.

"Yes, it was."

"You said that Pause for Paws began by placing ads on VHS tapes. What have they been doing lately?"

Chapman was silent for a moment. "That's a really good question," he said. "I'm not terribly sure."

"Any ideas at all?" prompted William.

"If I had to take a wild guess, probably something with the Internet and the World Wide Web or Free Cell or whatever people use on their computers."

"Could you clarify that?" asked William, a confused look on his face.

"Computers, Mr. Wright. Everything is computers nowadays, right? I've never used one myself. But everyone else in the world does."

"Why don't you use one, Mr. Chapman?" asked Doyle.

"I never wanted to catch one of those viruses I keep hearing about," Chapman explained.

"Makes sense," said Doyle with a mental roll of his eyes.

William gave Doyle an inquisitive look. Doyle shot back a glare as if to say, "Just go with it."

"Would your daughter know the current goings-on of Pause for Paws?"

"Well, probably. Though I can't imagine how it'd be relevant. Do you really think that organization could be affiliated with the robbery or the murder?"

"I really can't answer to that, Mr. Chapman. Anything's possible," said William.

"Especially when cats are involved," said Doyle. "They're very unpredictable creatures."

William darted eyes at Doyle.

"You've never owned a cat, have you William?" asked Doyle.

"Who licensed you?" asked William, holding a hand to his forehead as if he had a headache.

"Hey, not in front of the . . . uh, the uh . . . interrogatee? Is that a word?"

Timothy Chapman smiled warmly at them. "I find you both very amusing."

"Thank you," responded Doyle. "I find a sense of humor goes a long way. Of course, that's pretty rare in this profession."

"A sense of humor just isn't necessary in this line of work," retorted William. "In fact, it's much more of a distraction. Jokes don't get answers, only nonsense. Asking tough questions, now that gets the job done." William became silent, and scribbled down a note.

"Mr. Chapman, did you hear the one about the twelve-inch pianist?" Doyle asked.

Doyle and Chapman burst out laughing. William shook his head.

"Can we refocus, please?" asked William.

Doyle could have sworn William cracked a hint of a smile.

"Did you notice anything unusual from when your daughter arrived until when the murder took place?"

"Chad showed up drunk as a skunk, I had to change suits due to the large amount of vomit down the front, and there were dozens of people in my living room. I'd say it was a pretty normal evening."

"No one looked suspicious?" William asked.

"Only Tim Burton," Chapman said. "But he always looks that way."

Doyle laughed.

"Do you have any idea who would try to break into your safe?" William implored.

"I have no clue," responded Chapman.

"As far as you know, who had knowledge of the safe? After all, it was hidden behind a painting, correct?" William tapped his pen against the pad, ready to take down names.

"Well, the help always knows, so they can keep an extra careful watch over that area of the house. Marta and Darren knew of it, Kimberly knew of it, and I'm certain my ex-wife Suzanne remembers it. My lawyer knew of it. Arnold Schwarzenegger, too."

"Why would Arnie know about your safe?" asked Doyle.

"He once bet me five dollars that he could break into any safe with one fist."

"Did he do it?" asked Doyle.

"Yes," Chapman said with some asperity, "and it cost me hundreds of dollars to repair the safe." Then he grinned. "Of course, it cost Arnold several thousands of dollars to repair his hand. But all in all, it was still pretty amusing."

"Was this Chad aware of the safe?" asked William.

"Not that I know of, unless Kimberly told him. Which I pray to God she didn't. I've told her many times to keep all our family secrets safe from her boyfriends. That especially means Chad."

"You mentioned an incident that night with a drunken Chad. Could you go through that again, please? What exactly happened?" William continued jotting notes.

"I didn't exactly notice when he arrived. I was busy greeting my guests and making sure everything went smoothly."

"When did you notice him?" asked William.

"I didn't see him as much as I heard his voice rising above all the others. He was yelling jibber-jabber and slurring his words together. It was embarrassing."

"What kind of things was he saying?"

"He was saying lewd comments about various celebrities, some of whom were present at the party. He actually had the gall to say an off-color Pee-Wee joke right in front of Paul Reubens. The nerve!"

"And then?"

"And. . . hmm, that's funny." Timothy Chapman's eyes grew narrow.

"Funny ha-ha?" asked Doyle. "Did you remember the Pee-Wee joke? Was it the one where he—"

"No, it's not that. 'It always sucks when an actress dies.'" Chapman was lost in thought.

"Well, that's true. That's why we're investigating, Mr. Chapman," Doyle said.

"No, no—that's what Chad said. At the party, right before it happened. 'It always sucks when an actress dies.' Then he vomited on me, and then Marta escorted him out. No, that's not right—I asked Marta to escort him out, but Kimberly did instead. Marta cleaned up the mess, and I went upstairs to change my suit. That's the last time I saw her alive."

Doyle and William looked at each other.

"Mr. Chapman, would Chad have any reason to murder Marta?" William was scribbling furiously in his notebook.

"I don't know. I just don't know."

There was a rather uncomfortable pause in the conversation.

"If you don't mind gentlemen, I have an early morning tomorrow. I'd best get some rest."

William immediately stood up. "May we call you, sir, if we have further questions regarding this?"

"Absolutely Mr. Wright. I'll help in any way possible. I dearly miss Marta, and I want whoever did this to her to get what's coming to them."

"We understand. Have a good night, Mr. Chapman. Come along, Doyle."

The detectives headed toward the front door.

"Just one more thing, Mr. Chapman," said Doyle.

"Yes, Detective Malloy."

"What did you keep in your safe?"

"Nothing."

Both Doyle and William turned back to Mr. Chapman. Doyle said, "Nothing?"

"Nothing."

"Then why have a safe?"

"A safe can do much more than just hold things, Detective Malloy."

Doyle tilted his head in confusion.

"Good night, detectives."

9

A s DOYLE DROVE WILLIAM BACK to his peculiar office and temporary residence, he couldn't help feel both elated at having met one of Hollywood's greatest icons, as well as an overwhelming pressure to crack the case.

"Thanks for your help tonight, William. You were really awesome in there."

"I appreciate that Doyle, but I really didn't do anything extraordinary. I asked some basic questions and got some basic answers."

"You should learn how to take a compliment. It might make you a little more personable."

William began to smile, then held it back.

Doyle looked at William for a moment.

"You seem a little . . . stuck."

William lifted his glasses and rubbed his eyes. "Sorry, Doyle. I was just thinking about our conversation with Mr. Chapman. There's something itching my brain, but I cannot for the life of me figure out what it is."

"Perhaps it's a tumor."

Doyle was afraid William had taken him seriously, until William startled him with a thunderous belly laugh.

"I was starting to wonder if you were incapable of laughing. I'm glad to see I was wrong on that."

William nearly had tears escaping his eyes. "You're in the wrong business, my friend."

"That's funny. I hear that on a daily basis from Chief Burnside."

"Your boss?" William was still chuckling.

"If you want to be technical."

"I have a feeling I'll get along with him quite well."

"I sure hope not. I don't want you taking my job."

William continued laughing. "Please—I could do much better than that!"

"Thanks," said Doyle, turning his head with a scowl.

William eased up and caught his breath. "Oh, sorry, Doyle, I didn't mean it like that. I just mean I wouldn't work in law enforcement. I've done it before, and I won't do it again."

Doyle realized it was almost midnight as he parked along the curb near William's place.

"William, can I ask you a question?"

"Sure thing, Doyle."

"Earlier, you said you came to America because of a woman. What did you mean by that?"

William sighed. "It's not a terribly good story."

"Please, I'm intrigued. What lies beneath this gruff exterior?" Doyle asked jokingly.

"All right, Doyle. I'll give you a few seedy details from my past, but I don't want you thinking any less of me. You trust in my abilities, yes?"

"Sure I do," said Doyle. "From what I've seen so far, you're the most gifted detective I've met."

William briefly smiled. "Thanks, Doyle. I appreciate that."

"Although I should point out that I haven't worked with many private detectives in the past, so I don't have much to compare you to," said Doyle, with a smirk.

"Well, thanks just the same," said William, not letting a compliment go to waste.

Doyle said, "Okay, with all that build-up, whatever you have to say better be good."

"I'll try my best to keep you entertained," replied William. "I recall mentioning that I worked for Scotland Yard. Well, I didn't just work for them—I was the highest paid detective on staff. I had an absolutely flawless record. There wasn't a case I couldn't crack. Some of the boys used to say, 'Detective Wright can never be wrong.' I was doing so well, in fact, that I had the honor of courting the daughter of the Minister of Defense. She was an actress, plays and performance pieces mostly. Her name was Eva—and I'll tell you, Doyle, that she was the absolute world to me . . . *is* the absolute world to me, in fact, even though she's no longer with me. For now."

"What happened?" asked Doyle.

"Let me point out first that when we began dating, our relationship was filled with romance. Expensive dinners at fancy restaurants, wine by the fireplace at home, intimate conversations at all hours of the night."

"Sounds nice," said Doyle. "The closest I've come to that is when I took my mom to the Olive Garden."

William grunted. "It was nice," he agreed. "But as the months passed, I became more engaged in my work. I simply had to. I couldn't just let me job slip away from me."

"Oh, boy," said Doyle.

"And as I began to spend more hours at work, the romantic dinners occurred less often, our conversations decreased, and the fireplace was no longer being lit."

"How metaphorical," said Doyle.

"Yes, well, as time went by, it Eva was spending less time with me. I was so wrapped up in my work. She wasn't even bothering to come home some nights. It seemed altogether probable that she was having an affair."

"Oh, no," said Doyle.

"So, on one particular Friday night, I came home from work and Eva wasn't there. Friday night had usually been our night together, even when I got particularly busy. I tried calling her cell phone, but she didn't answer. So, I helped myself to a couple drinks, and waited around. As the minutes ticked by, I became agitated, and increasingly intoxicated. I called in a favor at work—I asked one of my boys in field tech to track any calls from her cell phone. As it turned out, she had made one outbound call from her cell phone earlier that evening, and it wasn't to me. The location of the call came from a restaurant, the very restaurant I took her to on our first date, in fact."

"Not good," said Doyle.

"After a couple more drinks, I drove straight to the restaurant. I should point out that I was not in a very good state of mind," William said.

"I figured that," said Doyle.

"I walk into the restaurant, and immediately I see Eva. She was with another man. He was older, even balding a bit. I couldn't imagine why she was with him instead of me."

"What did you do?"

"I approached the table and when Eva saw me, she seemed shocked. I figured she was surprised that I caught her in the act."

"What did you say to her?"

"I didn't say anything," responded William. "I just grabbed the man by his ugly bald head and shoved it face first into his bowl of soup."

Doyle chuckled. "That couldn't have gone well. Then what happened?"

"His eyes were so full of minestrone that he didn't see me punch him in the face."

"You didn't!" said Doyle. "In the middle of the restaurant?"

"Well, it wasn't really the middle—it was closer to the window. But close enough."

"Damn, William—you sure showed him!" Doyle slapped William on the shoulder. "Good job!"

"Don't start congratulating me until you hear the rest. The man wasn't a secret lover—it was her uncle Ricardo visiting from Sicily."

Doyle grimaced. "Ouch."

"Yeah, exactly. Apparently she had told me about her dinner plans the previous evening, but I was too busy researching my case to listen to her."

"Not good," said Doyle. "And you said that Eva's father was the Minister of Defense. So her uncle was his brother?"

Again, William sighed. "Exactly correct. I was jailed five days for assault and battery."

"Did you lose your job?"

"Not right away. But I may as well have. Eva left me. She flew to Los Angeles to try to get some acting gigs in American films. When that didn't work out, she moved to Minneapolis. Without me holding her back in London, she was free to do what she wanted. Although I would have followed her anywhere if that's what she wanted."

"So after she left, what did you do?"

"I drank more. I began requesting too many favors from my colleagues, trying to track Eva down. I was also useless as a detective. My head and heart just weren't in it. Eventually I was fired. It didn't matter —I had already lost all respect from my colleagues. And as for Eva, I still don't know where she is exactly, only that she's somewhere in this city. She may have changed her name."

"William—are you a stalker?" asked Doyle, seriously.

"No, I'm not a stalker. I just want to see her again and make things right. She's just made that awfully difficult."

"But, still, William, it comes off as a little creepy. You do realize that, right?"

William hesitantly nodded. "Yes, I suppose it does. But what else am I to do? I want to be with her."

"You could just let her go. Plenty more fish in the sea."

William shook his head. "Not like her."

"So, you come out to Minneapolis, start up your own detective agency inside an abandoned dentistry office in a dangerous part of town, and use your spare time trying to stalk—err, track down your old flame?"

"That's about right," said William.

Doyle nodded. "Okay, then."

"Do you think less of me?" asked William.

"I wouldn't say that. It explains a lot, actually."

William didn't say anything.

"Don't worry about it," said Doyle. "We both have our quirks."

"Thanks, Doyle."

"No problemo. Why don't you get some sleep . . . it's getting late."

"I don't think that will happen. I have a lot of research to do—I'll have to consult my resources."

"Sure thing, Giles."

William glanced at Doyle inquisitively.

"Oh, don't tell me you've never seen Buffy, the Vampire Slayer?" Doyle asked, shocked.

"We didn't have Buffy in England. We had Dr. Who."

"That's no excuse," murmured Doyle.

"Go on home, Doyle. I'll contact you in the morning." William opened the passenger door and stepped out.

"Thanks again for the help, William. I really appreciate it."

"You might want to wait until our investigation is done before you thank me."

"Why do you say that?"

"Because we have a lot of work ahead of us, and you haven't even seen my bill yet. Have a pleasant evening, Doyle. I'll see you shortly."

"Good night."

William walked the few steps up to his dental-office-turned-investigation headquarters.

As William disappeared behind the door, Doyle felt a pang of guilt. He knew he couldn't afford to pay William, not unless a miracle happened. William would become one more of the many, many people and/or companies that Doyle owed money. Doyle thought it would have been much easier if William was a much more successful detective who didn't need the money or more of an asshole. But, truth was, Doyle was beginning to like William. And, looking at the graffitied sign of the dentist office, Doyle knew William needed the money too.

Doyle drove off into the night, feeling exhausted. He wondered if he'd ever worked so many hours in a single day before.

"Nope," he whispered to himself. "Definitely not."

10

Despite the overwhelming day he'd been through and the exhaustion he felt, Doyle was surprised to discover he couldn't get to sleep. He lay in his bed for a long time, thoughts of the robbery, the subsequent murder, the people involved, potential motives, and everything else constantly popping into his mind. He would have far preferred to get at least a little much needed rest.

Maybe this is how real detectives get it done, he thought. They work, even when they're sleeping.

Doyle didn't like the feeling he was getting from the case. Maybe it would all turn out well or end in complete disaster—either way, Doyle didn't like the feeling of being a fish out of water. Had Burnside been wrong to assign this case to him? It's one thing to try to skate by in one's job and do the minimal work necessary to get by, but what if someone else dies, or the murderer gets away scot-free due to poor judgment or lack of effort on Doyle's part? Doyle couldn't comprehend how he would feel if such a thing happened.

Without expecting it, he began to think of his father. That was hard for him to do—his father hadn't been gone for that long. The fond memories of him were still fresh in his mind, but so was the pain of his loss. As Doyle began drifting uneasily into sleep, he remembered a particularly fond experience at the Heights Theater, only a matter of months before his father passed away. They had gone to a movie together a couple times a month since Doyle was a teenager. Always a classic film, preferably noir—whatever film the Heights happened to be showcasing. On one particular Friday, Doyle joined his father for *Double Indemnity*, one of his father's favorites. The movie was excellent, and Doyle and Senior Detective Harry Malloy left the theater in high spirits. They stopped off for a drink at Martiniapolis, not realizing they were walking directly into a domestic dispute. A man, older, maybe in his fifties, was yelling at his wife while slamming his fist on the bar. His speech was slurred, going on about how his wife was sleeping around town, probably even with the bartender. Meanwhile, the wife, also older but far more sober, repeatedly told him to calm down and that he was being ridiculous.

Doyle and his father sat at the bar near this couple. Doyle's father stared at the drunk with a look of pure contempt.

"I bet you eben slep wih her," said the man. "Slep wih my fuggin bitch wife."

"No, I haven't," Harry Malloy said.

"Eberyone slep wih her," he said. His arm flew out, striking his wife in the chest. She spilled onto the floor, crying out in surprise and most likely pain.

Doyle hadn't known how to react. He hadn't had much experience in this, although he knew his father had plenty of it in his many years of law enforcement service.

"We should call the police," Doyle said.

"We *are* the police," said Harry Malloy as he turned slightly, then spun and punched the man directly in the nose. The drunk hit the floor next to his wife, blood spurting like a fountain. The man cried out.

"We're not on duty," Doyle whispered to his father.

"We punched in five minutes ago," he responded. "Remember, you're always on call."

His father pulled a pair of handcuffs out of his jacket. Doyle never knew he kept handcuffs on his person when he was off duty.

"Put these on him," his father said. "I'll call Jimmy for a car."

Then Harry Malloy offered his hand to the wife, who was crying on the floor next to her bleeding husband.

"Do you need a ride home?" he asked.

The woman shook her head. "I have a car outside. But he has the keys." She pointed at her husband, but did not make eye contact.

"Do you have the car keys?" Harry Malloy asked the drunk.

"Fugg you," he responded.

Doyle's father popped the man in the nose a second time, causing a nasty cracking sound. The man's head hit the floor.

"Grab his keys," said Harry Malloy to Doyle.

Hesitantly, Doyle said, "Okay."

Doyle reached in the drunk man's pockets, which Doyle realized were somewhat moist from urine, and grabbed the keys. He handed them to the woman.

"Thank you," she said. Doyle's father helped her stand.

"He'll be in jail tonight, so you'll be safe for now. You may want to consider making some life choices," said Doyle's father.

She nodded, moving slowly towards the exit, being very careful to not look at her husband. She walked as though she were in a dream.

Doyle realized he felt much like that woman, not really knowing who he was or what he was doing there, just moving along listlessly as things happened. But it was in this moment when he also realized who he wanted to be. Doyle wanted the courage and the moral sense to pop a bad guy in the face if he knew it was the right thing to do.

As the memory faded into a dream, Doyle saw his father's hand punching the drunk's face over and over again. Soon this morphed into Amanda's breasts slapping Doyle in his face over and over again. Before long, Doyle was in much needed, very pleasant deep sleep.

DOYLE WOKE UP TO A LOUD KNOCKING on his apartment door. At first he thought he had overslept, or that the landlady had come to collect the rent that was now a few days past due.

Then he realized it was 3:30 a.m. and his apartment was pitch black.

He started to fear the worst—that his little sister was involved in a motor vehicle accident, or his grandmother had kicked off in North Dakota, or that he was under arrest for illegally downloading music. Or that friggin' creditor—the man in the white suit. *They can't serve papers this time of night, can they?*

These thoughts raced through his mind as he stumbled through his dark apartment, his left leg bumping into the edge of the sofa, his right shoulder crashing into a wall. When he finally got to the door, Doyle wasn't sure if he was relieved or pissed to see William through the peephole.

Doyle hesitated for a moment, wondering if it was worth opening the door or if he would be better off going back to bed. In the end, curiosity got the best of him, and he opened the door.

"William, what the hell are you doing here? It's the middle of the night!"

"I'm sorry, Doyle. But I've been doing some document searching online, and I've uncovered some information I think will help us."

"Couldn't it wait until the morning, for God's sake?"

William stared at Doyle with dismay and contempt. "Doyle, I know you haven't had much experience in these sort of situations, but this is a murder investigation. Time is of the essence. If we don't figure out who the murderer is, and fast, then the culprit may get away, rendering our entire investigation absolutely futile. Now are you going to let me in, or do I need to do this entire investigation myself?"

"Wait a minute—I never told you where I live. How did you find my apartment?"

William pointed to himself and mouthed the letters, "P.I."

Doyle grunted and let William in.

"So, tell me William, what do you have that's so utterly important that you wake me up from a very pleasant dream, which happened to include all three Charlie's Angels I might add, at 3:30 in the morning, which is a time that, up until now, I didn't even know existed? Can you answer that for me please?"

"In this dream, were you Bosley or Charlie?" inquired William with a smile.

"Bosley, of course. If I was Charlie, it would have been phone sex, and I can do that in real life. Now, what the hell do you got?"

William lit up with delight. "Chad Wilkinson. Boyfriend of Kimberly Chapman. Quite a sordid past. Trouble all throughout his school years. Few friends. It seems his opinionated personality got in the way of his relationships. He met Kimberly during his freshman year at the University of Minnesota. This was before he was kicked out after breaking into the film department's supply room. Apparently he stole equipment to make a short documentary about animal cruelty for PETA."

"Hope it was worth it—throwing away his academic career to make a film." Doyle went into his kitchen to make a pot of coffee.

"Apparently not. PETA chose not to use the film due to its poor direction, lack of cohesiveness, and completely unfounded allegations"

Doyle turned around. "The film was so bad, PETA wouldn't use it? That's saying something. What were the allegations?"

"That the U.S. government is placing bombs inside wiener dogs and using them as weapons in Iraq."

Doyle stood silent for a moment. "I'm not terribly sure how to respond to that."

"Nor was I," added William. "I saw the video. Fortunately he blew up donkey-shaped piñatas instead of wiener dogs. Obviously he shot the film on a beach somewhere instead of Iraq, as a lake was clearly visible in the background. Also, I'm pretty sure I saw a volleyball net."

"Okay," said Doyle, taking a sip of his coffee. "So what happened to Chad after he was kicked out of the U of M?"

"Well, frankly," said William, "Chad has done little else beyond mingle in downtown clubs."

"What do you suppose Kimberly sees in him?"

"That's a good question. I imagine they share similar political opinions, and perhaps he has an exceptional sense of humor." William sipped his coffee.

"With the wiener-dog video, I'd say that's a big 'yes.'"

"There's more," added William. "He's been accused of theft in the past. From a major celebrity's residence, no less."

"Whose residence?"

"Elizabeth Taylor. Chad was accused of stealing her Klimpt."

"That's disgusting," said Doyle.

William rolled his eyes. "It's a painting not a body part, and the case was dropped since there was no evidence against him, only suspicious circumstances."

"But, wait, Elizabeth Taylor doesn't have a residence in Minnesota, does she?" asked Doyle.

"No. This was actually in Los Angeles. Chad has family spread out across the country, and he tends to move around. That's the frightening part. For all we know, he could be developing a nation-wide criminal network."

"Well," Doyle said, "I somehow doubt he's that 'advanced' as a criminal. But it's interesting how similar the circumstances are. He just happened to be at a residence where a theft took place, he was intoxicated and caused a disturbance shortly beforehand, and if Kimberly told him about the safe, he would have been one of the few who knew its whereabouts."

"True, Doyle, true. But unfortunately, that's not enough to go on. We need evidence."

"Well, let's drive over to Chad's home and see what his alibi is."

"That's a terrific idea, Doyle," said William.

Doyle grinned happily at the reenforcement.

". . . if you want to be the absolute worst detective known to mankind. Sweet heavens, Doyle, you cannot just walk up to the suspect and ask him what his alibi is!"

The smile fell hard. "Why not? Then we can find out of he's lying."

"We find out if he's lying by asking everyone he knows *first*. Kimberly, the cab driver from the night in question, his roommate, his mother, gas stations and pizza joints, the used-clothes place he gets his duds—absolutely anyone who might know where he was every minute around the time of the theft and murder. *Then*, we get his alibi. And, if we're lucky, we'll, as you Americans like to phrase it, 'catch him with his pants down.'"

"I knew I hired you for a reason."

William smiled.

A jaw-cracking yawn burst out of Doyle, and he made no attempt to hide it. "If I pay you more, will you let me go back to sleep?"

"Absolutely not. Get dressed. We have work to do."

"What could we possibly do at this hour? We can't interview anyone. They'll be asleep. Besides, it's against police protocol to conduct interviews in the middle of the night."

"Are you certain of that, Doyle?"

Doyle hesitated. "Umm . . . not entirely. But there's gotta be some kind of law against it. Right?"

"While this should really be your area of expertise, Doyle, I do know a little about the Minneapolis police code of conduct. It's true, police cannot harass people into providing information. Of course, 'harass' is a rather loose term, and, as far as the courts are concerned, it means that the police officer cannot severely beat a potential informant. However, if you are concerned about your job and all-around well-being, it may be better for us to not waken people in the middle of the night to get information."

"Well, thank God we're in agreement on that."

"Absolutely. Fortunately, I know for a fact that Chad's roommate, Kyle Gordon, works the night shift at the McDonald's off of Twenty-Second Street and Washington. We need to go ask *him* some questions."

Doyle put down his mug. "First of all, William, how do you know Chad even has a roommate, and . . . and how did you possibly find out he works at this particular McDonald's on the graveyard shift?"

"I'm glad you asked," responded William. "Everything I learned tonight was perfectly laid out on Chad's MySpace blog. Terrific website, really. People completely expose their life stories, including all the incriminating information any good detective could want. It makes my job so much easier."

"Just when I think I have you figured out, you surprise me again."

William raised his mug. "Cheers."

"Fine. I'll get dressed. But I have one request."

"What would that be, Doyle?" asked William.

"You have to buy me an Egg McMuffin."

"If that'll make you happy, my young apprentice."

"I'm not your apprentice, William. Technically, I'm your boss."

William chuckled. "And you never cease to make me laugh. Get dressed. Let's go."

11

SO WHAT'S THE NAME OF THIS PUNK?" asked Doyle, still attempting to wipe the last of the sleep out of his eyes. William drove. He didn't look the least bit sleepy.

"Kyle Gordon," said William. "And the label 'punk' is actually quite accurate in this circumstance. I'm not joking, Doyle, when I say this young man has more metal in his face than the Liberty Bell."

"With or without the crack?" Then Doyle frowned, grumpy and irritated. "And stop making references to American things. It's not right. Say 'Big Ben' next time. It'd be much more British of you."

William chuckled. "I see. Would you like me only to speak in clichés and stereotypes from now on? Is that it? 'Perhaps some more tea and crumpets, govnuh?' That sort of thing? Well, forget it, Doyle. I'll speak however I damn well please. What? What is so funny?"

Doyle could get almost girl-giddy when he was really tired. He attempted to stifle his laughter. "The way you're getting worked up, William. It just so . . . British."

"Wonderful. I'm so glad I'm amusing you. Now do you have any other questions before we pull in and interrogate Mr. Gordon?"

"What are you going to ask him?" inquired Doyle.

"The obvious questions, of course," said William. "'How well do you know your roommate?' 'Where was he Friday evening?' 'Does he seem the violent sort?' 'Do you know if he robbed a supposedly empty safe and murdered a sweet, young Hispanic actress?' 'Can I have fries with that?'"

"Don't you think we'd be a little too obvious if we ask him all these direct questions?" asked Doyle. "I mean, we don't want him to tip off Chad that we're investigating him, do we?"

"That may be true, Doyle, but we still have to ask the questions, or else we don't get anywhere. Why?"

"Well, you seemed really against asking Chad direct questions."

"If we ask everyone indirect questions, we'll never solve this. Do you have a better plan, perhaps?" asked William.

"I think I might. How far are we from this McDonald's?"

"Only a few more blocks."

"Pull into that gas station. I have to pick up a couple things."

"What do you have planned?" asked William.

"You'll see." Doyle grinned.

"Good Lord," said William. "Doyle, what the hell are you doing?"

Doyle walked out of the gas station, wearing a backwards base-ball cap, sunglasses, and what William could only guess were bicycle chains hanging from his jeans, which were now pulled down several inches, exposing Doyle's striped undershorts.

"'Sup, yo. C'mon, Pops, move over up in dat. Dee-to-the-Oyle is driving this mo-fo."

"Doyle, I find you extremely disturbing. Perhaps you'd best check yourself into a mental institution as fast as humanly possible. Honestly, Doyle, what are you doing?"

"Simple, William. I'm going to get the information we need with-out blowing our cover. Now move over. I need to drive in order for this to work."

"I really hope you know what you're doing."

Doyle smiled. "Malloy in the hizzouse!"

AS DOYLE PULLED THE CAR into the drive-thru, he whispered to William, "Pretend like you're sleeping, okay?"

"Sure, Doyle, whatever you'd like me to do."

An unenthusiastic voice spoke out of the intercom, "Can I take your order please?" It sounded like more of a statement than a question.

"Yeah, man, I'd like two Big Macs, an order of fries . . . is it too early for Egg McMuffins?"

"We don't serve breakfast till six."

"Ahh, snap. I'll just take the Big Macs 'n' fries, bro."

"Please pull around."

Doyle drove past the intercom and whispered to William, "Snore."

"What?"

"Snore. You know, be authentic. We're undercover, for godsake."

"I don't understand why you—"

"Shh."

As Doyle approached the window, a kid wearing a polyester uniform was putting napkins in a bag. Doyle noticed the nametag read "Kyle." *Gotcha*, thought Doyle.

Kyle opened the window. "That'll be $5.50."

Doyle handed over a twenty. "Whoa, dude, aren't you Chad's roommate?" asked Doyle.

"Oh, yeah. Have I seen you before?" asked Kyle.

"I thought I recognized you from a party a few months back," said Doyle.

William let out an incredibly loud snore. Both Doyle and Kyle turned their heads to look at him.

"What's with the old guy?" asked Kyle.

"That's my drunk-ass Pops," said Doyle. "Just picked him up at the liquor store before the cops got there. I swear, he takes one sip and starts throwing shit and pissing himself."

"Bummer," said Kyle.

"So, where's Chad been? He was supposed to come to my party Friday night. Where was he?"

"Oh, man, he didn't get home till way late. I mean, later than usual anyway. I think he was at some other party. He was pretty freaked out when he got home."

"Yeah? Dude, why was he freaked?"

"I think his lady dumped him or something. He was pretty pissed about it."

"Really? Oh, man. That's harsh. I heard her dad was some rich dude," said Doyle, prodding to the best of his ability.

"Was he?" said Kyle. "I never heard that."

Doyle shrugged. "Oh, I could be wrong," said Doyle. "Maybe it was someone else I was thinking of."

"Could be."

"Hey, Kyle, is it true that Chad is a huge Timothy Chapman fan? It's just a rumor I heard."

"Isn't that the slide-whistle dude from Saturday Night Live? That's shit's fuckin' funny. 'I gotta have more slide whistle.' Funny shit."

Doyle waited. "Chad? No, I don't think so. I mean, he doesn't have any of his DVDs or shit. I never heard him mention it. Unless it's some weird, repressed homo-type thing."

"I guess you never know with Chad, right, dude?" asked Doyle.

"You got that right, man. Chad's the weirdest guy I know. Oh, here's your food, by the way, and your change."

William snored again.

"Shut up, old man," said Doyle. "Dads . . . what can ya do, right?"

"Right. Well, catcha later . . . what's your name, again?"

"Do—avid. I mean, Dave. Just call me Dave."

"Okay . . . Dave." Kyle looked at him suspiciously.

"Later, dude. Keep it real. I'm outty."

Doyle sped away and turned onto the freeway.

"Excellent job, Doyle, but you very nearly blew it," said William.

"*I* nearly blew it? What about those ridiculous snores?"

"You told me to be authentic! I was acting."

"Well, bravo, Olivier. But, hey, at least we have more information to go on. I'd say it was a rather big success for us," said Doyle.

"I'll agree with you on that, Doyle. Actually, I'm almost impressed. We did uncover some intriguing information. We now know that Chad has not been mentioning Timothy Chapman, which may suggest he's trying to keep it a secret."

"Yeah, I guess he was. I wonder why," said Doyle. "But it's not proof of anything."

"No,"

"But maybe potentially important."

"Precisely," said William. "Also, we know that, supposedly, his girlfriend broke up with him. This could be either Kimberly Chapman or some other girl. We won't know until we question Kimberly."

"Or," said Doyle. "The break-up was just an excuse for being 'freaked out' as Kyle put it. He could have been freaked out by the theft and murder he'd committed, not by a break-up."

"Actually, both could be possible. It might just so happen that Chad committed acts of theft and murder and broke up with Kimberly all within the same night. But what occurred when? What came first? And who initiated the break up? Did he break up with her just before committing the crimes? Did she break up with him?"

"Or did she break up with him because she found out about the crimes?" asked Doyle.

"It's an intriguing theory, but at this point we don't know enough about Kimberly to make a judgment. It sounds like she's awfully close to her father. I'd imagine if she found out anything about the theft or murder, she'd have told dear old dad immediately."

"Unless," said Doyle, "she was already so embarrassed by Chad that she wouldn't want to admit to her father that she was dating a thief and a murderer. One that she had invited into their home, no less. In fact, she may feel guilty about the whole thing. And she might be afraid of Chad. She could be too scared to go to either her father or the police."

"Of course, that all presupposes she knows anything about Chad's links to the crimes, if in fact he *has* links to the crimes. You must remember, Doyle, that right now we're only working on theories. Chad could be totally innocent. We need to get some solid evidence."

"Well, I have a wonderful theory. Let's say I drive back to my apartment. I go upstairs, crawl into bed, and then I sleep for several hours. Then, you come back and pick me up, let's say noon-ish, and we'll drive to police headquarters, and we'll find out what evidence has been uncovered from the scene by our field investigators."

"Fascinating theory, Doyle. We'll go with it for now. But remember that theories can always be refuted."

"Let's hope not," said Doyle.

Several minutes later, after parking the car, Doyle walked upstairs and tested his theory. Happily.

12

ONCE AGAIN, DOYLE AWOKE TO THE SOUND of knocking on his door. He opened his eyes just enough to see that light was coming in through his bedroom window, so he had slept, at least for a few hours.

Doyle sat up in bed and stretched. The knocking persisted. He yawned expansively and scratched his sides. He looked to his nightstand. The clock read 7:30. The knocking was growing more rapid.

"I'm coming, William," mumbled Doyle. "Couldn't have given me a couple more hours, could ya?" Doyle thought about getting dressed, but then decided his door might not stand it if William continued much longer. Doyle shuffled lazily through his living room in his boxer shorts and then opened the door.

"I told you William, I need—" Doyle stopped. It wasn't William on the stoop. It was, in fact, a pretty brunette with striking yet delicate features, features somewhat pulled into a look of surprise and shock. He blinked, then flushed bright red and bit his tongue. He jumped behind the door to conceal his nakedness. "I'm so sorry, I thought you were someone else. I didn't realize, I mean, I . . . who are you?"

The young woman wore a white summer dress. A brown leather bookbag was strapped across her shoulder. After noticing this, and studying her face, Doyle realized who it must be.

"You're Kimberly Chapman, aren't you?"

"Yes, I am. Are you . . . are you Detective Malloy?" she asked. She looked concerned.

"Yes, but please, call me Doyle."

"Okay, Doyle."

They stood for a moment in awkward silence.

"I'm sorry, would you like to come in?" asked Doyle.

Her face had reddened along her delicate cheeks. "Well, um, could you put some pants on first?" asked Kimberly. She kept her eyes diverted from Doyle's direction.

"Oh, yes, of course. I'm so sorry. I wasn't expecting anyone, you see, and . . ."

"It sounded like you were expecting a 'William.' Do you normally answer the door in your underwear for William?"

Doyle was thinking of how to respond when Kimberly said, "I'm sorry, that was rude of me. Here I come, early in the morning, banging on the door of someone I've never met, and then I start making implications on his sex life."

"No, no, no—there is no sex involved, I assure you," said Doyle.

"That's unfortunate," said Kimberly, and her mouth hinted at a smile.

Doyle stood silent for a moment, his mind seemingly unable to work or formulate even the rudiments of a cogent plan. Then he pulled himself together. "I'm going to close this door for a minute, Miss Chapman. When I come back, I'll be fully clothed. I promise. Then I'll open the door, and we can start fresh."

"Okay," she said.

Doyle eased the door soundlessly into its frame, then rushed at break-neck speed to his bedroom, threw on a pair of pants (which had to be peeled off and put on again with the fly in the front) and a dress shirt (which had to be buttoned twice as the holes ran out before the buttons on the first try), and, giving up the idea of finding matching socks, stuffed his feet into slippers. Then he ran to the bathroom, dragged a comb through his tangled bed-head hair, considered shaving but gave it up as a bad and bloody plan, then charged back to the front door, which he again tried to open with a modicum of smooth assuredness.

"My, that was fast," she said with a smile as he opened the door.

"I'm a guy. It doesn't take much. Please, come in."

Doyle led Kimberly into his apartment and offered her a seat on the living room couch, removing a sufficiency of magazines and dirty clothes so she was able to sit.

"I have to ask," said Doyle, "how did you find where I live?"

"I hope you don't mind," she said. "Daddy said you were the one investigating the robbery and Marta's murder. He said that, if I knew anything, I should go to you."

"Your dad's a smart man. How did you find my address?"

"I Googled it."

"Oh."

"Is that okay?" she asked.

"It's fine," responded Doyle, though he was feeling particularly computer illiterate at the moment.

Doyle picked up a notebook. "Now, you say you have some information that'll help me with the investigation?"

Kimberly looked uncomfortable. "Would it be okay if you put that down? I don't want this to be an *official* statement or anything. I just wanted you to know some things that might help."

Doyle tossed the notepad onto the coffee table, folded his hands in his lap, which covered his open zipper. "You got it. I'm all ears."

Kimberly looked around for a moment. "You sure have an awful lot of toys," she said. "Are those Ninja Turtle action figures?"

"Well, yes," said Doyle. "These are mostly collectibles from my childhood. Just sort of a hobby I have. It's a little embarrassing, to be honest."

"So why do you collect these things if you find it embarrassing?" she asked.

"Oh, I don't know," said Doyle. "I guess they just remind me of happy times. Of pure, unadulterated fun. You know?"

"I guess I can understand that," said Kimberly. "Do you have a girlfriend?"

Doyle squirmed. "Aren't you here to tell me something important?"

"Oh, gosh, I'm so sorry—I just thought that . . ." Kimberly began to say.

"No, no—don't worry about it. It's just that, well, my life isn't terribly interesting right now."

"But you're a detective!" said Kimberly, enthusiastically. "That's gotta be really exciting. Have you worked a lot of murder cases?"

"Some," lied Doyle. "Only if they're really high-profile."

"Wow," said Kimberly. "I'm impressed."

"Well," shrugged Doyle. "I'm not much of a bragger."

Doyle and Kimberly smiled.

"So, you were going to say . . ." prompted Doyle.

"Oh, yes. I take it you know who Chad is?" asked Kimberly.

"I think I've heard of him," said Doyle.

"We'd been dating a long time. Actually, we broke up on Friday." Kimberly looked down at her hands. Her lips quivered slightly.

"I'm sorry," said Doyle. "I'd offer you a tissue, but . . ."

"No, I'm fine. This is just hard, that's all."

"Take your time. Let it all out," said Doyle. He was using the best possible interviewing tactics he could muster.

"So, you were saying the two of you broke up," said Doyle.

"Yes, but it was after a long, awkward period. You see, we hadn't been getting along too well lately."

"Oh? Why? What was wrong?"

"He was so distant the past couple of weeks. I mean, he barely spoke to me. I used to see him every night, and we'd talk on the phone during the day. Sometimes I'd even cut class just so I could talk to him."

"He sounds like quite the guy," said Doyle.

"Chad was incredible. He has a brilliant political mind, and he cares passionately about things."

"Like animals?" asked Doyle.

She brightened. "Yes. How did you know that?"

"I'm a good guesser."

"Oh."

"So, you used to see him all the time, then suddenly it all stopped?" asked Doyle.

"Yes, it was so strange."

"Did anything happen, right before he stopped talking to you?"

"Yes," she said, quietly.

"What?"

Kimberly was silent.

"Did you mention the safe?"

Kimberly nodded. Tears welled in her eyes.

"Did he ask you questions about it?"

She nodded again. "Yes. He wanted to know what was in it, and what it was made out of, and what it would take to break in."

"Didn't you think that was suspicious at the time?"

"Not really—I just thought he was curious."

"Okay. What did you tell him? I mean, in response to his questions?"

"I told him I didn't know, and that was the truth. I have no idea what Daddy keeps in there, and I really have no idea what it's made of. I only know that Arnold Schwarzenegger tried to punch his way in once."

"Your dad told me that story."

"He loves that story," she said, and giggled.

"Did Chad ever say anything specifically about breaking into the safe?"

"No. At least, I don't think so."

"Do you believe he did it?" asked Doyle.

She drew in a quick, hard breath. "I'm not sure. It just . . . it would explain a lot, you know?"

"I understand. How did you first meet Chad?"

Kimberly rolled her eyes and her tension eased a bit. "It was at a bar of all places. Some friends and I were discussing fund-raising activities we could do for Pause for Paws. That's a charity I'm involved in that helps find homes for dogs and cats in local shelters. It started back in the early nineties with ads on videocassettes, and then—"

"Yes, I've heard of Pause for Paws. Was Chad in the organization?"

"Well, no, at least not at that time. But he had a lot of questions about it. He was involved with other animal-related charities, though to be honest, they were a little more extreme than Pause for Paws."

"How so?"

"Oh, he was involved with these groups who would do outrageous campaigns against companies who did animal testing, or rallies against farmers who injected steroids in cows and so on. It was all very dramatic, and all a little ridiculous if you asked me. Pause for Paws is much more down-to-earth."

"You said you met him in a bar. How did that happen?"

"He took our drink order."

"He was a waiter?"

"Yes."

"And you started dating him."

"Yes, I did." Kimberly sounded a bit irritable.

"Isn't it unusual that someone as well-off as yourself would date a waiter?"

She pulled herself up primly. "I don't judge people by how much money they make or what they do for a living. That would be completely shallow."

College angst permeated from Kimberly as thickly as her Paris Hilton perfume.

"I'm sorry, I didn't mean to offend you," said Doyle.

"It's okay," she said. "Daddy didn't care for him either. I guess he had good reason, seeing how things turned out."

"Though you don't actually know that he did anything of a criminal nature?" asked Doyle.

"No, I guess it's just suspicions. But why would he act that way, and why else would he break up with me?"

"So, *he* broke up with *you*, then? It wasn't mutual?" asked Doyle, eyebrow raised.

"Is it ever?" she asked, a sniff at the edge of her voice.

"Did he say anything to you when he broke up with you?"

"No, he just said it was something he had to do."

"That seems an odd break-up line. Had you seen him at all on Friday afternoon?"

"Just briefly. I was really busy getting decorations up for the fund-raiser gala, so I couldn't talk to him much. I guess I may have blown him off. But he barely talked to me the previous couple of weeks, so I didn't feel so bad."

"At what time did he break up with you?"

"It was about eleven on Friday night. He stumbled into the party, drunk. Maybe high, too—I don't know."

"Did he seem angry?"

"Ah, no," she said, thoughtfully. "Well, I guess a little bit. He didn't like Dad kicking him out of the party. We argued for a while, he dumped me, then he took off."

"Did you see him leave the party?"

She considered that. "No, I didn't. After he broke up with me, I tried to keep myself together and went back inside. I was in the bathroom—well, one of them—for probably an hour."

"Did you see Marta when you went back inside?"

"Yeah, I think she was still cleaning the carpet. He'd thrown up on it. It took her a really, really long time."

"I understand it was quite a mess," said Doyle. "Quite voluminous."

"Everyone knows about that incident now, too. It's the joke of the summer," said Kimberly bitterly. "In some ways, I'm glad he broke up with me. Especially if he did those awful things. But I still miss him. What really hurts is not knowing if I ever really knew him at all. Or maybe he was just acting the whole time he was with me." Her eyes began to well with tears.

"I should go," said Kimberly. "I hate barging into your apartment like this, but I just had to get this off my chest. I hate to think that, had I never told him about the safe, none of this might have happened. Marta could still be alive if it weren't for me."

Kimberly began crying.

Not sure what to do, Doyle looked around his apartment awkwardly, then finally opened his arms and put them around her.

"It's okay," he said softly. "And remember, he's innocent until proven guilty. At this point, we have no proof that Chad did anything besides throw up on the rug, although he is certainly a suspect in the break-in and murder of Marta. It was very good of you to come here and give me this information. It really helps."

Kimberly nodded. "Thank you. You're a sweet man."

"If you think of anything else," Doyle said, "don't hesitate to call, or stop in. I promise I won't answer the door in my underwear next time."

Kimberly laughed. "That's good to hear. Thank you."

"Don't mention it," said Doyle.

"Oh, and I really like your light-sabers. I always wanted one as a kid," added Kimberly.

Doyle felt his heart flutter a bit.

Doyle escorted Kimberly to the door and let her out, tears still clinging to her face. As she left, William was strolling up the walk.

They both stood on the porch watching Kimberly climb into her BMW and drive off.

"A crying girl leaves your apartment," said William. "Doyle, you certainly have a way with women."

13

S O WHAT WAS THAT ALL ABOUT?" asked William, handing Doyle a Starbucks coffee as he stepped through the door. "Did she find your collection of Star Wars action figures and realize what a pitiful loser she's dating?"

Doyle rolled his eyes. "First of all, William, they're not action figures. They're officially-licensed collectible miniatures. Secondly, that wasn't a date. That was Kimberly Chapman."

William nearly fumbled his own cup of coffee. "Sweet bloody hell, Doyle, why would you bring her here? Not only is that completely unprofessional, and utterly blurs the lines between business and recreation, but it also destroys our careful, meticulous investigation by exposing our involvement with the case, not to mention the area where you live. Honestly, Doyle, what were you thinking?"

Exhaustion had crept back into Doyle as Kimberly left, so he wasn't in the best mood. "Okay, William, I'm getting pretty sick of you jumping to conclusions about me. I did absolutely nothing wrong. Kimberly came here. I didn't invite her, set up an appointment—nothing. I had no choice in the matter. She got my name from her father and got my address, apparently, from Google."

"Yes, that is a terrific website. All right, Doyle, I apologize for making that assumption. But why did she come here? What was her purpose?"

Doyle motioned William inside toward the sofa. "Well," Doyle said, "it seems she came here to imply that Chad may be the guilty party."

"Since he's currently our primary suspect, her information could be quite useful. But, did you believe her?" asked William.

"I don't know," replied Doyle.

"You don't know?" asked William arching an eyebrow.

"I don't know," repeated Doyle, deep in thought.

"Would you care to expand on that?" asked William.

Doyle hesitated a moment.

"Everything Kimberly said made sense," said Doyle. "That she had told Chad about the safe, and then he began acting very strange around her. Then at the party he shows up drunk, gets kicked out, and then shortly thereafter the safe is broken into and Marta goes missing. And of course, we already know he's been at least accused of theft in the past. Unfortunately, Marta just seems to end up being part of a robbery gone bad. It all has a logical flow to it."

"However, you don't quite believe her," said William. "Why?"

"I've worked a lot of cases," said Doyle. "Nothing this high-profile, but a lot of cases nonetheless. And they all have something in common: none of them, not one of them, was ever cut-and-dry. And I can tell you why. Actors are never honest. Not even the ones here in Minnesota."

"But Kimberly Chapman is not an actor. She's only the daughter of an actor."

"I'm not so sure that makes any difference," said Doyle. "Dishonesty runs amuck in the acting community like pubic lice. Sure, you can try shaving down there, and perhaps scrub thoroughly with a loofa. But you just can't get rid of the itch."

William was silent, blinking rather sardonically at the image this had put in his brain.

"Okay, you lost me there, Doyle," he finally said.

"Sorry, I just remembered this episode of *Sex in the City* I saw the other night, and it got me thinking about how people present themselves, and the secrets they keep hidden. Maybe that wasn't the right metaphor, but what I'm really trying to get at is that I don't think we can really believe anyone we talk to in this case. Even Kimberly Chapman."

"You impress me, Doyle. Aside from the bizarre venereal reference, you're beginning to sound like a real detective."

"Yeah, I've been watching a lot of *CSI* lately. Anyhoo, if I want to keep my job, I best report in to Chief Burnside. He has this thing with showing up for work."

"He sounds like a real Emperor Palpatine, that one."

Doyle looked at William, surprised.

"Please, Doyle, everyone has seen *Star Wars*. Some of us just choose not to collect children's playtoys resembling the characters, that's all."

"Officially-licensed collectible miniatures," stated Doyle through clenched teeth.

"Right. But seriously, Doyle—how do you afford all these playthings on a cop's salary?"

Doyle didn't know how to respond to this. He knew damn well the answer was that he couldn't afford it. He just really knew how to get a lot of mileage out of a credit card.

"Trust fund," responded Doyle.

William nodded.

"Report in to work, Doyle, and we'll meet up later. Make sure you give me detailed notes on everything the other investigators have discovered. Do not leave anything out."

"What will you be doing?" asked Doyle.

"Exactly what you're paying me for," said William. "Investigating, and if all goes well, solving the case and saving your job. Give me a call when you can. You know the number. Good day, then."

"Later, dude," Doyle said, throwing his empty Starbucks cup into the trash receptacle, which, though half-full was surrounded with about two volumes of crumpled bills, old newspapers, and a few paper airplane's worth of misses. "Three points. Timberwolves score."

14

DOYLE DROVE TO WORK IN A HURRY, turning on the flashers of his unmarked squad, which he was under strict orders never to do, only when traffic seemed overly-congested. When conscientious civilians made way for a flashing police car, they assumed either an emergency was under way, or the cop was on a particular mission.

For Doyle, the only mission was getting to work on time.

Even though he was running late, at least he had a decent excuse. And a damned attractive one, Doyle thought to himself. Although she seems a bit nutty. And her ex-boyfriend might be a murderer. And her father had worked with Adam Sandler. Doyle shuddered.

"Hey, McNulty," Doyle called out as he walked down the main entrance. "So, what's the 411 on the investigation you guys did yesterday morning? Come up with anything I can use?"

Officer McNulty shook his head and kept walking.

"Hey, wait up," Doyle said, trying to catch up with McNulty as he walked in the opposite direction.

Doyle didn't love the fact he had to work with McNulty in the first place. The guy didn't have the best reputation. He had the appearance and attitude of a thug underneath his proper blue attire. He'd seen his fair share of action on the streets, and he had scars all over his face, and likely other parts of his body, to prove it. However, one opinion that was consistent throughout the department was that McNulty always got the job done. Perhaps that's what Doyle found so incredibly intimidating about him.

Doyle barely caught his breath as he approached McNulty from behind. "Seriously, what did you find out from Chapman and from the crime scene? We need to compare notes and draw some conclusions. I did some investigating myself and came up with some preliminary results, which, backed with your findings, should lead to a decent report to hand Burnside. Can you meet me in approximately half an hour so we can go over these things and—"

"I don't think so," said McNulty.

Doyle couldn't believe his ears. Granted, he wasn't used to working with other officers in the majority of his investigations, let alone a rough-and-tough street cop like McNulty, but he expected a little more cooperation from those assigned to the same case.

"Um . . . please?"

McNulty shook his head. "Well . . . no."

"Any particular reason?" Doyle asked. "You know, just out of curiosity?"

"I don't like you," said McNulty.

Doyle wasn't sure how to react to this. He always assumed many people didn't like him, but he'd never heard it so bluntly stated before.

"Okay . . ." said Doyle, the best response he could muster up.

"And, since you probably have no idea, I also don't want to 'come up with preliminary results' because the case is closed," said McNulty, almost as an afterthought.

"Oh. Could you just have said that and left out the first reason?" Doyle asked.

"I could have, but I wanted to make it abundantly clear that I don't like you."

Doyle could tell from McNulty's stone-like, unwavering expression that he was being completely sincere.

"I'm quite sure I don't want to ask this, but I will anyway. Why don't—"

"Because you're a shitty cop."

"Listen, despite what you may have heard—"

"You've never taken a difficult case in your life, and the moment you're given one, you hire someone else to do all the work for you."

For some reason, Doyle found he could not stop himself from reaching out his hand and slapping it across McNulty's face. The sound rang through the halls. To Doyle, the sound reminded him of a wet towel snapping against a bare buttocks.

The other cops in the hall turned towards Doyle and McNulty's exchange.

"He's not doing all the work, he's simply aiding the investigation," Doyle said hotly.

McNulty grabbed Doyle by the neck and squeezed. Doyle quickly began turning red.

"First of all, you idiot," said McNulty, "never slap a man who's much stronger than you. In fact, don't slap a man, period. What kind of a fighter are you? Secondly, it's against department policy to invite someone from outside into the investigation without the appropriate approval and documentation, which I'm certain you have neither. But don't worry, I've already filled Burnside in. I'm sure he'll want to discuss it further with you."

Doyle imagined he was somewhere near the color of radishes by this point. He wasn't sure when he'd take his next breath, but he knew that when it came, he would be most grateful for it.

"Oh, and in case I really need to mention it, if you ever touch me again, I'll kill you. Got it?" McNulty let go of Doyle's neck with a shove that slammed Doyle's shoulder into the wall.

Doyle gasped. The other officers turned back to what they were doing.

"Now you better head on upstairs, little guy. I think Burnside's expecting you." McNulty smiled. He turned to leave.

"Hey, McNulty," Doyle croaked. "Did you ever hear the one about the jerk-ass cop who didn't have a penis?"

Doyle's body vibrated with hatred, but he didn't look back. He stepped into an elevator and pressed the button.

"It's a funny joke, because the punch line is you."

As the door closed, Doyle saw the snarl of anger on McNulty's face.

Doyle smiled briefly, then grimaced at the pain in his throat.

I think that went well, Doyle said to himself, and coughed.

D OYLE ARRIVED ON THE FLOOR that housed Burnside's investigation unit. Burnside had the large office at the end of the hall, and each investigation officer, including Doyle, had a smaller office on the hall.

Although Burnside usually ended every meeting or performance review with the phrase, "My door is always open," this was quite untrue, in both literal and metaphorical terms. Burnside did not like talking to people, and his door was never open.

Except for today, Doyle noticed. He had a feeling that was probably not a good thing.

Doyle approached the open doorway carefully, like a frightened child entering a dark room.

"Hey, Chief," Doyle said, although speaking was still painful. "Chief, you in here?" Doyle knocked on the inside wall. He could see that Burnside was not at his desk, but his office also had entrances to a private bathroom and a separate storage room. "Hello? Chief?"

Doyle neared Burnside's desk, where he spotted one lone pencil sitting inside a ceramic coffee mug. Doyle stealthily snatched the pencil and tucked it inside the pocket of his sports coat.

Just then, Burnside walked out of the private bathroom, and Doyle shrieked with surprise.

"Sorry, Chief—you surprised me."

"Ahh, Doyle. Just the man I wanted to see. I take it McNulty gave you the good news?"

"Amongst other things . . ." Doyle said as he rubbed his neck.

Burnside laughed. "Yes, he does have a bit of a rough exterior, doesn't he? Though he sure knows how to take care of things. Well, just to reiterate any information he gave you, let me just state officially that this case is now closed. Period. Finito."

"I'm sorry, Chief, but I feel rather lost. How can the case possibly be closed? Who broke into Chapman's safe and murdered Ramirez?"

"A fellow you may have heard of—he was present at the party the night of the murder. A real weirdo, from what I hear. Had this strange fascination with wiener dogs in relation to the Iraq war. Don't ask me how that works."

"You mean Chad Wilkinson? He admitted it?"

"Not only that—he wrote a confession."

"Amazing," said Doyle. "What does this mean?"

"Simple, Doyle. It means the case is closed. And as the lead investigating officer, you'll be going through the investigation materials and preparing the final report."

"Okay, but—"

"Congratulations, Doyle. The opportunity to have your name on a case like this comes by only once in a blue moon. Not only did you do well, but you solidified your standing within the department, particularly in your association with high-profile cases. I must say, Doyle, that I was most impressed—"

"Why would he confess?" asked Doyle.

"What do you—"

Doyle ignored Burnside. "Why would Chad confess to the crimes if he was so careful to ensure there weren't any clues left behind? Unless, that is, he found out about Kimberly coming to speak with me, which could have made him nervous. But still, a guy like Chad is more likely to wait until he's caught rather than write out a confession."

"Listen, Doyle—"

"Of course, there's always the possibility that someone else is involved, and they put the pressure on Chad to either confess or ka-pow!" Doyle made a visual of a gun using his thumb and forefinger.

"Then again, if he's confessing anyway, why wouldn't he give up whoever else was involved? It's not like it would hurt him any. This just isn't adding up," Doyle scratched his head. He took out his notepad and scribbled some notes.

"Doyle, I'm going to say this just once more, and I'm going to say it very clearly. The case is closed. In this field, that doesn't happen too often, especially so cleanly. We have a confession. The confession meshes with the information we have for that evening. It fits. It adds up. Don't start stirring up trouble when there's no need. We have a closed case. Closed. Done. No more. Got it?"

"I want to speak with him."

"You can't," said Burnside, sternly.

"Why not?" asked Doyle.

"He's dead."

"As in, not living?"

"Is there any other kind of dead?"

"But how?" asked Doyle.

"Drug overdose. Heroin. Our reports state that Wilkinson was a regular user. He would often shoot up before attempting to steal something. He's been booked several times for various theft attempts. Often the drug charges were dropped as long as he confessed to the theft. I hear one time he tried to snatch Elizabeth Taylor's Klimpt."

"That's disgusting."

"You see, Klimpt is actually an artist, not a—" explained Burnside.

"No, I know, I just find it funnier that way. Was this overdose intentional or unintentional?"

"It's hard to say for sure. It was a large amount. Since he had just confessed, one could speculate he was trying to end it all."

"I'm not so sure speculation will sit well in my final report, sir. I have to take this further. I want to see the body. I want to see the confession," demanded Doyle.

Burnside started to go all cuttlefish, reds blending with purples. "You'll have access to the documents that the overnight investigators have already gathered for you. There, you'll find all the information you need to prepare your final report. The investigation at this time is closed. Repeat, THERE WILL BE NO FURTHER INVESTIGATING!"

Doyle was impressed with the height of color on that one.

"Go down to your desk, prepare your report, and sign it. Have it ready for me by tomorrow. Is this understood?"

Doyle remained silent. He couldn't keep his mind off the chain of events. Why would Chad write a confession and then kill himself on a large amount of heroin? And didn't that seem a little too convenient if someone else was trying to conceal the truth? Something just wasn't quite right about this.

"Doyle!" Burnside barked.

Doyle jumped. "What?"

"Do you understand?"

"Um . . . sure."

"What did I just ask you?'

"If I understand," Doyle replied.

"Understand what?"

"Everything you just said. Listen, I need to get on that report. After all, it may be the most important case of my career, like you said."

"Good, Doyle. Do that. Take these report files, and let me know if there's anything else you'll need. But it should all be there for you."

"Great, thanks. Oh, do you mind if I borrow a pencil?"

Burnside glanced at his empty mug. His jaw thrust out.

"Oh, never mind, I've got one," said Doyle, feeling the side of his sports coat. "I'll let you know if I need anything else, then. I'll just be in my office. Working on that report. For the closed case. I gotta go."

"Doyle, one more thing."

"Yes, sir?"

"If you ever use a detective from outside the bureau again, you're fired."

"I'm not sure what McNulty told you, but I assure you that—"

"Doyle, shut up. Get to work. Now!" That cuttlefish face rated only a seven on Doyle's bejesus scale.

Doyle grabbed the report files and scurried out of Burnside's office. Doyle walked down the hall towards his own office. He opened the door and stepped inside. Then he just stood there, counting down "Five . . . four . . . three . . . two . . . one . . . now." He stuck his head out the office door and looked towards Burnside's office. Burnside's back was turned. Doyle ran into the elevator and hit the ground level button, standing to the side so as not to be seen.

On his way down, Doyle dialed a number on his cell phone.

"William? I need you to meet me right away."

As the door opened on the bottom floor, Doyle was face to face with Superintendent Beth McDonald. Burnside's boss. The top dog.

"Hi, Beth. Err—Superintendent."

"Doyle—good job on the Chapman case. Burnside told me you have everything wrapped up."

"Yeah, well—" blushed Doyle. Although McDonald was an older, even gruff-looking woman, she has a certain attractive charm. Doyle couldn't help but feel a little tingly around her.

"I've actually got a meeting with him in just a couple minutes, so I should probably—" said McDonald, heading into the elevator.

"Oh, umm, just a moment," said Doyle, holding the elevator door open. "Listen, when you talk to Burnside . . ."

McDonald looked at Doyle suspiciously.

"Don't tell him you saw me down here," said Doyle. "If you don't mind."

"Why? What are you up to, Doyle?" McDonald's face looked stern, almost grim. Doyle didn't like seeing her like this. Typically, Doyle and Beth had a casual and pleasant relationship, mostly because they didn't work directly with each other, at least not often.

"Believe me, it's important. But he thinks I'm in my office, so if you don't mind keeping up that façade . . ."

"You know, Doyle—you really shouldn't be telling me this. You've basically just admitted that you're lying to your boss," said McDonald sternly.

"I know—but I have a good reason," said Doyle.

"I believe you do," said McDonald, "which is why I won't tell Burnside anything." She smiled a bit.

"Thank you," said Doyle, relieved.

"Just try not to lie to your superior officers too often. You could develop a poor reputation for yourself."

Doyle thought of his recent strangling from McNulty. "I think I've already done that."

"Oh, one more thing—when's the last time you took a vacation? I swear, I've never seen you not working," McDonald said.

Doyle didn't know how to respond to that. It was true, he had never taken a vacation. He wasn't really sure why—it just wasn't something Doyle even thought of doing. He had a couple ideas as to why: the amount of effort he put in on a daily basis was minimal at best, so he was at low risk for burn-out, and, also, if he did take a vacation, he didn't think he'd know what to do with himself. Or who to spend the time with.

"I don't like to travel much," responded Doyle.

"It's not about travel," said McDonald, "it's about getting out of the office and letting your mind relax. You didn't even take time off after your father . . . well, you know, except for the funeral. You have to take better care of yourself. And, whatever is going on here . . . I don't want you getting into trouble, do you understand?"

"Yeah, I do," responded Doyle. He actually felt rather touched—while she was his superior, it seemed McDonald really did care a great deal about Doyle. This was likely because she had been so close to his father. In fact, Doyle wondered if they hadn't been together, intimately, sometime after the divorce. Maybe even beforehand. And even then, Doyle wasn't sure if he could blame his father. McDonald was an incredible, strong woman.

"Just promise me you'll take a vacation after your plate is clear. Agreed?"

Doyle nodded. "Agreed. Thanks, Beth, for helping me out here."

"Don't mention it. Just be careful, whatever you're doing," she said.

"I will," Doyle said. "I will."

15

DOYLE PULLED INTO THE MORGUE PARKING lot just before William did. On his way from headquarters, Doyle realized that he had lost his notepad regarding this case, and that if he were told to present his notes on the case to anyone of authority, he'd be up you-know-which creek without a you-know-what. So Doyle had stopped off at the local K-mart for a handheld audio recording device, as well as some peppered beef jerky and a twenty-ounce bottle of Mr. Pibb.

He paid with a check. If he was really lucky, his direct deposit might come in before the check cleared.

"Hey, Doyle," Doyle said into his new toy as soon as he opened the package and inserted the batteries. "Stop losing things. And do not purchase Mr. Pibb again. It's a cheap knock-off of Dr. Pepper. The dude should not have started making soda before getting his degree. Over and out."

Getting out of the car to meet William, Doyle once again pressed the "record" button on his device. "Hey, Doyle, remind William to never wear a black-and-white checkered shirt. It looks ridiculous."

"Doyle, for God's sake, I'm right here. You don't need to record a message to remind yourself to remind me of something you just said right in front of me."

"I'm sorry, you lost me there," said Doyle, putting on his best dumb look. He played back the message. "Oh, yeah, this handy-dandy recorder here wanted me to remind you to not wear that shirt again. You look like a damn chess board."

William folded his arms and smirked. "Are you going to continue to insult me, or are you going to tell me why we're at the morgue? You've already seen Marta Ramirez, as have the medical examiners. At this point, beyond what we already have in our case notes, I can't imagine what else we could uncover with the naked eye."

"It's funny you should mention case notes. You see, I . . . never-mind, I'll get to that later," said Doyle, as he clicked a button on his recorder. "Note to self, tell William about missing case notes."

"Missing case notes? What missing case notes? Doyle, that's bad, very, very bad! What if we were court-ordered to present our find-ings immediately? Or, worse, what if crucial notes fell into the wrong hands! You could have jeopardized the entire case. Honestly, sometimes I cannot believe how imbecilic . . . "

"William, I said I'd get to that later. What we're dealing with here is far more important. First, let me point out that this has nothing at all to do with Marta."

"Nothing to do with Marta? Then why are we here, Doyle? That's our only case!" He ran a hand over his face in exasperation.

"Well, okay, it has *something* to do with Marta. But we're not here to look at Marta."

"We're not? What, did you lose your case notes here last time?"

Doyle thought about it for a minute. "I don't think so. Unless— no, I'm pretty sure I didn't."

"Okay, so what are we here for?"

"I'll give you one guess, and it rhymes with Dad Milkenson."

William narrowed his eyes. "Chad? We're here for Chad. What the bloody hell would Chad be doing here?"

"Just chillin', if you know what I mean." Doyle nudged William with his elbow.

"Very humorous, Doyle, but are you seriously telling me that Chad Wilkinson is now deceased?"

"Yup. I just found out from Chief Burnside. Seems Chad intentionally overdosed on heroin. Apparently he also left a note."

"He left a note? Are you sure?"

"No, I'm not sure. Which is one of the reasons why I'm here instead of in my office polishing off a final report and brushing my suspicions under a rug."

"A final report already? So soon after this news of Chad came about? That doesn't make very much sense," said William.

"Burnside was pushing for it. Supposedly in the note, Chad confessed to Marta's murder. It doesn't make any sense to me either. But Burnside told me the case was closed and that there was to be no more investigation. He said there's no more reason to investigate if there aren't any loose strings."

"Of course, if we can't fully investigate the confession letter and Chad's apparent suicide, how can we know that the strings are not loose?" asked William.

"My thoughts exactly," said Doyle.

"I don't think we could in good conscience end an investigation based on superficial conclusions drawn by someone other than ourselves, stemming from untested, unprocessed evidence. It would be immoral and unethical. We really have no choice but to continue our investigation."

"I agree," said Doyle.

"Excellent. Shall we go inside, then?"

"Yes," said Doyle. "But there's just one more thing I forgot to mention."

"What would that be?" asked William.

"I was told that if I was ever seen with you, I'd be canned."

"Oh, I see."

"It's a small matter—but, perhaps not so small."

Doyle felt ashamed bringing up the issue at all, but he felt he may be even more ashamed if he were to lose his job. Not that he ever worked too terribly hard, but lately he'd discovered it was somehow growing on him. He didn't want to lose it now.

"Doyle, if you're so concerned about this, why did you call me and tell me to come here?"

"I wanted your assistance. I thought you might see something that I wouldn't."

"That's it? You think I have good eyes? Don't you think you're being a little over-simplistic?"

Doyle sighed. "And, if you need to hear more, I think you make me into a better detective. I feel a little more professional around you. And to be honest, I've never felt this involved with a case before. I think that might have something to do with you."

William smiled. "Thank you, Doyle. And don't worry about losing your job. That's not going to happen."

"How can you be so sure?" asked Doyle.

"Because, if your Chief Burnside is eager to close this case, so eager in fact that he's willing to allow an unknown thief and murderer roam free, then he's going to have to do a lot of explaining to his superiors once we find out who the culprit is," said William.

"That's all great in theory," responded Doyle. "But who's to say? We could solve the case, and then Burnside takes the credit for it. Presuming, of course, that we even solve the case at all. We might not be able to, not in the short term anyway. Burnside's resourceful. I have no doubt he could find a way to pin any mistake on me. Not to mention he's pretty much got me on the whole 'don't use outside help' policy. I don't have much wiggle room there."

"Doyle, you said that Burnside is resourceful. Tell me, what makes him resourceful?"

"Well," said Doyle. "He's my superior, so obviously he has access to all my files and does all the reporting on my behavior and abilities in the position. Not to mention he has friends all throughout the department. If he reports that I messed up somehow, people will tend to believe him."

"But what if you were to tell others that Burnside screwed up, that he tried to pin a murder and a theft on a dead guy without a full investigation?"

"Why would they believe me, William? Believe it or not, I've been reprimanded more than once. And other officers tend to not put a lot of faith in me. They tend to see me as an idiot or a slacker who somehow got into a cushy position because of the clout his father had. Now I know what you're thinking, William: 'Doyle? Not seen as a Holmes-like genius of investigation and detection?' Well, it's true. Truth be told, William, I haven't put a whole lot of effort into this job until just recently, and that's only because my job was on the line."

"Now I don't believe that's true, Doyle. Well, the words 'idiot' and 'slacker' do have a ring of truth, now that I think of it, but the rest is just rubbish. I don't believe you're doing this just because your job is on the line. If that's all that mattered to you, you'd be up in your office right now completing that final report so you could head home, drop your trousers, and watch *Star Trek* reruns all night long."

"I'd rather you not make fun of my hobbies, William."

"The point is, there's something more than employment driving you, and I think it's that you have the desire, and, whether you like it or not, I know you have the abilities to be a really good, top-notch detective. Maybe not quite Holmes-esque, but maybe somewhere along the lines of Fletch, perhaps?"

"He is pretty good," said Doyle, smiling. "Thanks, William. I appreciate the confidence booster. But I still don't understand how you're so confident that I won't get fired."

William cleared his throat. "Doyle, what did you just purchase today?"

"I bought a Mr. Pibb. It wasn't very good though—it tasted like a flat Dr. Pepper. I'm pretty sure it has something to do with their respective levels of education."

William rolled his eyes. "Doyle, what else did you buy today?"

Doyle hit record on his device. "Note to self, stop using Mr. Pibb joke. No one is laughing. I am no Mitch Hedberg."

William stared.

"Oh, you mean this recorder. What about it?"

"Doyle, any kind of audio or video surveillance is a detective's best friend. Now, you choose to use your recorder for the sake of taking notes, which is all well and good, and does serve a purpose. But just think of what good you could have done should you have recorded your conversation with Burnside."

Doyle thought about what William was suggesting. "I would have had proof that Burnside was trying to close a case before a thorough investigation was complete. It would have shown negligence on his part. Heck, I could even argue that I had to hire you because of a lack of resources and support from my own department. That's pretty brilliant, William."

William nodded appreciatively.

"Only one problem there, William. It wasn't recorded."

"Are you sure?" asked William, with a coy smile.

Doyle cocked an eyebrow. He rewound his recording device and pressed "PLAY."

"*Note to self,*" Doyle's recorded voice emanated from the machine, "*next time, purchase boxer shorts. Tighty-whities have a tendency of pinching my testicles.*" Doyle hit the stop button.

"Yeah, I'm pretty sure it's not on there," said Doyle.

"True, it probably isn't," said William.

William grabbed the side of Doyle's jacket, put a hand into his inner coat pocket, and pulled out what looked like a small, quarter-sized plastic button with several tiny holes.

"Absolutely everything you've said or that's been said to you has been recorded and filed on my personal computer. I guarantee, you will not be fired."

Doyle's eyes widened. "But you might! You've been recording me? Without telling me? Why would you do that?"

"For a couple reasons, Doyle. First and foremost to protect myself. I have to know that you are exactly who you say you are. This is a very shady business, Doyle, and I've had more than one client hire me with the intentions of pinning me with crimes. I'm sorry, but I felt it was something I had to do."

Doyle shook his head in disbelief.

"Furthermore, it's served some other beneficial purposes. For example, we now know you have the tendency of losing notes. Well, at least any interviews you've conducted we have safely stored. And as we've now discovered, we've recorded a conversation that could be pivotal in saving your job. So, while you may be angry with me, which I do understand, realize that it will ultimately serve higher purposes."

"Was it recording all of the time?" asked Doyle.

"If you're wondering if I had recorded your conversation with what I can only imagine was an adult phone line, then yes, Doyle, it was recorded and deleted as fast as imaginably possible."

"Good, good," said Doyle, uncomfortably.

"Sorry," said William.

"It's okay," said Doyle.

Uneasy silence followed, as Doyle tried to think of how best to continue. He was angry at William, although he couldn't blame him entirely. Doyle had just never been in a situation where he felt he had to record someone without their prior knowledge. It felt cheap and under-handed. But Doyle also thought of what William said about becoming a better detective. Maybe Doyle just had a lot to learn. Maybe being under-handed is necessary at getting to the truth.

Truth. There was a loaded word. What was the truth in this case? Did Chad really break into the safe, kill Marta, then off himself when the heat was on? Or did someone set Chad up to take the fall? What did that damn note say? And if Chad was set up, who did it? And how about Kimberly, how was she involved in all of this? To Doyle the case was expanding way too fast and morphing into something very different than what he thought he was dealing with.

"I never thought I'd say this," said Doyle, "but can we go look at the dead body now?"

16

DOYLE AND WILLIAM HEARD LAUGHTER as they approached the examination room of the morgue.

"I've never met a morgue man who didn't have a great sense of humor," Doyle said, nudging William. "They all have killer wit. I'm dead serious. Eh? Get it? Oh, nevermind."

The morgue looked much like it had the day before, except for the fresh new body lying on the metal slab, and the drunk photographer with his hand on Dr. Sylvester's shoulder.

"Hanratty, you got my message!" said Doyle, as he approached and knocked fists with Hanratty in a friendly albeit juvenile fashion.

"Hey, anything for you, Doyle. Although I usually don't like to go this far. My legs get tired. And then I get thirsty." Hanratty hiccupped.

William approached Hanratty and sniffed the air around him. "I assume it wasn't tea you used to quench your thirst," he said. "Good God, if I lit a cigarette, you'd likely explode."

Hanratty stared at William and blinked repeatedly. "Heeey," slurred Hanratty. "Who the hell are you? You're not a cop. And you talk funny, like Monty Python. Say something funny, Python man." Hanratty slapped William's shoulder.

William looked down at his shoulder and brushed his shirt off, as though it had been contaminated.

"Let's get to work, Doyle. Where's the body?"

Hanratty laughed, then paused. "Wait a minute, that's wasn't funny."

"Very insightful. Who are you, and what are you doing here?"

Hanratty lifted up his department-issued Nikon camera and snapped a picture of William.

"I take da pictures." He snapped another photo of William. "That one will look nice," said Hanratty. "I don't get many angry poses from the corpses."

William tried to wipe the flash out of his eyes. "And Ronald," he said, looking at Dr. Sylvester, "how have you been lately?" William offered his hand, and Sylvester shook it.

"I've been better," said Sylvester. "I've developed a rash. You know . . . downstairs. I think it might be from a . . ." he coughed, "business woman from a couple weekends ago. If you know what I mean."

"I know very well what you mean. I thought you would have learned after the last time I assisted you in finding out the cause of your venereal issues. I need to learn to stop asking questions," said William.

"That pretty much sums up my approach to detective work the past few years," said Doyle. "Dr. Sylvester, could you show us the body of Chad Wilkinson, please?"

Sylvester looked downward, as if considering pumping more air into his Reeboks.

"Yo, Sylvester, what is it?" asked Doyle. "Don't tell me he's still at the hospital, too? Oh, boy, if I have to go through this all again . . ."

"No, Doyle, it's not that. The body's actually here, it's just that— well, I'm under strict orders to not let you see it."

"You are? Is that possible? I'm the lead detective on this case. I don't think I can be restricted."

"Well, you are," said Sylvester solemnly. "Sorry, Doyle, you know I like to help you whenever I can."

"Under whose orders?" asked William.

"The orders came from a Chief Oliver Burnside of the Minneapolis P.D. I wasn't even supposed to say that much. He threatened I would lose my job. He wasn't very nice, Doyle. He insulted my shoes."

"Trust me, I feel your pain. He's my boss, and a royal pain-in-the-ass. But don't worry—he won't ever know I was here."

"But how can you be sure of that?"

"Just trust me."

"Doyle, you know I want to trust you. But still, this is *my* job. This isn't something I can just play around with. You know?"

"Tell you what," said Doyle, "If Burnside finds out, and you lose your job, I'll owe you a Coke."

"That's not terribly convincing, Doyle," said Dr. Sylvester.

"Listen, I'll let you in on a little secret," said Doyle. "I'm actually well acquainted with Beth McDonald, Burnside's boss. Now, that doesn't mean we can do whatever we want, but I do luckily have some evidence that Burnside's been negligent. It's not exactly fail-proof security—but it sure makes me feel a little fuzzy. I think if anything were to happen, we could work it out well enough."

Dr. Sylvester considered Doyle's words.

"I'm still trying to see what's in this for me," he said.

"Tell you what," said Doyle. "If we learn anything substantial from this, I'll make you a very happy man—and I think you know what I mean."

Dr. Sylvester shrugged. "The usual?"

Doyle patted his own coat pocket. "You know it."

17

DOYLE GAZED DOWN AT THE STARCH-WHITE, gangly body of Chad Wilkinson, pure as alabaster except for the track marks peppered up and down his arms, and he thought to himself, *Maybe I should start working on a tan.*

But the odds of that were as likely as Chad being a cold-hearted murderer. Doyle just couldn't wrap his head around it. Chad was a thief, a self-admitted thief according to his MySpace page. And sure, he was a little nuts, what with the whole wiener-dog thing. But for the life of him, Doyle couldn't visualize Chad, having just gotten sick in a crowded room, moving on to robbery and murder within a matter of minutes. Chad seemed far more like the type to pass out on the lawn rather than commit a crime on a whim.

"Those are some serious dreadlocks," said Hanratty, as he snapped a photo of Chad.

"I know what you're thinking," said Dr. Sylvester. "Does the carpet match the drapes? Shockingly, the answer is 'yes.'" Sylvester lifted up the white sheet, exposing Chad Wilkinson's braided pubic hair.

"That's nauseating," uttered William.

"It sure is," said Hanratty, as he snapped another photo and readied for more.

"Is that really necessary?" William asked Hanratty.

"It's for my personal collection," said Hanratty, as he hiccupped. "And I'll thank you to stay out of my private affairs, Prince William."

"Ha! British joke!" Doyle said, as he high-fived Hanratty, although Hanratty was slightly off-balance and nearly missed.

William pointedly ignored them.

"Now, down to business," said Doyle. "Dr. Sylvester, obviously you've had more than sufficient time to play around with Mr. Wilkinson's body. Did you notice anything unusual?"

"You do realize I don't actually conduct physical exams, right?" asked Sylvester.

"Well, I . . . I assumed you didn't. I'm really asking in more of a general sense," said Doyle. "You see a lot of bodies come in and out on a regular basis. Was there anything unusual about Mr. Wilkinson, other than the pubic braids?"

"Wiener dreads?" offered Hanratty, with a dumb grin on his face. "Cock locks?"

"Can we stay focused?" asked William. "You people are ridiculous."

"Please, if we were in Britain, there would've been a midget and a transvestite in here a half hour ago filming a porno," said Hanratty.

"What the bloody hell are you talking about?" said William, folding his arms.

Dr. Sylvester lowered his glasses. "Gentlemen, if I may."

Doyle, William, and Hanratty turned their attention to Dr. Sylvester.

"Thank you. To answer your question, Doyle, I didn't see anything unusual other than that this man clearly did a lot of drugs. As you can see, there are needle wounds all over his arms, most commonly referred to as 'track marks.' As I understand from his report, this man's death was due to an overdose. Certainly not a surprise judging from his appearance. But I did pay special attention to his arms. Take a look at this."

Dr. Sylvester pointed to one particular mark on Chad's right arm. "This is the wound where the alleged overdose was injected. You can't see it now, but there was the smallest bit of dried blood covering the wound when he arrived here."

"Excuse me, but I thought you said you don't do physical exams," said William.

Sylvester looked at William for a moment. "I don't. But I'm a curious person. And I had a bit of a feeling Doyle would be coming here."

"That's awfully kind of you," said William.

"Oh, I don't just do it for friendship. Speaking of which, before I continue . . ." Sylvester looked over at Doyle. "You were saying something about 'making me happy?'"

Doyle nodded in recognition. "Yes, yes, I almost forgot." Doyle reached into his inside jacket pocket, pulled out a white envelope, and handed it to Dr. Sylvester.

"Third row?" asked Dr. Sylvester.

"Second," replied Doyle. "Mid-court. You'll be able to see the Timberwolves in all their glory."

"You're a beautiful man, Doyle," said Dr. Sylvester, as he kissed the envelope and put it into the pocket of his lab coat. "Now where was I?"

"The blood on the wound," said Doyle, as Hanratty took a snapshot of Chad's arm.

"Where is the blood now?" asked William.

"I removed it so I could examine it," said Dr. Sylvester curtly.

"Doesn't that go against procedure?" asked William.

"The fact that I'm examining anything, yes, that goes against procedure. Typically I just clean up the bodies and store them. Terrific use of a masters in Forensic Science, I tell you. But since the authorities have not requested any further investigation or autopsy, it doesn't much matter how I alter the body at this point. The blood, especially, would have been washed off when the body was prepared for storage and eventual burial. Now, I was about to say something that would have been really useful. But if you're going to keep pestering me . . ."

"I do apologize, but I—"

"William, just be quiet for a few minutes, please?" asked Doyle.

"Very well." William again folded his arms in discontent. He then mumbled something about "Americans" and "dimwits."

"I'm sorry, Dr. Sylvester, what were you going to say?" asked Doyle.

"Well, like I was saying, I removed the blood so I could examine it. As one might expect, there was indeed a trace of heroine. But a little more surprising was the presence of calcium."

"Why would there be calcium in the blood?" asked Doyle.

"I doubt there was calcium in the bloodstream itself," said Dr. Sylvester. "But most likely, when the heroin was injected, the needle went so deep it hit bone. When the needle came out, some of the calcium deposit at the tip of the needle must have stayed within the blood."

"Isn't it awfully strange for a seasoned drug addict to hit his own bone?" asked Doyle.

"I would say it's quite strange," said Dr. Sylvester. "Normally someone injecting heroin is just looking for the most accessible vein. But, if he was indeed trying to kill himself, it's probable that he could have been a little more 'dramatic' with this injection."

"Another thought," said Doyle, "what if someone who had no idea about injecting drugs did it for him. Maybe even stabbed him with a syringe. Possibly against his will."

"Of course it's possible," said Dr. Sylvester. "But that's impossible to determine for sure. Nothing we have here rules out suicide."

"Though it doesn't rule out murder, either," added William.

"True," said Dr. Sylvester thoughtfully. "That is true."

Hanratty took one last snapshot of Chad Wilkinson. He reached into his pocket and pulled out a flask.

"Hold it there, buddy. I need you in top form. We have a little mission, right now," Doyle said, as took hold of Hanratty's flask.

134

Hanratty's grip was surprisingly solid, but he accidentally let go after he hiccupped.

"Aw, dammit," said Hanratty. "What are we going to do?"

"We're going to gain access to the evidence locker," said Doyle, "And we're going to take a photograph of the supposed suicide letter. I have a damn good feeling our Chad didn't write that note."

"Excellent, Doyle," said William.

"And I have a feeling we're starting to run out of time on this. We need to multitask. William, I need you to find Kimberly Chapman. She's in a vulnerable position right now. If she knows anything, if she's going to let anything slip, now would be the time. I'd recommend you use some of that audio recording mojo. If she gives us anything we need, let's have it as evidence. Am I right?"

"Quite right. You become more and more impressive every day, Doyle."

"No kidding. I just spent nearly a half-hour with a dead body and I haven't yet had the urge to vomit. I impress myself sometimes."

18

AFTER THEY EXITED THE MORGUE, Hanratty told Doyle and William, "Listen, I gotta run across the street. It'll only take me a minute or three."

Both Doyle and William turned in the direction of the Squeaky Clean Bar and Grill, a local establishment that catered mostly to government employees. The bar was located right in front of the Hennepin County Courthouse.

"Hanratty, dammit, we're in the middle of a major investigation!" said Doyle. "I'm not kidding around here."

"I get that, Doyle. I really do. But I don't do good around bodies. If I don't have a little drinky-drinky here, I'm gonna have the image of that dead kid's dreaded pubes in my mind for the rest of the week. Maybe longer. I just can't take that risk."

"But, Hanratty—" growled Doyle.

"I'll be right back!"

Before Doyle could say anything more, Hanratty had disappeared.

"Very reputable friends you have here," said William. "I take it he's not made chief investigator."

"No, he's not," said Doyle. "He has his issues, but he is a great friend."

William laughed.

"No, trust me—he is," added Doyle. "He's always been around when I needed him. However, he can be a little—well, unpredictable, I guess—when it comes to work."

Doyle and William stood silent for a moment.

"While we're out here, Doyle, I thought I might need to talk to you about something," said William.

"Sure. What's up?"

"When I left my house—"

"Dentist office?" inserted Doyle.

"Yes, well, my place—" continued William, "I'm pretty sure I saw an undercover cop car parked across the street. I think I may be under surveillance."

"What?" said Doyle. "Oh, shit—if the department knows I'm still working with you, I could be incredibly screwed."

"I know—that's why I may need to lay low for a while."

"What does that mean?" said Doyle. "I kinda need you here. I mean, that's what I'm paying you for."

"No, you're paying me to help you solve the case, and I will continue to help you do that. Have no worries."

"Okay," said Doyle. "Can I still call you and everything?"

"I'm sure that won't be a problem—but if I feel that's being monitored too, then I may switch out phones. I'll let you know."

"Okay," agreed Doyle.

Doyle and William stood in silence once again.

"How long will this take?" asked William, looking in the direction of the bar across the street.

"Should only be a few minutes," said Doyle. "He can knock 'em back pretty fast."

William nodded.

"Hey, Doyle, I've been meaning to ask—what is that?" asked William, pointing at Doyle's brown wristband.

"Oh," said Doyle, "it's just a little something my dad gave me. Shortly before he was shot, that is."

"He's a cop, yes?" asked William.

"Yes, was. Senior detective," said Doyle. "Known through the department as the best detective in decades. "

"So he was shot . . . and killed?" asked William, as delicately as possible.

Doyle nodded.

"Was it in the line of duty?" asked William.

"Yeah, it was," responded Doyle somberly. "Someone, they don't know who, but probably some young punk, shot him in the middle of a drug raid in the Phillips neighborhood. They never tracked him down."

"Did they have any leads at least? Anything?" asked William.

"No, nothing," said Doyle. "And honestly, I don't know if it really matters. Chances are, whoever shot my dad will get shot himself by some other drug dealer. Maybe he already has. Typically not a long life expectancy in that business. At least, that's what I usually tell myself. Helps me cope with the situation, you know?"

William nodded. "I can understand that, absolutely. And frankly, I think you're right. Violent criminals generally don't die of old age."

Doyle chuckled briefly before returning to a somber mood.

"Oh, but it would be nice if I could have caught the guy," said Doyle. "I would have locked him in the slammer and thrown away the key. That's how it always works on TV. The protagonist is always able to avenge the death of a loved one—even if it's through some strange twist of fate that inevitably leads him directly to the perpetrator."

"Too bad we live in reality, eh?" said William. "But I know what you mean—things get wrapped up so nicely in movies and on TV, when in the real world there are hundreds, maybe even thousands of unsolved cases. And as a detective, you have to be satisfied that you can't solve every crime. You can only do the best you can—and hope that eventually the criminals get caught for something else and eventually get what's coming to them."

Doyle nodded.

"How long ago did he die?" asked William.

"About a year," said Doyle.

"Do you feel proud that you're following in his footsteps? Being the brave detective, solving crime, helping the city?" asked William.

"Please, I'm not half the detective my dad was," said Doyle. "I wish I was the big brave cop, but I've intentionally taken the easiest cases. Granted, I've carved out a nice little niche for myself in the department—but it's nothing to brag about."

"But you can say you learned from the best, right?"

"That's what really gets me, William. I had the American equivalent of Sherlock Holmes in my home for years, and I never bothered to learn anything from him. It's not that he didn't try to show me things—methods of detection, logical steps in finding a prime suspect—he did all that, but I was too busy with other things to really take it in. I swear, William, that I paid far more attention to Dragnet than I did to my father."

"You're still really upset by this, aren't you?" asked William.

"Is it that obvious?" asked Doyle. "Amanda's right. I've had no ability to move on since his death. I just feel like I'll never be what he was. And I feel like everyone sees me as a screw-up as a result. I'm in a very uncomfortable situation that I can't get myself out of, no matter how hard I try."

"Until this weekend, how hard have you tried?" asked William.

"Not very," Doyle said, laughing a bit. "This is the hardest I've worked in my entire career."

"Don't you think if you continue to work this hard and solve major cases that you just might make your father proud? Mmm?"

Doyle looked at William curiously. "When did you become all Dr. Phil over here?"

"Doctor who?" asked William.

"Not Dr. Who—Dr. Phil. You know—Oprah's bald psychologist friend? Never mind—it's not important. But I do appreciate what you're saying, William. If I actually solve this without getting fired, sued, killed, or beaten to a pulp by McNulty, I might be able to make my dad proud."

William smiled.

"Oh, I also wanted to know—what do those letters on your wristband represent?" asked William. "WWCD? I don't get it."

"It means 'What Would Columbo Do?' Dad and I used to watch *Columbo* all the time while I was growing up. It was our favorite show."

"It sounds like your father shared your rather unique sense of humor," said William.

Doyle eyed William again.

"It's funny—you can actually be a rather nice guy when you want to be," said Doyle.

"Well, I am human, Doyle."

"Really?" said Doyle. "I thought you were British."

"Ha ha," said William. "Very funny."

"Hey, guys," said Hanratty.

"Ahhh!" yelled both Doyle and William, surprised by the sudden appearance of Hanratty.

"And you call yourselves detectives? I walked across the street in plain view." Hanratty cocked a thumb towards the street and almost lost his balance.

"You didn't have too much, did you Hanratty?" asked Doyle. "Please tell me you didn't."

"Too much is never enough," said Hanratty. "Never enough."

"Doyle—I need to head home and pick up some items," said William. "That is, assuming everything hasn't been confiscated by the Minneapolis P.D. or the Minnesota B.C.A. Then I'm going to track down Kimberly Chapman and ask her some questions. I'll be in contact later."

"Thanks, William—I appreciate it. I'll be heading back with Hanratty to headquarters. I need to see that confession letter," said Doyle.

"Are you sure he's in good enough condition?" asked William. "He does look a little . . .

"Intoxicated?" asked Doyle. "Don't worry—they're used to that. They'd be more concerned if he went to work sober."

"Yup," agreed Hanratty.

"Good luck, Doyle," said William. "I think you might need it."

"Thanks, William. And umm . . . thanks for our little talk here. That was nice," Doyle said.

"Consider it a portion of my services rendered," said William. "But don't worry—I won't show it itemized on my bill."

"I wouldn't think so," replied Doyle.

"Can we go now?" asked Hanratty. "I'm bored."

19

I DON'T THINK THIS IS A VERY GOOD PLAN," said Hanratty, as Doyle drove his squad much faster than the street limits allowed. "Actually, what *is* your plan?"

Hanratty had been crabby since he had left the bar. Doyle caught him trying to drink out of a flask again in the passenger seat, which was against the law in so many ways. But Doyle managed to nab the flask away from Hanratty. Taking away Hanratty's flask was like taking a lollipop from a toddler. It was undoubtedly easy; Hanratty had all the dexterity of a penguin in an oil-wrestling match. But he sure put up a fuss.

"My plan is brilliant, yet simple," said Doyle. "All we need to do is go into the evidence locker and photograph all we can."

"You mean the evidence locker you're not allowed to go anywhere near because the case is closed and Burnside specifically banned you from doing any further investigating?" asked Hanratty.

"That's the one. Like I said: brilliant, yet simple."

As courageous as Doyle was being, a feeling he hadn't had since he snuck into *Indiana Jones and the Last Crusade* at the Grandview Theater, he couldn't shake the nervousness that sat in his gut. If things didn't go perfectly, that was it. He'd be out of a job, he wouldn't be able to pay his rent, and eventually he'd be smelly, homeless, and begging for change, which he'd probably spend on Magic: The Gathering cards rather than food.

"All right," said Doyle, as he pulled the car into headquarters. "Let's do this thing."

"Oh, goody," said Hanratty.

It was approaching late afternoon, which was a good time to sneak into headquarters. Most of the cops working the night shift were already out on the streets, and any who'd been on day shift had already gone home to their families. If Doyle was right, there shouldn't be too many cops walking in and out of the building.

Doyle was pleased to see he was correct. Aside from one pair of officers pulling along a haggard man in handcuffs, no other cops were near the front entrance.

"Are you ready for this?" asked Doyle as he got out of the car.

"Of course I'm ready. What do I care? It's your ass," Hanratty mumbled.

"I didn't mean for you to get so emotional," said Doyle with a smirk.

"F.U." responded Hanratty. "I have a headache."

Doyle and Hanratty walked casually up the stairs into the front entrance of the building. Hanratty had his photographic equipment in a bag at his side. Doyle had nothing except his badge and a generous cache of verbal one-liners, which he was mostly relying on to get him through this.

"Detective Malloy, Officer Hanratty," said Amanda from the front desk, which she manned most evenings. Doyle was disappointed that she wasn't being given anything more than the role of a glorified receptionist. He knew she'd get her chance. Oh, and she sure was also very attractive. Doyle had been thinking more and more lately that maybe he should seriously date her . . . someday. When he wasn't so busy.

"Hi, Amanda," said Doyle, still consciously walking at a steady pace.

Doyle saw her eyes widen as if she suddenly remembered something.

"Hey, didn't you . . ." she began to say.

"Forget something upstairs? I certainly did. I'm gonna go grab it. Be right back down, promise."

"But, Doyle?"

Unsure if he was doing the right thing, Doyle stopped in his tracks and turned to Amanda.

Hanratty whispered under his breath, "May Day, May Day, going down . . ."

"Amanda," Doyle said quietly to her, "I promise I'll be back down in five minutes. No harm done."

Doyle was pretty sure that had done the trick. The last thing he wanted was for every cop to be on alert that somehow Doyle was disregarding authority and needed to be brought in to Burnside.

Just to be sure, Doyle added, "Please?"

"Just tell me you're not screwing up your one big case, Doyle. I know you like to play by your own rules and all that other cliché detective BS, but try not to land yourself in jail, okay? I was kinda hoping we'd be able to go out after you got a big promotion or something, not when you get bailed out."

"I won't be going to jail," said Doyle. "I've just bent a couple rules here and there, and disobeyed Burnside's orders, which I've never been real keen on anyway. Amanda, please, please, please with sugar on top—I could really, really use your help here."

Amanda looked down and sighed.

"Okay, Doyle. Just don't get me in any trouble, okay?" Amanda said, concern washing over her delicate features.

"Ditto," responded Doyle. *Ditto?* he thought. *Who says "ditto"?*

But, fortunately, Amanda just smiled. Doyle and Hanratty began walking.

"Oh, Doyle—one more thing."

Doyle turned around. "Yeah?"

"If you need any help from me, just meet me at the Rabbit Hole. You know my number."

Doyle nodded. "Sure."

Doyle and Hanratty continued on.

"Now that you've sufficiently flirted, are you ready to get on with whatever it is we have to do here?"

"Trust me, that wasn't flirting. It was more likely getting a stiff reprimand from one of those nuns in Catholic school. Besides, it was necessary. I didn't need her blowing this whole thing."

Hanratty chuckled. "Amanda wouldn't blow anything. Although I don't know her that well, so I can't speak to her personal life, but from your ridiculous display there, it sure seems you'd like to find out what she would and would not blow."

"You disgust me," said Doyle.

"That's what all the women say until they get to know me better," said Hanratty.

Suddenly, Hanratty grabbed Doyle by the arm and pulled him into the men's room. The door swung shut with a loud thud.

"What's going on?" asked Doyle, massaging his arm.

"Shh," said Hanratty. "McNulty's out there. In case you don't know it, that guy has a serious grudge against you. If I were you, I'd stay as far away from him as possible."

"That's great," said Doyle. "But you know, it'd have been even better if you coulda told me that earlier today before he put a strangle hold on me."

Hanratty looked at the bruises on Doyle's neck. "Oh yeah, I was meaning to ask you about that."

From behind them, a toilet flushed, and to Doyle's sheer horror, Burnside himself stepped out of the stall.

"Fuck!" said Hanratty, far too loudly. Burnside turned his head. Then, to save himself, Hanratty added just as loudly, "I really have to pee!"

Doyle was pretty sure he felt something die inside as Burnside approached.

"Ahh, Doyle, there you are. I didn't see you in your office. How's that final report coming along?"

"Very well, sir," said Doyle, feeling the sweat dripping down his back. "Just had to take a little pee break before I head upstairs to finish 'er up."

"Glad to hear it. I knew you'd come to your senses." Burnside looked over at Hanratty as he peed in the urinal. "And Officer Hanratty, you haven't damaged any more of our bicycles have you? That can be a real expense to our department, you know."

"No, sir. Same bike." Hanratty then hiccupped.

Burnside sighed. "I'll just pretend that was just a normal, every-day hiccup as opposed to something even potentially alcohol-related."

"No alcohol here, sir. No, siree." Hanratty zipped his fly.

"Wonderful," said Burnside. "Doyle, come with me. I want to talk to you about something." Burnside turned to the bathroom door.

"Sure," said Doyle. He then whispered to Hanratty "follow me, but stay back."

Hanratty nodded.

Doyle and Burnside were alone in the elevator. Doyle wished to God there'd have been someone, anyone, in the elevator with them, but, no, it was just Doyle and Burnside. Of course a security guard watched them from somewhere else in the building.

"I just wanted to tell you, Doyle, that I respect how much hard work you've put into this case. I've been your superior for several years now, and I worked with your father even longer than that. Your father was also a good man, and a darned good detective. And let me tell you, he knew when to put a stamp on a file and move on to the next case. We have a lot of work to do in this department, Doyle. We always have, and we always will. It's our jobs to continuously and progressively work our way through it as much as we can."

Burnside took a couple steps closer to Doyle, and the move had a hint of threat to it. "This was not a small case I handed to you, Doyle, I know that. But you've done a stunning job with it. You've worked longer hours than I've ever seen you work. You've put forth more effort than I've ever seen you put forth. And if this case finally wraps up tonight, with the help of your report, of course, there might just be a promotion in it for you. Same work, but higher pay. Possibly even a bonus. I'd like to make you my senior-level detective, Doyle. That was the same level as your father, you know. Of course, it took him twenty-five years to achieve that. It would be only, what . . . seven for you? That's impressive by anyone's standards. And something serious to think about."

Doyle was thinking about it. He'd worked under Burnside for seven long years. He never liked the man, and he'd always been certain that Burnside hadn't much cared for him either. But he never realized until now that Burnside was the absolute scum of the earth. Sure, there was probably worse. Hitler. Stalin. Russell Crowe. But right now, Burnside was the only one Doyle really wanted to slug in the face.

"I certainly will think about that, sir. Thank you." God, Doyle hated himself right then. But it was for the greater good. Soon, once he brought the truth into the open, once he really solved the case, then he could say what he really felt. But for now, he had to play the game. "Let me know if there's anything more I can do, sir."

"You're a good detective, Doyle. Don't you forget that."

What Doyle said was: "I appreciate that, sir."

What Doyle meant by that was: I'm going to steal every last one of your pencils and stick them all up your nose.

The elevator door opened. Burnside headed off towards his office. He turned around and said, "Good luck with the rest of that report, Doyle. Let me know if there's anything else you need."

An idea struck Doyle. It was unlikely, but it might work.

"Actually, Burnsie—erm, sir, I mean, I want to include some of the photos that Hanratty took with my report. If that's okay."

"Absolutely," said Burnside. He reached into his pocket and pulled out a keychain that had numerous keys attached. Burnside took one of the keys off the chain and threw it at Doyle. "Have at it," he said.

Wow, thought Doyle, *that was much easier than expected.*

Burnside continued walking towards his office. "Remember," he called out, "my door is always open."

Burnside then stepped into his office and slammed the door shut behind him.

D OYLE WAS STANDING IN FRONT of the evidence locker, which was really a full room dedicated to the storage of evidence, when the elevator behind him opened with a ding. Hanratty's head popped out. "Is he gone?" Hanratty whispered.

"Yup, he's gone, and he's given me the key to the evidence locker," said Doyle, wiggling the key in front of Hanratty's nose.

"That's a little peculiar, don't you think?"

"It is, but maybe I did a really good job of convincing him that I'm eager to finish that report."

Hanratty knitted his brows. "Well, let's hope you're right," he said. "I don't need any more problems."

"Only one way to find out," said Doyle, as he slowly placed the key into the doorknob of the evidence room.

Doyle turned the key. There was an audible click. Doyle turned the knob, and the giant steel door swung open with ease.

"Huh," said Doyle. "It worked."

"Doesn't this make you a little suspicious?" asked Hanratty.

"Suspicious of what?"

"Oh, I don't know. Maybe someone's gonna slam the door shut and lock us in. Or, maybe what we're looking for isn't even here. Maybe you're being set up. Maybe we'll open that specific locker and BAM! A bomb goes off. You're starting to get yourself into some deep shit, Doyle. Anything could happen."

"Thanks, Hanratty. I needed that little boost of confidence."

With the thick metal door of the evidence locker swung open, the men looked into a room consisting of several rows of high-school style lockers. Each locker had a tag with a number corresponding to a particular case number. If an investigator didn't know the case number off-hand, a computer was installed towards the entrance of the room which contained a database of all cases in progress and historical cases from the past two years. Everything prior was then archived in a separate area.

Doyle had written down the case number at some point, but he couldn't remember exactly where or when that had taken place. Doyle was not known for his organizational skills.

He entered his User ID and Password, which let him into the database. He then entered "Chapman" and "Ramirez" into the search field, which populated case #1207-011.

"Did you find it?" asked Hanratty, who had begun to pace. "I'm getting claustrophobic in here. Hurry up, will you?"

"Cool it," said Doyle. "This should just take a minute. Get your camera ready."

Hanratty was a bit shaky as he unzipped his camera bag. Doyle wondered if it was nervousness, or one-hour alcohol withdrawal.

"It should be down this way," Doyle said, gesturing for Hanratty to follow.

Doyle found the eleventh row of lockers and looked for his case number. The lockers were roughly numerical by case, but it usually took a little searching. Doyle remembered he had once spent two hours looking for some pills that were seized from Corey Feldman's garage.

Soon enough, he managed to find the right locker for the case. The locker swung open with ease. Locks were only instituted when there was a clear danger that evidence could be tampered with.

Hanratty snapped a photo from behind Doyle. He moved in closer to the locker.

"I don't know, Doyle. I'm not seeing too much in there."

Indeed, there wasn't much in the locker. Only a large manila envelope and an index card.

Doyle looked at the index card first. It read, "Storage 259786B—Rug with bloodstains. Property of T. Chapman." The rug that Doyle and Hanratty had initially discovered concealing blood underneath it was being stored in an offsite storage facility, which was not uncommon for larger items. The evidence locker within police headquarters only had limited storage capacity.

"Take a picture of this, just to be on the safe side," said Doyle.

Hanratty did as instructed.

Doyle moved on to the manila envelope. He undid the metal clasp and peered inside. Within the envelope were several documents and the stack of photos Hanratty had taken on-scene in Chapman's office. Doyle flipped through them, but there was nothing unusual. It was exactly what they had seen that day.

Doyle looked through the documents, hoping the supposed suicide note would be there, but he knew it was doubtful since something so important was usually enclosed within plastic or some other protective material, and nothing of the kind was in the envelope.

Hanratty took a photo of the documents.

"Don't bother," said Doyle. "There's nothing here but notes from other officers and interview transcripts. No suicide note."

"Are you sure they would include it in this case?" asked Hanratty. "I mean, I'm no professional investigator, at least, not anymore, but it seems to me if someone off-ed himself, that would be kept in a separate file from a burglary/murder case. Especially if it took place on a different day and at a different location. Am I right?"

"Yes, of course!" said Doyle. "You're brilliant, Hanratty!"

Hanratty snapped a photo of Doyle's face, nearly blinding him.

"Ow! What was that for?" asked Doyle.

"I just wanted to capture you saying I was brilliant," said Hanratty. "That one's a keeper."

Doyle headed back to the computer terminal, and Hanratty followed.

This time, Doyle searched simply for "Chad Wilkinson." A number of cases populated on the screen, more than a few relating to burglary or attempted burglary of paintings.

"Look at that," said Hanratty. "It says that Chad once tried to nab Joan Rivers' Ruebens."

"That's disgusting," said Doyle, laughing to himself. "Ahh, here we go."

The final listing on the page was labeled "Suicide," and referred to case number 1207x019.

Doyle and Hanratty quickly scuttled toward row nineteen, which was toward the far end of the room. Hanratty repeated the number over and over again so he wouldn't forget it.

Doyle knew the locker he was looking for before even looking at the case number. It was the only locker with a giant padlock.

"Son of a . . ." mumbled Doyle. This was why Burnside had no problem with his getting into Evidence.

A laminated label clung to the front of the locker which read "Restricted Access—Investigating Officer Thomas McNulty and Chief Investigator Oliver Burnside."

"Wow, that's pretty rare," said Hanratty. "It's been awhile since I've been an investigator, but they hardly ever padlock evidence. Usually the door lock is considered sufficient. That's already restricted access. But a padlock inside that?"

"Gee, I wonder who they're trying to keep out?" asked Doyle, sarcastically.

"Unless you have a key that I don't know about, I'm guessing it's you," said Hanratty.

"What do I do?" asked Doyle. "I can ask Burnside for that key, but I have a feeling that wouldn't go over so well. We can keep investigating without knowing what's in that locker, if we really have to."

Hanratty stared at Doyle for a couple long moments.

As if picking up Hanratty's telepathic message, Doyle said, "We have to get in that locker."

They both looked at the padlock.

"Say, Hanratty, you sometimes hang out with less-than-stellar individuals. You haven't, by any chance, picked up on the art of lock-picking have you?"

Hanratty grimaced. "First of all, Doyle, the people I spend my time with are decent people. They just like to have a few drinky-poo's after work. Or during work. Or as a midnight snack. But I do not associate with criminals, I assure you."

"Could you start? That'd have really been helpful in this situation. You disappoint me."

"Doyle, you're starting to sound like my ex-wife. Every day she told me I was going to get fired if I didn't stop drinking. Well, I showed her. I only got demoted, instead. Whore."

"Hanratty—you're a genius!"

"I haven't heard that one before. I call a woman a whore, and suddenly I'm a genius?"

"No, no—you said 'fired.' You know, 'fire.'"

"Okay . . ."

Doyle pointed at the wall. "Fire extinguisher!"

"I'm not on fire, Doyle."

"I know that. We're going to take the fire extinguisher, and slam it down on the lock. Bam! Broken lock!"

Hanratty hiccupped. "Sweet Peter, Doyle, this isn't a movie. You'd have to be Rambo to bring down the extinguisher with enough force to bust open a lock."

Doyle was still smiling.

"You're going to try it anyway, aren't you," said Hanratty.

Doyle nodded.

"Let me ask you this, Doyle. Would your sophisticated British friend use a fire extinguisher to open a lock?"

"Of course not, he's British. He'd probably try to convince the lock through brilliant rhetoric to open itself up."

"Fair enough," said Hanratty. "Be my guest." Hanratty motioned Doyle toward the fire extinguisher.

Doyle hesitated a moment, then lifted it from the wall and squared himself in front of the locker. He was hoping since they were the only ones in the room that the sound wouldn't be so loud as to attract attention.

"You've gotta bring it down with all your force, Doyle," advised Hanratty. "Just be aware that it's going to be all resistance, so you could end up pulling or breaking something. Your arms, for example."

"Thanks, Hanratty. I appreciate the advice."

"It's what I'm here for," said Hanratty. "And for taking pictures. But I'll avoid that now, since you're committing a potentially criminal act 'n' all."

"Be good, and I'll buy you an O'Doul's after this," said Doyle.

"Not funny," said Hanratty. For some reason, non-alcoholic brew was not Hanratty's forte.

Doyle readied himself. He held the extinguisher above his head.

"One . . . . " said Doyle.

Hanratty's eyes were wide open with excitement.

"Two . . . " Said Doyle.

Doyle breathed hard.

"THREE!"

Doyle slammed the extinguisher down on the lock with all his force. It was immediately clear when he made contact that the lock did not break. The shock up his arms told him that much. He also realized in the same instant that it was a mistake to be holding the trigger device at the top of the extinguisher. Doyle was fine except for two sore arms. Hanratty, however, looked like the Stay-Puft Marshmallow Man.

"Not cool, Doyle," said Hanratty sadly. "Not cool."

"I really wish I were the photographer right now," said Doyle.

"You cover me with the entire contents of a fire extinguisher and you don't even break the damn lock. Why am I even here? Dammit all!" yelled Hanratty.

"Shh," said Doyle. "Keep it down. I'm sorry. I didn't mean to do that. It just sort of . . . happened."

"Whatever, Doyle. Let's get out of here. You're not getting in that locker."

"One more time."

"You have to be shitting me. You're not going to break the lock!"

"I am going to break the lock."

"I'm not standing anywhere near you for this," said Hanratty.

"Keep your distance then," said Doyle. "But this lock is going down."

Hanratty wiped some of the white foam off his brow and took several steps back.

Doyle held the extinguisher with both arms again, except this time with his hand off the trigger. He didn't bother counting down. This time, he slammed the extinguisher against the lock with three consecutive blows.

After the third time, the lock dropped and hit the floor with a clank.

"Holy shit," said Hanratty. "We got Rocky friggin' Balboa in the house."

"Yes, I'm the man," said Doyle. "Now let's hurry this up, I'm guessing we have limited time."

Doyle opened the locker. It looked similar to the contents of the Chapman/Ramirez locker, containing a plastic bag with photographs, a manila envelope which likely contained police reports and interviews, a plastic bag with a syringe, and a plastic bag holding one sheet of paper.

"Hanratty, I think this may be the confession."

"Look at these photos," said Hanratty, flipping through the photos. "Whoever did these was a real shoddy photographer."

"Don't get any foam on those, Hanratty."

"Sure thing, Italian Stallion."

"Wait a minute, this can't be right," said Doyle. He looked into the manila envelope and went through all the contents. He then went back to the plastic bag that contained the lone sheet of paper.

"This just can't be right," said Doyle again. The bag was clearly labeled "confession letter." The trouble was with the letter itself.

"What does that even mean?" asked Hanratty.

"Anything. Really, it could mean absolutely anything."

Both Doyle and Hanratty continued to stare at it.

The document had three words scribbled on it in large, upper case letters: "I DID IT"

20

OYLE AND HANRATTY RUSHED TO DOYLE'S CAR in a hurry, and with good reason. They had illegally broken into a restricted evidence locker to take pictures of the evidence, and if Doyle were caught he'd ultimately be fired, if not put in jail. Hanratty looked as though he had bathed in Cool Whip, which was strange and suspicious by anyone's standards. Most importantly, Doyle needed to talk to William. He had too many questions and didn't know what to do with them.

Doyle dialed William's cell.

William answered. "Wright."

"Wow, William—you're starting to sound like a real American detective. None of this, 'Hello there, sir or madame, this is William Wright, formerly of Scotland Yard, how may I be of service.'"

"I've never said that," said William.

It was hard for Doyle to hear William with all the background noise.

"William, what's going on there? Are you driving through construction?"

"Not quite, Doyle. I'm at the Humphrey terminal, waiting to catch a plane to Hawaii. Surprise."

"What are you talking about? You're working on a case. I'm paying you. You can't just leave!"

Doyle was hating himself more and more—he didn't want to keep lying to William that he could actually pay him. But, right now he was more concerned as to why William was ditching him.

"Doyle, I'm still on the case. I'm following one of our most important leads. It turns out Kimberly Chapman went to Hawaii, immediately after her former, now late boyfriend either committed suicide or was murdered. A little suspicious, don't you think, Doyle?"

"Yes, yes I'd call that suspicious," said Doyle. "But listen, I need to talk to about the supposed suicide note. I don't know if it even refers to suicide. It just says, 'I did it.'"

"What was that Doyle?" William said loudly. Doyle could hear a plane pass in the background.

"It says, 'I did it,'" yelled Doyle.

"You did what now?" William shouted.

"No, the suicide note!"

"It says you did it?"

"No, it . . ."

"Doyle, I'll have to call you later," yelled William. "I can't hear a thing."

"But this is important!"

"You'll be fine, Doyle. You're a great detective."

"Thanks, William."

"Pardon?"

"THANKS!"

"Did I mention you're covering business expenses?" asked William.

"To hell with that," said Doyle.

"Sorry, couldn't hear you there. Oh, my plane's boarding. I must go now. Ta."

Doyle heard a click, and William was off the line. He shut his phone with a *snap*.

Shit, thought Doyle. *Except for incessantly drunk photographer, I'm on my own on this one. Shit.*

"Doyle, I think I'm heading home now. I'm tired," said Hanratty.

Double shit, thought Doyle.

"Come on, Hanratty," said Doyle. "I know you're tired and everything, but I still need you. William just left the continental U.S., and I still need to find out who's behind all this. Please, won't you consider helping me out here—just a little bit longer?"

Hanratty shook his head. "Nope. I'm tired. Time for bed."

Doyle looked at his watch, then back at Hanratty as if he were crazy for wanting to go to bed so early in the day. Hanratty shrugged.

Doyle didn't want to let Hanratty go that easy. "I'll buy you alcoholic beverages if you help me."

Hanratty laughed. "I'd be buying my own liquor, and you know it! Besides, I can't be any help right now. I'm out of it. I'm sorry."

Doyle didn't have much else to say to that. He popped his trunk so Hanratty could get his bike out.

Getting into his car, Doyle waved good-bye to his friend.

"If you wake up and you have no plans, give me a ring," said Doyle.

Hanratty nodded and waved back. "Take it easy, Doyle."

Realizing that Hanratty was still covered in fire-extinguisher gunk, Doyle left his friend with one very important piece of advice as he sped away:

"Hanratty, be careful on your way home," shouted Doyle out of his car window. "You look like you just stepped out of an all-male porn video."

21

DOYLE DROVE HOME IN SILENCE. Normally he sang along to eighties power ballads as he cruised the roads at night with his windows down, but he just didn't feel like it tonight. Besides, he was thinking. And that took serious concentration. He had a headache.

"'I did it,'" Doyle muttered to himself. "What does that mean? 'I killed Marta Ramirez'? 'I broke into Timothy Chapman's safe'? 'I dumped Kimberly Chapman'? 'I ate a club sandwich for lunch'? 'I made top score on Tetris.' Good God, it could mean anything."

Doyle kept driving, staring at the road in front of him. "What am I going to do?" he asked himself. That's when he caught sight of his bracelet. It was a thin, brown leather bracelet his father had given him years ago, when Doyle first began training for the academy. Doyle and his father were never that close; he was a tough, commanding man, and Doyle was a silly, smart-aleck boy. They didn't always get along well, except for maybe when they were watching old cop shows on television.

When Doyle entered the academy, it had made his father proud, far more proud than anything else Doyle had done in his life. Doyle, however, wasn't so much trying to please his father as just trying to be like one of the guys from *Get Smart* or *Dragnet*. But Doyle accepted his father's affection, along with the bracelet which his father presented to him on his graduation day from the academy.

"What is this?" young Doyle had asked a beaming Lieutenant Malloy.

"It's inspiration," his father had said.

"But what does it mean?" Doyle had asked.

"Son, you're not a detective yet. But I have no doubt you will be, if that's what you want. When you make it, I want you to look at this whenever you're in trouble, and it'll help you out. I promise."

"But, Dad, 'WWCD.' What does it stand for?"

Although Lieutenant Malloy rarely smiled, he did at that moment. "It means, 'What Would Columbo Do?'" His father let out a hardy laugh and slapped his son on the back.

It was one of the best memories Doyle had of his father.

Doyle seriously wondered if his father was proud of him or not. For the most part, Doyle felt like a screw-up. But then again, it was hard not to feel like a screw-up when your father was the best there was. How could Doyle even try to compare? Now that he was really working hard on a case, he felt like how his father must have felt every day he was working out on the street and busting not just petty thieves and dog-nappers but real, dangerous criminals like murderers, rapists, and drug lords.

Suddenly, Doyle missed him. He also suddenly—barely—missed a giant semi truck as he whipped a U-turn and crossed a median to go the opposite direction. Cars angrily honked at him, but Doyle couldn't care less.

"I'll tell you what Columbo would do," said Doyle. "He'd visit the scene of the crime and get some friggin' answers."

Doyle flipped open his cell phone and called headquarters. He prayed Amanda would answer. If it was anyone else, Doyle probably had caused several near-collisions for nothing.

"Minneapolis Police, how may I direct your call?" said a young, remarkably sweet female voice.

"How's my favorite girl in the whole wide world tonight?"

Amanda whispered in the phone, "Doyle, is that you?"

"You mean you're someone else's favorite girl, too?"

"You better get in here. You're in big, big trouble. Burnside looked like he was ready to kill you."

"Hey, it's okay. I have things under control. Trust me."

"Somehow I don't believe you," she said.

"I need a favor."

The line was silent.

"Amanda?"

"Sorry, Burnside just walked past. What kind of a favor? Doyle, don't make me lose my job. I can't handle that right now."

"It's a small favor. An itty-bitty teenie-weenie little favor."

"What do I get out of it?" asked Amanda, playfully.

"A movie?" suggested Doyle.

"And?"

Doyle sighed. "Dinner?"

"Okay," happily agreed Amanda. "One more thing."

"What's that?" asked Doyle

"I'm on break in fifteen minutes. Can you meet me at the Rabbit Hole?"

"Uhh . . ." Doyle hesitated. "I'm in the middle of a . . ."

"Just meet me at the Rabbit Hole, Doyle. I think I deserve that, right?"

"All right, I'll meet you there," said Doyle.

"Excellent!" she said. "Now, what's the favor?"

"I need an address for a Kyle Gordon."

"Who's that?"

"No one in particular," responded Doyle.

He heard typing on the other end of the line.

"Got it. Fifty-three Wilshire Court, Apartment 6B, Dinkytown. Hey, isn't that the suicide address?"

"I'll see you at the Rabbit Hole. You're the best, Amanda."

"Hey, I . . ."

Doyle snapped his phone shut and stepped on the gas.

Things were looking better by the moment. He had a new plan and a date with an attractive young officer. He was more excited by that than he'd expected.

"Thank you, Columbo," said Doyle with glee.

He rolled down the window and hit "play" on the tape deck.

"Take it on the run, baby!" sang Doyle as he sped off towards his favorite hang-out.

22

I T WAS LATE EVENING WHEN DOYLE PULLED into the Rabbit Hole parking lot. Shay usually kept the place open until 10:00 or 11:00, as long as there were enough customers to support it. The parking lot was still close to capacity, so Doyle didn't think he'd have anything to worry about.

When he walked in the door, Amanda was sitting in the same chair he'd been sitting in during their previous encounter.

"Thanks for coming, Doyle," she said. "I know you're super busy right now, but I just really needed to see you."

"No, it's fine. I always have time for you."

"Fuck!" she yelled. A few heads turned, looking in her direction.

"What?" said Doyle, taken aback.

"That's exactly the problem, Doyle! You're always nice and fun and there for me and all that great stuff. Oh, and you're very, very flirty, which I'm sure you're aware of. But for some mysterious reason, you never want to be in a *relationship* with me. What do I have to do? Huh? What the hell do I have to do to be with you? Am I not attractive enough?"

Doyle could barely speak. "No, you're very attractive."

"Do I bother you? Am I not pleasant to be around?"

"Well, right now you're not terribly pleasant," he said.

Shay walked over from the coffee bar. "Is everything okay here?" she asked.

"I don't know, is everything okay?" Amanda asked. "I have no idea. Hey, you've known Doyle for a while, right? What's his problem? Why doesn't he want to be with me?"

"I'm right here," said Doyle. "You two don't need to talk about me."

"Shhhh," said Amanda. "Shay, what do you think it is?"

"Well, he is awfully shy when it comes to interpersonal stuff. Despite his quick wit, he seems rather fragile inside."

Amanda looked at Doyle and nodded. "Yeah, I can see that."

"He hasn't had a lot of experience with women. Since we were together back in high school, I haven't known him to date too many other women," said Shay.

"You two were together?" asked Amanda.

"Before I turned her into a lesbian," said Doyle with a sigh.

"You never turned me into a lesbian," said Shay, frowning. "I just realized back then that I found you shockingly boring naked."

"Oh, now I feel better," said Doyle.

"For once, this isn't about you. This is about me," said Amanda. "Why the hell don't you want me? What is it about me that you don't like? Shay, do you find me attractive?"

Shay nodded. "Yeah, I would definitely want to . . ."

"Let's not even go there, okay?" said Doyle.

"Wow, Mister Insecurity," said Shay.

"I'm not insecure, I just . . ." he looked at Amanda, "I take awhile, you know?"

"Do you like me?" Amanda asked.

"Well, yeah," said Doyle.

"Would you conceivably want to date me?"

"Yeah, sure," he said.

"Will the upcoming dinner and movie you owe me be more than just a 'friendly' date?"

"Yeah, whatever you want. Can we please stop drawing all this attention to us?" Doyle was more than aware of the numerous eyes and ears taking in their little exchange.

"Kiss me," Amanda said.

"What?" asked Doyle.

"Kiss me. I've been waiting too damn long."

Shay mouthed the words *Kiss her!*

Amanda closed her eyes and puckered up.

Doyle had never been more embarrassed than he was in that very moment. Despite that, he moved in for the kiss.

First he gave her a little peck on the lips, then pulled away. But then he smelled the perfume she was wearing. He couldn't pinpoint what it was, exactly, but it smelled really, really good. So he kept his face close to her, and moved in for another kiss. A much longer, more passionate kiss.

The patrons of the Rabbit Hole hooted and clapped for them. Soon, the establishment was filled with a thunderous applause.

"You're crazy—you know that, right?" whispered Doyle.

"You're not so normal yourself," Amanda replied. And then, "Thank you."

"No problem," he said. "But next time, can we have intimate moments that are not quite so public?"

Amanda laughed. "Sure."

She looked at her watch. "Shoot, I should probably get back to work."

"Me too," said Doyle. "I still have a major crime to solve."

Doyle TURNED DOWN THE CAR STEREO as he pulled into the apartment complex's parking lot. He remembered Wilshire well from his early days as a patrol cop. The apartment complex was one of the many areas on the northern side of Dinkytown that had been beautiful when it was built, a perfect layout for the University of Minnesota's college residences. But, as decades passed, Dinkytown attracted its fair share of crack whores and drug lords.

Wilshire wasn't horrible by any means, at least not during the daytime. The buildings that lined the street were run down and dirty, and the occasional bum asked for change. Usually a respectable person could walk by without fear of getting mugged. At night, however, less-than-stellar individuals came out of hiding with guns, drugs, and unfathomable language.

"Hey, fuck face," a voice said as Doyle got out of his car. "Can I have some change?"

A dirty, smelly man with a long, straggily beard was staring at Doyle with wide eyes and an empty jar in his hands.

"Well, since you asked so nicely," said Doyle. He reached in his pocket and then flipped a coin towards the bum, a coin Doyle himself had found on the ground that same day. At the moment, it was the only cash Doyle had to his name.

"Wow, a quarter. Maybe I'll buy myself a gumball. Thanks, fuck face."

"Welcome," said Doyle. *Ahh, it feels good to be back on the streets*, he thought to himself.

Doyle walked up to the front entrance of the apartment complex. Upon closer inspection, Doyle could see the building had been pink at one point in its history, but had turned to more of a smeared gray. Not much different from the bum.

He pulled on the door handle. Nothing happened.

Dammit, thought Doyle. Doors have locks on them, sometimes. "Okay, brain, let's think."

Doyle looked at the buzzer system attached to the wall. It had a number of buttons corresponding to residents of the building.

Doyle pushed a button next to the name "Sanchez." It made a loud, screechy noise, and a man's voice quickly answered.

"*Hola?*" said the voice.

"*Hola, senor. Necisito druggas, por favor.*"

"You police?" asked the voice.

"Uh, no. No, I am not. I just want some good drugs. My friend Phil said you were the mad hook-up in the hood. Yo."

"You police. Fuck off, policeman. We got no drugs here." The intercom went silent.

Shit, that didn't work, thought Doyle.

Doyle pushed the same button again.

"Man, what the fuck do you want?"

"I'll give you twenty dollars to open the door."

"You a policeman, ain't you?"

"Maybe."

"'Maybe' ain't no fuckin' answer, gringo. Either you is or you ain't. Know what I'm sayin', bitch?"

"I hear what you're saying, and I'm totally down with that, yo," responded Doyle. "And yes, I am a police officer. A police officer who wants to give you twenty dollars to open a door."

"You gonna arrest me?"

"What am I going to arrest you for?"

"I just called you a bitch," said the voice.

"I don't think that's illegal," said Doyle.

"Are you going to raid my apartment?"

"Why would I? You said you don't have any drugs."

"Yeah," said the voice. "I did say that."

"Are you gonna let me in now?"

"Let me think about it," said the voice.

The intercom went silent.

Doyle waited.

He hit the buzzer again.

"*Ay, policia loca.* Come in, crazy bastard," said the voice.

Doyle heard a clicking noise near the door. He pulled on the door handle, and he was in.

Within seconds, a fat Mexican man came running down the stairs at an impressive speed for his girth.

"*Vente dolares, gringo,*" said Sanchez.

Doyle held out a bill, but pulled it back when Sanchez reached for it.

"Don't ever call me bitch again. Unless we're having relations. *Comprende?*"

Sanchez gave Doyle a skeptical look and grabbed the bill out of his hand.

"*Punto,*" said Sanchez.

"I know what that means," said Doyle, but Sanchez had already began walking up the stairs back to his apartment.

Within seconds, Doyle heard Sanchez's voice call, "*Punto,* this is fake money. George Bush is not on currency, gringo bastard!"

Doyle realized he was out his last twenty-five cents and his mock currency all within ten minutes. *This is starting to get expensive,* Doyle thought.

He approached apartment 6B. Doyle had no idea whether or not Kyle Gordon was working at the McDonald's drive-thru tonight or if he was in his apartment.

Only one way to find out, thought Doyle.

He knocked on the door. Silence from inside. He tried one more time just to be sure, but again, no sound.

Dreading that the door would be locked, Doyle reached out and turned the knob. To his surprise, the knob turned very smoothly, at least until the entire knob itself fell through the hole in the door and clattered onto the floor within the apartment.

Hmm, wasn't expecting that, thought Doyle.

He looked inside the apartment through the hole in the door, but saw nothing but darkness. As far as he could tell, no one was there.

Doyle pushed the door open and stepped inside. Upon turning on the light, Doyle saw pretty much what he expected the apartment to look like. Dirty clothes and discarded food products were lying in random areas, the furniture looked like lower-end thrift store merchandise, and the air held a faint scent of moldy cheese.

Moving from room to room, Doyle looked for anything of interest. He realized he was in Kyle Gordon's room when he noticed a mustard-stained McDonald's uniform on the floor. The Nine Inch Nails and Marilyn Manson posters seemed to fit Mr. Gordon's affinity for piercings and tattoos.

Doyle had a feeling that Kyle knew more about his roommate than he'd led Doyle to believe in the drive-thru. If Kyle knew something, Doyle wanted it. Needed it.

Doyle's eyes fell on the laptop in the corner of the room, sitting on a small desk piled with magazines, crumpled papers, and half a pastrami sandwich, probably a couple days old from the look of it.

For some reason, Doyle had a really good feeling about this. A computer held everything about a person these days: their life history, their hobbies, their shopping habits, their sexual tendencies, and if Doyle had any luck at all, this one held knowledge of Chad's crimes and/or murder.

Please, God, I could seriously use a break here, thought Doyle.

It seemed that God took this request quite literally. As Doyle reached to turn on the computer, a sound from behind him made Doyle turn his head, only for him to come face to face with the base end of a metal, industrial flashlight, which made a gristly cracking noise when it made contact. Doyle's face burst into pain, but he was still aware enough to see, albeit blurrily, the panicked face of Kyle Gordon.

"Hey . . ." Doyle started to speak, although he wasn't terribly sure what he intended to say. Unable to think through the pain, it was almost merciful when a second blow from the flashlight, ironically, turned out the lights.

23

A s Doyle slowly gained consciousness, a few things struck him as peculiar. One: he was outside. He knew this because it was raining, and judging from how wet he already was, chances were he'd been outside for some time. Two: He smelled something foul. After registering this, he prayed to God he hadn't had any excretive accidents while he unconscious. Fortunately, he had not. After examining the soft, albeit angular material beneath him, he realized he was lying atop a large pile of garbage. When Doyle searched for his wallet, to see if it was stolen, he had the third and most frightful revelation: he was not wearing any pants.

Cautiously, Doyle pushed himself up. As soon as he moved his head, he felt a throbbing pain that seemed to go all the way into the center of his skull. Doyle touched the top of his head, and his hand came back with a little blood. But the top of his head felt fairly intact. He didn't think he'd have to worry about a concussion or any serious brain damage, at least none that anyone could notice.

Well, it could have been a lot worse, thought Doyle.

That's when he had a dreadful thought. He reached down his soaked undershorts and felt his parts, which were shriveled from the cold rain. To be on the safe side, he also brought a finger down to his nether regions. *Thank God*, thought Doyle. *My innocence was not taken from me.*

"Hey, Fuck Face," he heard a voice say.

Doyle sat upright. Over the edge of the green trash dumpster, Doyle saw the same bum from earlier looking at him.

"Yeah, you," said the bum. "Get the fuck out of my house."

"Sorry . . . I'm . . . I'm sorry." Doyle attempted to stand on wobbly legs. He realized he must be right outside Kyle Gordon's apartment building, so at least he knew where he was. *Kyle Gordon, that little bastard*, thought Doyle.

"What the fuck! Were you jerking off in my house?"

Doyle realized a bit too late that his right hand was still down his undershorts.

"No, I . . ."

"Just, get out!" said the bum. "Fuckin' pervert. Jerkin' off in a guy's home. And people call *me* sick."

"You don't understand," said Doyle. "You see I was investigating this guy, and before you know it I was thrown out into the garbage without my pants."

The bum flipped a quarter at Doyle, which landed squarely between Doyle's eyes.

"There you go, Fuck Face. You obviously need that more than I do. Now get the fuck out."

For the first time in his life, and Doyle prayed it was the last time he climbed out of a trash dumpster with the rain beating on his back, ran past a crotchety old bum who currently had the social upper hand, and made his way onto the city street, without any pants, only to realize he also didn't have any car keys.

Thunder rolled and growled above him. Rain ran down his brow into his eyes. The throbbing in his head seemed to grow louder and heavier every second.

Doyle leaned again his car, looked up into the sky, and yelled with complete and utter sincerity, "FUCK ME!"

"PERVERT!" the bum screamed from down the alley.

Doyle tried again and again pulling on the handles of his car door, but to no avail. Not typically an angry person, Doyle felt awkward about kicking his own car, but he needed to let out some steam. On a scale of one to ten, this day was somewhere near a zero in Doyle's book.

It was right around when Doyle's foot made contact with his car door that he heard the police siren only a few yards away from him, and suddenly Doyle's day went from bad to a whole lot worse.

24

I had a feeling I'd find you around here at some point," said Detective McNulty gleefully from the front seat, speaking to Doyle through the metal mesh wire that separated the two of them inside McNulty's police car. "I just had no idea I'd find you without any pants, attempting to harm a motor vehicle. Let's see here, we could include disorderly conduct, indecent exposure, attempting to flee the police—"

"Hey, I never attempted to flee—"

"No, but you should have," said McNulty, "because as it is, right now, you're in some major shit. And I don't even mean, 'goodness, I might lose my job' type shit. I mean, 'I've lost everything worth living for, my life is a living hell' type shit."

"I take it you're pretty familiar with that one," said Doyle. His wrists were throbbing from how tightly McNulty had put on the handcuffs.

"Fuck you, Malloy. I've been after you a long time now, just waiting for you to screw up big. For years now, Burnside's been handing you easy case after easy case while me and the other guys get shot at, spit on, assaulted, verbally abused, harassed. Meanwhile you sit in your little office watching movies and occasionally hand in a report. I don't know how you ever became Burnside's little pet, but it's all over now. Even Burnside doesn't want your ass around anymore. I heard some of the shit you pulled today. You're done, Malloy. Done."

Doyle could see McNulty staring at him in the rearview mirror. His eyes were hard and unwavering. They also weren't watching the road.

"Hey, McNulty," said Doyle conversationally.

"What the hell do you want?"

"Car."

McNulty quickly swerved, narrowly avoiding a white Toyota that honked as they passed.

"Shit," spat McNulty, his hands tightening on the wheel.

"Listen, McNulty," said Doyle. "You can do whatever you want to me, charge me with whatever, try to ruin my job and my life, but it won't matter. I'm cracking this case wide open, and once I do, I'll be promoted and I'll make damn sure that once I am, you'll be scrubbing the floors around the station. Maybe I'll let you do the occasional rectal exam. You should be pretty familiar with those, what with being an asshole 'n' all."

"Don't push me, Malloy. You're not in any position to do so."

McNulty took the exit towards headquarters.

"Hope you're prepared, Doyle. This won't be your finest hour, I assure you," McNulty smirked.

"That may be," said Doyle. "But things could always be worse."

"I'd like to know how things could possibly be any worse for you," said McNulty.

"Well for one, I could have been without my undershorts. That would have been embarrassing."

McNulty shook his head. "You'll never change," he said. "You'll always be the same old idiot Doyle Malloy."

"I wouldn't be so sure," said Doyle.

After a moment of silence, McNulty said, "So, Doyle, how well do you know that Amanda girl that works the front desk?"

"I know her pretty well," said Doyle.

"If I ask her out, think she'd say yes?"

Doyle didn't respond. McNulty looked back at him.

"What, no answer?" asked McNulty.

"I guess I wouldn't know," said Doyle. "I really doubt it, though."

"Why not?" said McNulty sternly.

"I don't think you're her type," said Doyle. He decided to reserve the information that he, as of a few hours ago, was already dating her. He wanted to see where this conversation was going first.

"Oh, yeah? And what type is that, exactly?" asked McNulty.

"Do you really want me to answer that?" asked Doyle.

"I suppose you think you're her type, huh, Malloy? Well let me ask you this—how many times have you spoken with her, you know, little girlie chit-chatting here and there, and not asked her out? What's wrong with you? She's smokin' hot!"

"I know," said Doyle.

"You gay?" asked McNulty.

"I'm not gay. I'm just big-boned."

"What does that mean?"

"It means you're thick-skulled, and she wouldn't be interested in you because of it," said Doyle.

"Is that so?" said McNulty. "Well, we'll see about that. While you're sitting in jail, I think I'll ask her out. Maybe take her out to a nice dinner, take her back to my place, maybe play cop and criminal—what the heck, I got the handcuffs, right?"

"Not a chance, asshole," said Doyle.

"What was that?" shouted McNulty.

"Car," said Doyle.

McNulty narrowly avoided direct contact with a sportscar.

"Don't even bother trying, McNulty—she won't be interested."

"Well, we'll see about that, Malloy. We'll see."

McNulty parked the car and stepped out. He opened the rear door and yanked Doyle by the handcuffs, which sent a sharp pain up Doyle's arms. Of course, McNulty had decided to bring Doyle in through the front entrance, just to make sure Doyle was humiliated as much as possible.

McNulty had his hand on Doyle's back and pushed him forward. Doyle stumbled along in his sport coat, dress shirt, and boxer shorts, now dried, which allowed the dirt and grime from the garbage to become visible.

Amanda was the first to see Doyle, and she quickly lowered her head, likely to save Doyle some embarrassment, and also to save herself from having to repeat the image over and over in her head. Doyle very much hoped she would not remember this all that well. He didn't think his chances were very good.

Other cops turned to look at Doyle. The ones he didn't know stared at him as he passed. The cops who knew him quickly looked away. No cop wants to see one of their own fall, no matter what the cause.

McNulty led him to the east side of the building, where the holding cells were located.

As he was being pushed along, Doyle said, "I need to know exactly what you're charging me with."

"Burnside'll let you know," said McNulty. "I think he has some other things he wants to discuss with you. He's not too happy."

"Thanks for the warning," said Doyle.

"Oh, I wasn't trying to help you," said McNulty. "I was trying to add a little extra fear, sort of add to the suspense, you know."

"Again, I appreciate it."

"I have to admit, Doyle, you're handling this pretty well. I thought for sure I'd have you in tears by now. Perhaps begging me to just let you go."

"I hate to say it, McNulty, but this isn't the first time I've been led down a long hallway in my underwear. High school sucked."

"I should have guessed," said McNulty, laughing since it was at Doyle's expense.

McNulty took a keychain out of his pocket and flipped keys around until he found a tiny one. He stuck it inside Doyle's handcuffs and released the locks. Doyle quickly rubbed his wrists in relief.

McNulty opened a cell door and shoved Doyle inside. It was an empty cell, which was a pleasant surprise as it was starting to get late into the night, and a number of other cells were likely already filling with drunks and domestics.

"Hey, Doyle, don't go anywhere," said McNulty, and laughed mischievously.

"Don't worry, I'll be right here. Hold my calls, will you?"

McNulty narrowed his eyes, turned and left.

Doyle put his hands around the steel bars. This was his first time in a jail of any sort, and he always imagined what it would be like to be behind bars. Without a doubt it was disappointing, but he couldn't help but feel a surge of energy from somewhere within him. It was as though he finally felt what it was like to be a villain in a classic cop crime show. Put behind bars and brought to justice. Except instead of being booked by Dan-O, he was thrown in by that douche bag McNulty. Not to mention, Doyle wasn't actually guilty of anything. Well, not much anyway.

A few minutes passed before Doyle heard footsteps approaching. Doyle's powerful surge of energy flopped rather rudely into dread. Doyle had worked for several years with Chief Burnside. They had always had a suitable, albeit unsavory working relationship. But Doyle had been continually impressed by the forceful and dominant way Burnside dealt with others. When Burnside was your enemy . . . well, you didn't want Burnside as your enemy.

But now, it seemed, Doyle was Burnside's enemy. It wasn't a good feeling. He gulped.

"Doyle," said Burnside, as he stepped in front of Doyle cell. "Detective Doyle Malloy."

Doyle shuddered. Not just because he was cold and still a little wet, but because when Burnside repeated your full name and rank, thinks were going to slide downhill, real fast.

"Hi, Chief—"

"What the living hell do you have to say for yourself?" spat Burnside, his face growing redder by the second as he cuttlefished his way through the spectrum of mad.

"I can explain—"

"Explain what, Doyle? Explain what?"

"You see, I was out investigating this Kyle Gordon, and I ended up in my underwear here, and . . ."

"Doyle!" hollered Burnside. "I don't give a flying fuck why you're in your underwear. I don't give a fuck where you were. I don't give a fuck why you were kicking in your own car door. I don't give a shit about any of that. What I want to know is why you deliberately disobeyed my specific orders. Furthermore, I want to know why you broke into the evidence locker and forcefully gained access to sealed evidence. I have no idea what you tampered with, what you destroyed, or in how many ways you completely ruined any sort of credibility our department had. Doyle, you fucked up more tonight than I ever thought was possible. I gave you this case, which I knew was big and thought if you pulled all your shit together you might be able to handle it. But as it turns out, I was wrong. Incredibly wrong to think you had any chance of completing this case in a reasonable manner. I honestly don't know what the hell to do with you."

Doyle attempted to respond, but realized he had no voice to respond with. It was as if all the air in his lungs had suddenly vanished.

"Well?" asked Burnside. "What do you have to say for yourself?"

"I'm sorry," croaked Doyle.

"You're sorry? That's supposed to make up for it?" Burnside's eyes seemed to glow, and Doyle realized why every perp turns to mush when they're thrown against Burnside.

"I didn't think the case was done yet. I still don't. Kyle Gordon assaulted me."

"Did you go into his home without a warrant?" asked Burnside.

Doyle didn't respond.

"I want to make it very clear that you're not going anywhere tonight. Maybe not for a while. I really haven't decided what I'm going to do with you yet in the long term."

"What are you charging me with, exactly?"

"As far as what happened in the evidence locker, I'm not charging you with anything for that. I wouldn't want anyone to think I have rogue cops on my force who can't be trusted."

Doyle laughed, but Burnside pretended to ignore.

"McNulty's charges will be good enough for the time being. One count of indecent exposure and one count of improper conduct. Judging from your appearance, I don't think anyone will have a hard time buying either of those two charges."

"How soon will I get out?" asked Doyle.

"Don't worry, you'll get a fair trial in a couple of weeks or so. I'm sure by then we'll have everything nicely wrapped up. I'm assuming you have all of your case notes organized in your office?"

"You can't do this," said Doyle.

"I've pulled some strings with Judge Nelson and D.A. Reichert, they both agreed that a bail of $100,000 was justified, given the circumstances."

"Circumstances? I'm still working on a case! You can't do this," Doyle repeated. "Kyle Gordon was involved with Marta's murder, and he was probably involved with Chad's death, too. Even if I'm in here, you have to keep investigating. There's far more that you're not looking at."

"Doyle, there is no evidence for either of those accusations. That being the case, I don't see one good reason to push this further."

"He bashed me over the head!"

"You were trespassing, which you're very fortunate he didn't charge you with. Now get some sleep. Maybe in the morning, you'll be a little more rational and willing to face things like a man."

Doyle had worked with Burnside a long time, but he never felt the hot, burning loathing he did right then.

Burnside turned to leave.

"Hey, Burnsie," said Doyle.

Burnside looked back at Doyle.

"You're making a big mistake," said Doyle.

Burnside shook his head. "You were a colossal waste of my time," he said, and left.

Doyle sat on the bench and listened to the drunken ramblings and yells coming from cells near him. Finally, he stretched out and lay down, his head resting on the firm, cold pillow.

As the gravity of his situation settled in, Doyle wondered how he had gotten himself so deep into this mess. He wondered if he had just handed Burnside the report if things would have been much better for him. Instead of being in jail, he could be in Burnside's office discussing the terms of his promotion, a raise, and the future of his career. Doyle saw flashes of medals, beautiful anchorwomen interviewing him, very large bonus checks . . .

"No point in thinking about that now," Doyle muttered to himself, although it was all he could think about, even as he drifted off to sleep.

WHEN DOYLE MALLOY WAS ELEVEN YEARS OLD, he went to school dressed like a popular TV detective. It was only one day, but it was one that stuck with him for a long time. Had it been Halloween, he would have been fine, but a random Tuesday, not so much. What made him do it, he wasn't sure.

Assembling the outfit was easy. He had the white dress shirt and black slacks from a cousin's wedding the month before. The trench coat and tie were his father's. The coat dragged behind him as he walked, the sleeves twenty times wider than they needed to be, and the necktie hung down well below his crotch. He also carried one of his father's shoes.

"Who are you supposed to be? Dick Tracy?" asked Kenny Schmidt, his classmate who had far more muscle than brains.

"No. I'm Maxwell Smart. From TV," said Doyle defensively.

"Why are you holding a shoe?" Kenny asked.

"It's my shoe phone," Doyle responded matter-of-factly. "It lets me talk to headquarters."

Kenny rolled his eyes. "Let's see you talk on it, then."

"What?" asked Doyle.

"You heard me. Talk on your shoe phone," he said. Other students had gathered around to witness their interaction.

Doyle brought his father's size-ten dress shoe up to his ear. "Headquarters?" Doyle asked.

Doyle saw Kenny's fist swing out at him with plenty of time to spare. He dodged the meaty hand and spat out, "Missed me by that much!" Doyle didn't see the second fist headed directly for his jaw. It made contact with a loud crack.

Doyle's head thudded onto the ground. He heard his fellow students gasp as he went down.

As far as Doyle was concerned, that experience in grade school summed up his entire career as a detective. Doyle would have continued to consider how pathetic his life had become, but his thoughts were interrupted by the noise of footsteps coming down the jail's hallway.

"OH, GOD, DOYLE—WHAT ARE YOU DOING HERE?" he heard the voice say.

It was Amanda.

"It's a long story," said Doyle with a heavy sigh.

"Rumors have been spreading around that you were streaking and breaking into cars. What's gotten into you?"

Doyle could see a mixture of worry and sadness in her face.

"Believe me, Amanda—those rumors are grossly exaggerated. I wasn't naked—I was wearing boxer shorts. And I was kicking my own car because I was upset."

"What made you so upset?" asked Amanda.

"Getting knocked out and having my pants stolen by some punk. And I've been under a lot of pressure," said Doyle. "But it'll all work itself out, I'm pretty sure."

"But you're in jail!" said Amanda. "How are things just going to work themselves out? You have to do something."

"I'm a little tied up at the moment, but trust me, there's nothing more I'd like to do then get out of here," said Doyle.

Amanda looked at Doyle with pity.

"Oh, Doyle—what happened? Here, I thought things were going to be perfect! I'd finally convinced you that we should be an item, and more or less made you kiss me in front of dozens of people at the coffee shop. I told my mother I'd actually bagged myself a boyfriend . . . and you wouldn't believe how pleased she sounded on the phone! Now my boyfriend is a jailbird—the kind of scum I'd be throwing behind bars myself. Why couldn't you have just been an honorable detective?"

"I am!" retorted Doyle. "You wouldn't believe the kind of detective work I've been doing—I mean, real hard-boiled kind of stuff. I've never felt more alive!"

"You call this being alive?" asked Amanda.

"Well, yeah. I tell you, Amanda—I'm so close to cracking this case wide open. And when I do, there are going to be people going down. I swear, it feels like even Burnside and McNulty are in on this thing."

"You mean because McNulty arrested you for indecent exposure and Burnside threw you in jail because of it? I don't think that means they're 'in' on anything. I think it just means their doing their jobs, which right now you're not doing."

"Sure, take cracks at the guy in jail—very nice," said Doyle.

"Maybe I should take McNulty up on his offer. At least he's a little more put together."

Doyle jumped up from his seat and put his hands around the steel bars.

"McNulty? What offer? Did he ask you out?"

"Yes, Doyle, he did. What are you getting so bent out of shape for?"

"Don't go out with him, please! He's a jerk. A dillweed. He's pure poison. You don't want to go out with a guy like him. He won't treat you right."

"That's real sweet, Doyle. But he's actually asked me out. And that hasn't happened to me for a long time. A real long time. If I remember correctly, I had to ask you out."

"I'm sorry, Amanda—I'll take you out as soon as I'm out of here. I swear. Just don't go out with that guy. I couldn't live with that."

"It's not your choice, Doyle. You've made your choice over and over again, and it's always been 'no.' I want to be with a guy who will actually say 'yes.'"

"But I did say yes!"

"You mean before you became a jailbird? Wow, what a guy you are."

"Now you're just being insulting."

"Well, what do you expect, Doyle? You let me down," said Amanda.

Doyle felt an awful pang of guilt.

"Okay, okay. I'm really sorry this happened. But, believe me, I'm just as honorable as you always thought I was. And how about that dinner and a movie? I owe you from before, remember?"

"It's kind of tough to take me out when you're in jail, Doyle."

"Here we go again with the whole 'jail' thing."

Amanda sighed.

"Just . . . when you're out of here," said Amanda. "Try to stay out of trouble. Okay? We'll talk later when things are going a little better. If you still have a job after all this."

"You sound like Burnside," said Doyle.

"That's not scoring you any points," said Amanda.

"Sorry," replied Doyle. "You're much more attractive than he is, if that helps."

"It does," she replied. "Maybe I'll stop by and see you again."

"Okay," he said.

Amanda walked down the hall and out of sight.

Doyle lay down again and tried to get some sleep.

25

DOYLE WAS HAVING A NIGHTMARE about working in a murky, industrial steel mill, with Burnside as his whip-cracking boss. Doyle felt weak, exhausted. He could feel the sweat drip down his back. Inexplicably, he was slamming a heavy sledgehammer against a small block of metal again and again. Meanwhile, Burnside continuously yelled his name: "Doyle! Doyle!"

Doyle knew something was amiss when Burnside yelled, "Doyle, wake the fuck up!"

Burnside had been rattling a nightstick against the metal bars of the jail cell, making the loud bangs.

With much effort, Doyle opened his heavy eyelids. The cell was still dark, except for minimal fluorescent light.

"What's going on?" asked Doyle in a weak morning voice.

Burnside responded dismally, "Your bail's been posted. You can leave."

Doyle blinked unbelievingly. "Come again?"

"You heard me. I don't know who you know, or if you were just born with a horseshoe up your ass, but your bail's been fully paid. Get out."

Standing up slowly, Doyle looked at Burnside apprehensively.

"After everything you said last night, you're just going to let me leave, just like that?"

"I really don't have much choice. BUT . . ." Burnside continued, "IF you give me ANY reason to arrest you, I will. I'll have people watching you twenty-four/seven. Go home and stay there. And don't bother coming to work the next few days. You're on temporary suspension until we decide what to do with you."

"With pay?"

"Unfortunately."

Doyle nodded. "Sweet. It's kind of like a vacation then."

Burnside grunted. "I'd like to reiterate, once more, that you are NOT to piss me off in any way. I'm basically not leaving here until everything's wrapped up. I'm sleeping in my damn office while you get to go frolick back to your apartment. That in itself makes me very angry."

"Are veins supposed to get that big?" asked Doyle, staring intently at Burnside's neck.

"Leave. Now."

Doing as he was told, Doyle exited his jail cell for what he hoped would be the last time in his life. As he walked down the hallway towards the lobby, Doyle thought he heard Burnside letting out a heavy sigh.

26

Wearing state-issued attire, Doyle took a cab back to his apartment, as his car was still near Kyle Gordon's apartment, partially kicked in. Doyle wondered if Kyle had yet attempted to take it out for a joyride.

The cab driver didn't say anything to Doyle the entire way back to his apartment, but he watched him cautiously. Doyle assumed cabbies were not too keen on having convicts and troublemakers in their vehicles.

Doyle had no idea who posted his bail, and was a bit overwhelmed to even consider who it could be. Rather than dwell on it, he thought his mental resources might be better spent deciding what to do next. First, he definitely wanted to go home. Not just to keep any potential police on-lookers at bay, but also because he desperately wanted to get into something much more comfortable. And dry. And clean.

After that, Doyle wasn't sure what his next move would be. He'd like to call William and get his advice, but he didn't know if he could get through to him or not. He also thought it might be a good idea to get some more background on Kyle Gordon. Doyle had seen the look in Kyle's eyes—he was afraid of Doyle. And not just in the typical, "Oh my, there's an invader in my house," sort of way. No, Doyle was certain it went much deeper than that. He would have to do some further poking around.

The cabbie pulled to the curb in front of Doyle's retirement complex.

"Have this charged to the Minneapolis police department," said Doyle.

The cabbie eyed his jail fatigues suspiciously.

"Trust me," said Doyle with a warm smile. "I'm a cop."

Doyle got out of the cab and headed to his apartment. It was starting to get light out. From what Doyle could tell, it was probably around 5:30 or 6:00 in the morning. He'd take a nice, hot shower, maybe catch a few extra winks, then continue his work. He was finally starting to get into this all-work no-play routine. No wonder William was always bent out of shape.

The fluorescent lights in the apartment hallways were dim. Doyle turned the corner to his apartment and nearly stumbled over the woman sitting in front of his door, her hair hanging loosely over her face. She was snoring.

Hesitantly, Doyle said, "Excuse me, miss?"

The woman snorted rather inelegantly, then jolted awake. She flipped her hair, revealing the unmistakable face of Kimberly Chapman.

"Oh, boy," said Doyle.

"Thank God you're here, Detective Malloy, I badly need to talk to you," she said with a pleading urgency in her expression. Then, studying his appearance, she said, "Did you just get back from a costume party?"

"Something like that," said Doyle. "Aren't you supposed to be in Hawaii?"

"No," said Kimberly curiously. "Why would you say that?"

Doyle pondered silently for a couple moments. "No reason, I guess. Here, let's go in, and you can tell me whatever it is you need to say."

"Oh, thank you so much. I got here around midnight, and I thought maybe you were working late, so I hung around, and then I must've fallen asleep, and . . . goodness, what's that smell?"

"Sorry, it was a pretty wild party. Why didn't you just go to the police station and give them this vital information—it may have been a lot faster."

"I know," she said. "But, I have a hard time trusting anyone, and for some reason I feel I can trust you."

"You trusted Chad Wilkinson, didn't you?"

Kimberly looked taken aback.

"Sorry—perhaps that was inappropriate of me," said Doyle. "I'm not very good around women. Or people for that matter. But still, I think I had a point there."

Doyle led Kimberly inside his apartment, and motioned her to have a seat on the couch. "After all, you trusted Chad with your father's secret safe, and, according to you, he misused that trust, betrayed you, broke into the safe and maybe even murdered Marta. So, forgive me if it seems your trust might be a little out of place."

Kimberly nodded, solemnly. "No, you're right. I did trust Chad. Then he broke up with me, and I stopped trusting him. But Detective Malloy—I don't think he did it!"

Doyle rubbed his forehead. "So you came over a couple days ago, panicked because you believed he *was* responsible for the burglary and the murder. Now you come believing he didn't do it. Why should I believe you at all, or even listen to what you have to say?"

"Because! Before he died, Chad e-mailed me!" Kimberly looked at Doyle with wide, stressed eyes.

Doyle took this in. "Chad was found dead yesterday morning, which means you must have received that e-mail prior to that. Why are you only coming forward with this now?"

"I didn't receive it until around 10:00 o'clock tonight! I swear! I just got the new Windows program, and it's completely slowing down my e-mail service. Every time I tried to log on, everything stalled or rebooted. It's a complete hassle. I just don't know what to—"

"Okay, okay, I get the picture," said Doyle. "Now what did the e-mail say exactly?"

Kimberly reached into her purse a pulled out a printed copy of it.

"It's nothing that big. It's actually very chit-chatty," said Kimberly. "He said he wanted to get together next weekend to talk, and he also wanted to apologize to my father for how he acted at the party. He seemed to be in a pleasant mood."

Doyle scanned the e-mail. "You're right. He doesn't sound very guilty, does he? Or suicidal. But how can you be sure it's not just a front, an attempt not to look guilty? Protect himself, if you will?"

"It could be, I guess. It just—it's doesn't seem like it. I feel like such an idiot. I mean, a couple days ago, I so badly wanted him to be guilty. I mean, how can a guy dump this?" She drew attention to her nearly perfect body.

"Point taken," said Doyle.

"But anyway, I thought it could've been him, since I did tell him about the safe. But after thinking about it, I realized, he could've told someone else about the safe. He could have told anyone, really."

"You know, Chad does have a history of stealing things. Paintings, mostly."

Kimberly laughed. "I know, but that was just silly college stuff." She started snorting. "One time," she snorted again, "he pinched Rosie O'Donnell's Botticelli."

"That's disgusting," said Doyle, smiling.

Kimberly burst into laughter. But her laughter soon died. Doyle assumed because she realized Chad was gone for good.

"He was a lot of fun, Mr. Malloy. You probably would have liked him," she said.

"You never know," said Doyle. "And thanks for this," he said, referring to the e-mail. "This helps. It's may not be enough to clear his name, but it helps."

Kimberly nodded.

"Now the important question," Doyle said. "If you don't think Chad did it, do you know anyone else who might have?"

"Do I have suspicions? Sure, I do. If I had to take my best guess, I'd say Chad's roommate would be a deadringer. Kyle is . . . how shall I put this . . . a little mean. Unpleasant. He's kind of a jerk. And he has a lot of facial piercings. It's really gross. And he smells like marijuana and Big Macs like all the time."

"Is it anything more than a suspicion?"

She shrugged. "No, I never talk to him. He's the reason I never go . . . never went, I should say, to Chad's apartment. I just didn't like being around Kyle. He creeped me out."

"He's sort of a sore spot for me, too," said Doyle, rubbing the bruise on the top of his head.

"I really don't know if he did anything, but if Chad had told anyone about the safe, there's a good chance it was his roommate."

Doyle nodded.

"I should probably go," said Kimberly. "I have class in a couple hours, and I sooo need a mocha."

"Thanks for stopping by, Miss Chapman. It was helpful."

Kimberly glowed. "Anything I can do to help."

Kimberly went out the door, leaving a lingering scent of perfume, which nicely commingled with Doyle's scente de garbage.

"Okay," said Doyle to himself. "Take a shower—then I may have to pay Mr. Gordon another little visit."

27

AFTER GETTING OUT OF THE SHOWER, Doyle toweled himself off, put on a fresh pair of trousers and sports coat, and shaved his very scruffy face. Doyle was pleased he was now looking like a civilized man, not like a convict just released from the slammer.

Doyle was going to attempt calling William, only to realize he no longer had his cell phone. As far as he could tell, he must have had it in his pants pocket before his noggin got a floggin' from Kyle Gordon, who then so rudely stole his pants.

"Bastard," said Doyle into his empty apartment.

Then Doyle realized he'd be on his own for a while. Even if Doyle had his phone, he wouldn't attempt to call William—at least, not right now. If there was any chance that his calls were being monitored, Doyle couldn't risk putting himself into any more hot water than he was already in.

No more jail for me, thank you, thought Doyle.

He made himself a cup of coffee, opened his apartment door, and picked up the morning paper. He had no intention of reading the paper; it was merely a prop he was using. Doyle took the paper and his coffee and walked out to the railing that overlooked his building's parking lot. Doyle looked around, but casually—he wouldn't want anyone to think he was nervous about being watched. Out of the corner of his eye, Doyle saw an undercover squad. It was easy to spot, especially within that lot—it was the only car that didn't have any rust spots, window cracks, or missing parts. And there was a cop inside.

Doyle leaned against the railing, sipped his coffee, and pretended to read the paper. He wanted to make it clear that he wasn't go anywhere—he was just enjoying a relaxing day off.

Of course, that was far from his plans. After giving the undercover cop a little show (long stretch, exaggerated yawn), Doyle strolled back to his apartment. As soon as he got in, he locked the door, went to his dresser, and removed his police-issued handgun from his underwear drawer. The last time he had even held the gun was three years ago, when he was investigating Snoop Dogg's Beanie Baby collection that went missing from his Minneapolis hotel room. (Doyle had a feeling the dolls held more than just beans, and that things could get a little rough. To his surprise, Snoop was just an avid toy collector. Fo-shizzle.)

Doyle stuck the gun in the back of his waistband, and headed to his bedroom. He lifted up the window, and looked around. He didn't see anyone nearby or in the distance. Then, he stared intently at the tree five feet away.

Oh, shit, thought Doyle. His plan had seemed really smart in his head, but looking at the tree, he was starting to reconsider.

Well, no time like the present, Doyle told himself.

Doyle jumped, fell about a foot, but managed to wrap around his body around the tree. He shook a bit out of fear, causing some of the leaves to shake and tumble off the limbs. He was still a good twelve feet off the ground. Doyle was expecting to just slide down, but he quickly found it didn't quite work that way. He slowly inched his way down, trying his best to not tear or smudge his pants, but was having a difficult time doing so.

When Doyle was about four feet off the ground, he released himself and hit the ground on his butt. He stood up, wiped himself off, and then jumped back in surprise.

"Good morning, Mr. Malloy," said the man in the white suit.

"What the hell are you doing here?" asked Doyle.

"Since it appears you're being watched by the police, it seemed this would be the most likely place for me to find you. Turns out I was quite correct."

It occurred to Doyle that the man in the white suit, the loyal employee of Gaff and Gafferty collection agency, looked startlingly like a weasel.

"I already told you the other day, I don't have any money for you. Now tell your collection agency to leave me the hell alone! Besides, I'm really, really busy right now."

"I'm sure you are, Mr. Malloy. Escaping the law, it seems. Perhaps I should tell the nice policeman down the way that I found you leaving your apartment. How might he react, I wonder?" The man in the white suit smirked with pleasure.

"What do you want?" asked Doyle, feeling downtrodden.

"My employers at Gaff and Gafferty require minimum payment by tomorrow at the latest, or we are going to court. Liquidate any assets you feel necessary. I understand you have some very nice toys hanging on the walls."

Without realizing what he was doing, Doyle reached out and punched the man in the white suit directly in his weasel face. The man didn't see it coming. He fell down like a sack of potatoes. He was out. To Doyle's grim satisfaction, his white suit was a bit bloody.

What did I just do? Doyle thought to himself. *I just assaulted a guy*.

But then Doyle realized that the man, somehow, at sometime, had been in his apartment, or at least knew in good detail the contents of his apartment, and this made Doyle angry again. Doyle knelt down and slapped him in the face. The man was still unconscious.

Nervous and scared, Doyle looked around to make sure no one was watching, then ran. Like Forrest Gump, in regards to both speed and appearance, Doyle ran and ran until he was several blocks from his apartment.

This is where Doyle's brilliantly thought-out plan, for all intents and purposes, ended. He was still several miles from Kyle Gordon's apartment, and he had no car, nor money to pay a cab. And it was only a matter of time before even more police were looking for him due to accusations of assault and battery. Doyle considered his options.

This could go really bad, thought Doyle.

Doyle took out one thing he did have—his badge.

He ran to a nearby stoplight. A few cars were stopped on a red. He ran up to a silver SUV with a middle-aged woman inside. She was chatting on her cell phone, and when Doyle approached, she merely looked away.

He then went to the car behind her. It was an old tan Chevy with tinted windows and a fair amount of rust. Doyle knocked on the window. A balding, fat black man rolled it down.

"Whatchoo want?" he asked.

"I'm confiscating your car. I'm with the Minneapolis Police."

"Wha the hell you talkin' 'bout?" The man looked at Doyle as if he were speaking a foreign language.

"Your car—I'm taking it," said Doyle.

"Not a damn chance," said the man. "I know for a fact you can't do that 'cept for extreme circumstances, and I don't see no damn emergencies anywhere. Do you? C'mon, man, my brother's a cop. I know this shit."

Doyle sighed. He reached behind him, pulled out the gun, and pointed it at the man. "Get the fuck out of the car!" yelled Doyle.

"Oh, sweet blood of Jesus, save me now," said the man, as he pulled himself out of the car.

Doyle took his place in the driver's seat. He nodded to the man.

"Thank you, sir. Your cooperation with law enforcement is most appreciated. You have a nice day, now."

"I'll get my car back, right? If I go home without our car, my wife's gonna kill me, man."

"I promise, you'll have it back in no time." Doyle then cranked the wheel to the right and sped off through the streets of northern Saint Paul.

28

DOYLE ARRIVED BACK AT THE PLACE he had become all too familiar with—Kyle Gordon's and the late Chad Wilkinson's apartment on Wilshire in Dinkytown. He didn't like coming back here, but he had unfinished business. First and foremost, Doyle did not appreciate getting slammed in the head with a flashlight. That wasn't very Minnesota Nice. He also didn't like having his pants stolen and then being thrown into a dumpster, while it was raining no less. As far as Doyle was concerned, Kyle was a bigger ass-hole than McNulty. And that was saying something.

This time, Doyle parked to the rear of the building, just in case Burnside had cops planted in the parking lot out front looking for him. Doyle didn't want to take any chances. At least, not any more than he had to take. He didn't notice any suspicious vehicles, so he went through the rear entrance, as opposed to something idiotic, like climbing up a tree.

Doyle pulled on the door, which of course was locked. The rear entrance had the same buzzer system as the front entrance. Once again, Doyle pushed the "Sanchez" button.

"*Hola,*" responded a voice on the intercom.

"Hey, remember me?" asked Doyle.

"*Ay, policia loca!* Do I get real money this time?" asked Sanchez.

"*Si, senor.*"

Doyle heard a buzzing, and the door unlatched. He opened it and went inside. Sure enough, Sanchez came running down the stairs.

"*Donde es mi vente dolares*, crazy police man?"

"Here's your twenty dollars, *punto*," said Doyle, pointing a gun at him.

Sanchez's eyes went wide, and he backed up. "Oh, you are loco. *No es bueno, senor. No es bueno.*"

"Why don't you go back up to your apartment and pretend like I was never here. How does that sound?"

"I no buzz you up anymore, *senor*," said Sanchez, sternly.

Doyle aimed the gun towards Sanchez's heart.

"I go now." Sanchez quickly retreated up the stairs.

Doyle put his gun back behind him and approached Kyle Gordon's door, which was still missing its doorknob. Doyle peeked inside, but didn't see anything.

Feeling an incredible surge of energy, Doyle attempted to kick the door down, only to find that he did not have any of the strength or muscles in his legs to make that happen. Doyle let out a muffled cry. Then he pulled on the rim of the hole where a knob used to be, and door opened right up.

Doyle ran into the apartment. He wanted to come at Kyle with the element of surprise, just like how Kyle snuck up on him earlier.

"Kyle Gordon? Where the fuck are you?" screamed Doyle. He felt more powerful than he had ever felt in his several years of criminal investigation. Doyle thought he might be able to get used to this.

Doyle ran through the living room and into the kitchen, but there was no sign of Kyle. The rooms looked just as they had previously. Untouched by man or vacuum.

Doyle backed up and went towards Kyle's bedroom.

"Kyle!" screamed Doyle. "You're going down, right now!"

Doyle thought he'd try the kicking routine one more time. To his surprise, he was successful. The door burst open.

And then Doyle threw up. It was involuntary, to be sure. It was a mixture of adrenaline, over-stimulation, and visual stimuli. Undoubtedly, the visual issue was the true cause of Doyle's sudden illness: Doyle was staring at the body of Kyle Gordon, lying on the floor of his bedroom, blood trailing off from the hole in his skull. There was a gun in his hand.

This is bad, thought Doyle. *This is really, really, really bad.*

Doyle scanned the room for clues, evidence, anything. And he found it: lying on the bed was a confession letter similar to the previous one. It also said, "I did it," except on this one, the "I" was circled.

Then Doyle noticed something else.

Christ, he thought, he's wearing my pants.

Doyle removed a tissue from the nightstand on Kyle's nightstand and carefully reached into Kyle's pocket. Doyle kept his eyes closed the whole time so he wouldn't have to look at Kyle. He didn't want to throw up again. Doyle pulled out his car keys, reached into the other pocket, and pulled out his cell phone.

There was a lot more Doyle thought he should do, but sticking around could be even worse. He had done some yelling—the police could potentially be on their way already. He looked at his own lunch laying on the ground and decided to leave it—if McNulty or another investigator wanted to sift through that for evidence, they were free to do so.

I have to leave here now, thought Doyle. *Right now. Now! C'mon legs, why aren't you working?*

Doyle thought about last night and the uncomfortable few hours he'd spent in the slammer.

No way I'm going back there, he thought. That was enough to motivate him to move his legs and run out of the apartment. He hoped Sanchez wasn't keeping an eye on him. Unfortunately, that was a risk Doyle would have to take.

Just in case there were cops around, Doyle headed for the confiscated Chevy instead of his own car. He'd have to worry about that later. Right now, all he wanted to do was leave the scene of the second murder and call William.

To hell with my calls potentially being monitored. I need help, dammit!

Doyle could feel himself losing control. He realized he had done things in the past twenty-four hours that he had never fathomed doing, and he wasn't sure if it was all good. Well, especially punching the weasel-faced white suit-wearing collection agent. He really shouldn't have done that. Although he had to admit, it did feel good.

But Doyle knew he needed William.

William was the expert. The professional. He would know what to do. He always knew what to do.

"Please, William," Doyle said to himself. "Please answer your phone."

ILLIAM DID NOT ANSWER. Doyle hit redial over and over as he sped through the streets towards his apartment. He continued to question whether running from the apartment had been the wisest thing to do, or if he should have just stayed put and taken the heat for investigating under strict orders not to. But, he had made his decision, and there was no going back now. Besides, he didn't trust Burnside or any cop under his supervision. Doyle could smell something fishy, and it wasn't just the Long John Silver's on the corner.

Doyle was discouraged to see his apartment was absolutely crawling with cops. Squads were parked out front, cops were walking in and out of the main entrance, and when Doyle drove around back, he could see a cop parked, looking through a pair of binoculars at his apartment window. He couldn't tell definitively from the distance, but Doyle was pretty sure the cop with binoculars was McNulty. When Doyle saw this, he pushed down the accelerator and headed for the highway. Doyle felt fairly comfortable that he hadn't been noticed. And if he had been— well, he'd know about it soon enough.

Doyle was sweating profusely. It wasn't just because the cheap-ass vehicle he'd confiscated didn't have working air conditioning, but he realized if there were that many cops roaming around his apartment, either they (a) figured out he wasn't at home, which would be the best case scenario, or they (b) found out he'd recently barged into an apartment with a gun, and left behind a body with a large cranial hole in it. If it was the latter, Doyle could end up in a jail cell for a very, very long time, through no fault of his own. Well, maybe a couple of missteps . . .

Not knowing where else to go, Doyle headed for what he hoped would be sanctuary. Someplace to stay just long enough to figure things out, and hopefully avoid any future mishaps.

Doyle hadn't been to William's humble abode since they first met, but Doyle was hoping that, as clever as William was, he wouldn't be officially listed as the owner of the former dental office, hence making it harder for undesirables to find him.

Trying to remember the directions to the best of his ability, Doyle slowly drove down the side streets, hoping to remain inconspicuous. He pulled his cell phone out of his pocket and dialed William. He didn't get an answer, but it did go to voicemail, which it hadn't done before. If anything, it was progress.

"William, this is Doyle," he said into his phone. "I really, really need you to call me back. Things have gotten . . . complicated here. I spent some time in jail, Kyle Gordon's dead, the police probably think I did it, I can't go back to my apartment, and I think I may have stolen a car. Do you know if I'm allowed to confiscate things? Oh, and Kimberly Chapman came to my apartment again—aren't you supposed to be looking for her out there? Well, she's here. So if you're still there, come here. Because here is where she is. Who told you she was there? Well, anyways, I'm headed toward your place right now. I'm probably going to steal some of your clothes, because I can't get to mine, and I smell pretty bad. Hey, do you think my phone's being tapped? If it is, then this is kind of awkward. Just for the record, I haven't done anything illegal—except for maybe the car thing I mentioned, but I'm pretty sure that's just a misunderstanding. And I really don't smell that bad. Umm . . . . Malloy out."

Doyle hung up and shoved his phone back in his pocket. As much as Doyle would love to think he was a professional detective, the last forty-eight hours had been a giant blow to his ego. His mistakes helped him realize that he still had a lot to learn. William would never have busted into Kyle's apartment, vomit, then run away from a body without calling the authorities. Doyle, on the other hand, was frightened and inexperienced, so he ran away like a child, putting him in a drastically vulnerable position.

Doyle hit the brakes. He was still a few blocks from William's place, but he decided it was time to start making some smart decisions. He would watch the location, just to see if anyone, particularly cops, drove by or approached the door. This time, Doyle wasn't going to be caught with his pants down. Figurally or literally. Which reminded Doyle of Kimberly Chapman. *I wonder if she liked how I looked in my underwear?* thought Doyle. He would have continued contemplating this if it weren't for the sudden movement ahead of him.

A police squad peeled around the corner a few blocks ahead and sped towards William's home. The squad pulled onto the sidewalk and screeched to a halt directly in front of the former dental office. An overweight cop Doyle didn't recognize stumbled out of the car and ran towards the front door. The cop shouted something, but Doyle couldn't make out what it was. He then slammed his tree trunk of a leg into the door, taking it down like a bulldozer crashing through a house of cards. Doyle made a mental note: *gain weight, crash through doors.*

After a couple of minutes, the overweight cop waddled out of William's office and spoke into his walkie. Within seconds, another squad came in from behind Doyle and pulled alongside the other squad. Doyle didn't think he'd been seen, but he hunched down lower behind the wheel to be on the safe side. Two leaner cops came out of their squad and joined the overweight cop. They spoke for a moment then went back into the office.

Time ticked by, but the cops didn't leave the office. Doyle was fearing they'd camp out there all night, but, if that were the case, they likely wouldn't have left their squads so visibly parked in front. After nearly twenty minutes, the overweight cop carried out William's desktop PC in his arms and placed it in the backseat of his squad.

Oh shit, thought Doyle. William had said he had recordings of Burnside on his computer. As far as Doyle knew, it was the only evidence they had proving his boss was being neglectful of the case, and pushing Doyle to wrap it up prior to a full investigation being completed.

The two leaner cops carried out armfuls of files and also put them in the overweight cop's squad. They spoke to each other for another moment, then the heavy cop got back into his driver's seat and drove in Doyle's direction. Doyle hunkered down and tried to press his entire body against the floor of the car. A minute later, he lifted his head and looked about. The overweight cop was gone, but the lean cops were sitting in their squad car, not moving.

Doyle didn't know how long they intended to stay there, but he couldn't keep waiting much longer. Not only did he need to figure out what to do next, but he was also feeling a familiar sensation in his bladder. Sometimes, the call of nature was more powerful than the call of sensibility.

Doyle drove forward a block and made a sharp right. It's possible the cops noticed Doyle's car, but it would be unlikely they'd leave their post unless they had a really strong suspicion. It was a risk, but one Doyle felt was worth taking. Besides, a guy's gotta take a leak.

After driving a few miles and consistently looking in the rearview, Doyle felt sure that he wasn't being followed. When he was a safe distance away, he pulled into a Super America gas station to use their facilities.

When he was finished and got back into the car, he considered the gravity of the situation he was in. Not only did he not have William's assistance, but once William got back, they wouldn't have access to any of William's resources, since the police department found it necessary to confiscate the computer and what was likely his most important files.

Doyle once again looked down at his bracelet. What Would Columbo Do? One answer: squint. The other: go back to the scene of the crime.

Yes, thought Doyle. The scene of the crime.

Doyle hoped a certain someone might be willing to lend a hand.

30

DOYLE PRESSED THE INTERCOM BUTTON outside the closed gates of Chapman Manor on Grand Avenue. A familiar voice asked, "Yes, who is it?"

"This is Detective Doyle Malloy," yelled Doyle, with great urgency. "I need to speak with Mr. Chapman. Please."

"Come in," the voice responded. The gates leading to the mansion opened, allowing Doyle to drive through. As soon as his car passed through, the gates closed again. Doyle parked on the driveway, but off to the side in case anyone needed to come in or leave. Chapman owned a quadruple garage on the east side of the mansion, and Doyle didn't want his blemish of a vehicle to block anyone from coming or going.

As Doyle stepped out of his vehicle, it dawned on him that he was really in no condition to be speaking to anybody, particularly someone of Timothy Chapman's social stature. Doyle hoped that Chapman was so used to the grotesqueness of Tim Burton's appearance and odor that he wouldn't think twice of Doyle. Regardless, Doyle was embarrassed to have such excruciatingly bad body odor and clothes that had been ravaged from sweat and dirt from running and slamming into things. A world of difference from Doyle's usual life of sitting at his desk and watching B movies, and occasionally filing a report. Surprisingly, he found he didn't really miss that former life.

Doyle approached the front door and knocked. The door opened, and the butler, Darren Brookes, motioned Doyle inside. Brookes was very well dressed as he had been the previous times: a formal tuxedo, neatly polished dress shoes, perfectly tied and centered bowtie. Something was a little different though, Doyle thought, but he wasn't quite sure what.

"I apologize for not telling you on the intercom," said Brookes, "But Master Chapman isn't currently home. He's at a script reading for a new comedy with Eddie Murphy and Jackie Chan. I believe they're supposed to play triplets."

"Oh, okay," said Doyle.

Dammit, thought Doyle. He had really felt sure that Chapman would be able to help him somehow. Mostly because Doyle thought it might have been Chapman who paid his bail. He didn't have any particular reason to think this, other than the fact that Doyle didn't have any wealthy friends, and Chapman really seemed to appreciate him, or at least get a kick out of him on a visceral level. A good sense of humor went a long way.

"So, why didn't you just tell me that on the intercom?" inquired Doyle.

"Because I'm also supposed to tell you that you have free reign over his house while he's gone. Whatever you need is at your disposal," said Brookes.

"Really? And why's that?" asked Doyle, intrigued.

"He stated that he wanted to be in full compliance with the investigation and didn't want his work schedule to interfere with it. He only asks that you respect his property, and that only you and Mr. William Wright are allowed to have open access to the house."

"I hate to repeat myself, but . . . why?"

"Don't ask me," said Brookes. "I'm just the butler."

Doyle nodded. "Very well, then."

"Do you plan on staying long, Mr. Malloy? If so, I can have some supper prepared for you. It's getting late, but I'm certain I can make arrangements."

"No, no, I won't be long. Is there any possibility of contacting Mr. Chapman, perhaps via phone?"

Brookes shook his head. "I'm sorry, but absolutely no calls while Master Chapman is working. However, he should be done with this evening's work in a couple hours. He usually calls around nine o'clock to check up on things if he's staying out of state."

"He's in Hollywood?"

Brooks nodded.

"Do you think I might be able to speak to Mr. Chapman after nine?"

Brookes seemed to think about it for a moment, then nodded. "Yes," Brookes said. "Master Chapman is most dedicated to the completion of this investigation. I'm certain he'll have no qualms about speaking with you."

"Excellent," said Doyle. "So then, umm, should I just take a seat in the living room?"

"I might suggest, and please don't take offense to this, that a shower may be in order if you wish to sit upon any of the furniture here. It seems you've had a . . . busy day," said Brookes, eyeing Doyle with slight distaste.

Doyle blushed a little with embarrassment. "Oh, yeah. I mean, yes, of course. Sorry, I got into a fight today with a grizzly bear. I kicked it's ass."

Brookes didn't respond.

"I'm kidding, of course."

"Yes, I assumed," said Brookes.

"It was a Kodiak."

"Will you be requiring a change of clothes, Detective Malloy?"

"I don't require it, but it would be most appreciated."

"If you follow me upstairs to the guest bedroom, I'll show you the guest wardrobe."

"Guest wardrobe? Does Mr. Chapman have many people showing up at his home without clothes or in the process of losing their clothes?"

"Do you expect me to answer that?" asked Brookes.

"It would help with my tell-all biography of him," responded Doyle.

Brookes' eyes swept Doyle's face, looking for signs of seriousness.

"Kidding, of course," said Doyle.

Brookes' face eased with a slightest bit of relief. "You're a funny man, Detective Malloy."

"Yeah, I'm a regular Jim Belushi," mumbled Doyle.

Doyle followed Brookes up the stairs towards the guest room.

Like most of the furnishings in the mansion, the guest room itself was grand and eccentric. Much like Chapman himself, come to think of it, considered Doyle.

As Brookes dug through the closet for clothing, Doyle tried to imagine the vast array of celebrities who had likely slept within these walls. Doyle was in the midst of imagining Al Pacino and Beverly D'Angelo naked when he was interrupted by his cell phone emanating, "Bad boys, bad boys, whatcha gonna do . . . "

Doyle answered his phone, and said to Brookes, "The ringtone's funny because I'm a cop."

Brookes nodded and turned his head back to the closet.

"Detective Malloy here."

"Doyle?" said the voice on the other line.

"William, is that you?" asked Doyle, as he sat on the bed.

Brookes looked at Doyle as he took a shirt and a pair of pants out of the closet.

"Yes, Doyle, thank God you're okay. Listen, I think you may be in grave danger."

"No shit, William. I'm in big trouble. You know Kyle Gordon?" Brookes was close by, so Doyle lowered his voice. "Well, I think I may be the number one suspect."

"I know, Doyle, I heard your message, but that's not what I'm talking abo—"

"Hey, William, are you back from Hawaii? Why were you even there—I mean, Kimberly Chapman's been here in Minneapolis the whole time. Who told you she went to Hawaii?"

"Dammit, Doyle, that's what I'm trying to tell you. The butler—Darren Brookes. He's responsible for everything. Almost everything. I mean, he didn't kill Marta, of that I'm certain, but I'm positive he killed Chad and Kyle too. And there's more—Doyle, his name isn't really Darren Brookes. It's Darren Burnside. *Burnside*, Doyle. He's your bloody boss' son. Have you been wondering why you've been given such a hard time lately? Doyle, where are you?"

Doyle gulped. Brookes was behind him, breathing. Doyle said into the phone, loudly, "Wow, that sounds like some wacky mix-up William—" but before he could finish the sentence, the phone was smacked out of his hand. Doyle tried to turn, but Brookes' hands closed over his throat. That's when Doyle realized why Brookes had looked different today—he was wearing white gloves. They had looked natural with the tuxedo, but Doyle couldn't remember Brookes having worn them before. They were a soft felt material, and under different circumstances would seem rather pleasant. However, currently those gloves were stopping any air from reaching his lungs.

Aside from being without oxygen, Doyle was in dire pain. Brookes was squeezing into the same bruises that McNulty had left on his neck the day before. Doyle grappled and clawed at Brookes hands, but as he did so he could feel his strength diminishing by the moment.

As Doyle went from distinct pain to bleary lightheadedness, he had just seconds to appreciate how neatly the puzzle pieces seemed to fit together. Doyle could hear William's voice coming from the phone, quietly but distinctly, shouting "Doyle? Doyle are you there? Are you all right?"

As Doyle's body went loose, he thought to himself:

The goddamn butler. That's so fucking cliché.

31

OYLE DIDN'T LOSE CONSCIOUSNESS, although Brookes certainly thought he had. Unbeknownst to Brookes, Doyle had learned from an episode of *Law and Order* that it's possible to fool a strangler by simply letting go of the struggle and pretending not to breathe, which is naturally no easy feet, and Doyle had little expectancy that he could pull it off. But, Doyle had the benefit of being former superintendent of the swim team in high school, and was able to hold his breath for a lengthy amount of time. And Doyle was pleased to discover that, a few seconds after he allowed his body to go loose, Brookes released his grip from Doyle's neck.

It took great strength to keep from choking or gasping for air, though that was what Doyle desperately wanted to do. After holding his breath for approximately sixty seconds, but what felt like forever, Doyle could hear Brookes pacing about the room, seemingly in circles, before leaving the room altogether. Doyle quickly took breaths while he could, knowing he may have to hold his breath again real soon.

Sure enough, Doyle heard footsteps coming back into the room. Doyle held his breath. He could hear movement not far from his head. Then he heard Brookes voice say, "Aloha."

Fear surged through Doyle before realizing Brookes wasn't speaking to him but rather to William on the cell phone. Doyle could hear William's voice but not what he was saying.

"If you want to see your partner alive, you'll come directly to the house. You know which one. And you will not tell anyone. If you tell the police, your partner is dead."

Nice move, thought Doyle. Dragging William here to save me, when Brookes thinks I'm already dead. He'd make a good Bond villain.

"And don't do anything stupid, like bringing a gun. Not that it would do you any good. I could kill you with my bare hands."

Nevermind, thought Doyle. He's no Bond villain. He's just a douche bag.

"Shut up, or Malloy's dead!" yelled Brookes.

Excellent, William got at least one good insult out.

Doyle could hear Brookes slam the cell phone to the ground. It didn't sound like it was in one piece any longer.

"Okay, Malloy. Stand up."

Doyle remained frozen.

"Yes, you. I know you're still alive. I saw you breathing, you idiot. Now stand up."

Doyle opened his eyes, and saw he was looking straight up the barrel of a handgun.

Brookes looked far less prim and proper than he had minutes ago. His forehead was covered with sweat, his hair was a mess, and his face had taken on a feral snarl.

"I'd shoot you right now," said Brookes," but it'd be awfully diffi-cult to make it look like an accident."

"You mean like Chad and Kyle?"

"The doper who OD'ed and the goth freak who shot himself? I have no idea what you're talking about," Brookes said with a sinister smile.

"Why did you do it?" asked Doyle. "You didn't have to, you know. We know you didn't kill Marta—you couldn't have. You were up here with Chapman when the murder took place. So why kill those two stupid kids?"

"Simple answer—they knew too much."

"I'm surprised you were even worried about them knowing too much. Your daddy's a cop. It doesn't seem like you had much to worry about."

Brookes laughed. "You're right, I didn't have to worry about going to jail. That's never been a problem. But Dad doesn't like covering up for me, and when he does, he makes me pay for it. I would have preferred he hadn't found out."

"But I'm guessing he put two and two together?" asked Doyle.

"Right away," responded Brookes. "Nothing slips past him. That's why I studied to become an actor in the first place—to fool him. It's never worked."

"You're an actor?" asked Doyle. He'd never come across this information before.

"Yes, of course," Brookes responded. "Chapman hires all of his help from acting schools. Lets them earn a living while trying to get acting gigs."

"He seems like a pretty nice guy," said Doyle. "Why did you feel the urge to mess with his life."

"You're right—Chapman's a phenomenal person. But he involves himself with idiotic charities. Pause for Paws? What the fuck is that all about?" spat Brookes. "They're cats, for Godsakes. They don't need donations, they need drownings. Absolutely ridiculous—rich people giving money towards the well being of furry pests. It makes me sick."

"I take it you're not a Garfield fan," said Doyle.

Brookes moved the gun closer to Doyle's forehead.

"Fuck Garfield," said Brookes, looking furious and disgusted at the same time. "And fuck Jon Arbuckle for owning that little orange asshole."

"So you're an Odie fan. Is that what this is all about?" asked Doyle.

"This has nothing to do with comics. It has to do with large amounts of money going to stupid causes, money that could be better utilized by yours truly."

"But you didn't get any money, did you."

Brookes growled. "No, I didn't. I never got a single dime from that hippy dickhead Wilkinson. He was supposed to give me all the money from the safe the morning after, but he refused. He swore the safe was empty, but I don't believe that. If it was empty, why did Chapman always tell me to watch it very carefully? He was scared someone would break in and steal his money. I guarantee it, that safe was loaded."

A safe serves more purposes than just holding things, Chapman had said. Doyle was starting to understand what he meant by that.

"You thought Chapman was putting all the Pause for Paws donations into the safe? Did Chapman ever make trips to the office?"

"No, but Marta made a few. I figured maybe she was doing it for him. I don't know. Frankly, I don't really care if it was donations or if it was Chapman's family loot. I'll be honest with you—I just wanted some fucking money. But instead, I got nothing but a broken safe, a stoner running away with my money, and a dead maid that was indirectly due to me."

"You asked Chad to break into the safe," said Doyle. "It was all your plan."

"Yes, and that's exactly what he would have told the police, too. He knew about the safe—Kimberly had told him about it. But he wouldn't have done anything if I hadn't influenced him to do so."

"How did you influence him?"

Brookes paused. "You know, normally I wouldn't be telling you any of this. But, since I intend to kill you, I'm really not too worried."

"Fair enough," responded Doyle. One thing he knew about actors. Every one of them wanted to be on stage. That meant time.

"But to get back to your question, I simply told Chad that if he doesn't break into the safe, I would tell Chapman that I caught him trying to pilfer his Picasso. That freaked him out. One more theft charge would have kept him in jail for an awfully long time. He didn't want that."

"So let me make sure I have this right," said Doyle. "You get Chad to break into the safe, he gets scared and kills Marta on impulse, he takes off with your money, he refuses to give you any of it, so you kill him, but set it up as an overdose."

Brookes nodded, as though it sounded reasonable. "I figured he probably spent my money on his heroin, so it was only fitting that it should be his undoing. Rather poetic, don't you think?"

"Oh, sure," said Doyle. "And the reason for killing Kyle?"

"Information control," said Brookes. "I had no idea how much Chad had told Kyle. They were roommates, so it could have been a great deal. And I had seen you, Doyle, going into his apartment, which made me rather concerned. Though I was happy to see you lost your pants and your dignity in the process."

"Good times," Doyle responded.

"So, I shot him in the head, not unlike what I'll be doing to you and your colleague when he gets here, and then I set it up like a suicide, nicely covering my tracks."

"But you didn't cover your track so well. William and I found out. And if you kill us, how are you going to cover that up? A little too suspicious, the two detectives working on the case suddenly get shot to death in this house while you're the only one here. I wonder who the killer could be . . . hmmm . . ."

"First of all, I'll thank you to not mock me. Secondly, I wouldn't be too quick to compliment yourselves. I knew right off the bat that I was a prime suspect."

"Oh, yeah? How's that?" asked Doyle.

Brookes took a notepad out of his pocket. "Does this look familiar?"

"Hey, I was looking for that!" said Doyle. "Where was it?"

"You dropped it in the office, the first time you came here. Pretty clumsy, if you ask me," said Brookes. "And you call yourself a professional detective? Is that right?"

"Mistakes are made," said Doyle. "Besides, I highly doubt I stated that you're a prime suspect in that notebook."

"Well, you did write down my name and circled it. I thought that was a strong allegation," said Brookes.

"Hardly," said Doyle. "I do that for everyone. In fact, that's pretty much all I do with the notebook. Write down names and circle them."

"Why?" asked Brookes.

"I'm not very good with names," responded Doyle.

Brookes rolled his eyes. "Well, regardless, I hardly think I can cover myself at this point. Which, unfortunately, means that after I kill you and William, I'll have to move away and create a new identity for myself. Meanwhile, Darren Brookes will be found responsible for the murders, but he'll be nowhere to be found."

"You really think it will be that easy?" asked Doyle. "Just running away and creating a new name?"

"Why not?" asked Brookes. "I've done it before."

Suddenly, a tapping sound coming from the window drew both Doyle's and Brookes' attention.

A bright flash nearly blinded him.

When the blurriness in Doyle's eyes dissipated, he was able to make out the face of his now most trusted ally Hanratty, who briefly smiled until Brookes pointed the gun at him.

Brookes fired. The window shattered in a sudden burst. Doyle saw fear in Hanratty's face in the instant he began his descent of two stories to the ground.

He must have been on a ladder, thought Doyle. And that's a long way up. He could have hit the pavement, and . . .

Surging with adrenaline and fear for his friend, Doyle took that strength and utilized it has he drove his right foot directly into Brookes' balls, sending him cowering to his knees. Doyle smashed his arm down on Brookes, causing the gun to clatter against the wall and then to the floor. With speed and agility that surprised even Doyle, he grabbed Brookes by the hair and smashed his snarling face into his knee repeatedly, bruises appearing almost instantly.

"If you just killed my friend, you're more dead than you realize," said Doyle, feeling an anger he'd never felt before.

"You won't kill me—you're a cop. You have to obey the law 'n' shit," said Brookes.

Dammit, he's right, thought Doyle. *Stupid police code.*

"That may be so, but I can make damn sure you spend the rest of your life in prison."

"My Dad would never let that happen," said Brookes.

"Don't worry," said Doyle. "Your dipshit father will be joining you."

For the first time, Brookes looked genuinely concerned.

"You can't do that—what did he do? Don't get him in trouble, he was just covering for me. If he gets in trouble, he'll really be mad. I don't want to see him that mad. Please, I . . ."

Brookes started whimpering. All aspects of Darren Brookes, the aristocratic Saint Paul butler, were gone in a flash, leaving behind the frightened, weak fledgling actor. A thirty-something child, really.

"You're pathetic," said Doyle.

Then Doyle remembered Hanratty and thought to himself, What the hell, as he lifted his foot and kicked Brookes squarely in the jaw. His head flew back and hit the ground. He was out for the count.

"I learned that from Chuck Norris, bitch," said Doyle, knowing full well that neither Brookes or anyone else could hear him. But hey, it sounded good.

Then, in the silence, Doyle heard a muffled scream.

32

ITH A RENEWED FOCUS, DOYLE GRABBED the gun and his cell phone off the ground. He removed the gun's magazine, tossed it into a bureau drawer and kicked the gun under the bed, then placed the phone in his jacket pocket. Before investigating the strange muffled sound coming from the hallway, Doyle rushed to the bedroom window to see if Hanratty was badly injured and/or dead. If he was seriously hurt, Doyle was going to make sure something equally horrendous happened to Brookes. But since Doyle had already given him a mighty kick to the nuts, Doyle wasn't sure how he was going to top that.

Doyle looked through the window, which had shattered into large shards, some of which had fallen outside. He saw Hanratty laying on the grass two stories below. His eyes were closed.

"Hanratty!" Doyle yelled. "HANRATTY!"

Doyle was panicking now. He could feel his heart race and his hands shake. Doyle glanced at Brookes, who was still down. Doyle decided to temporarily ignore the muffled noise coming from the hallway and make sure first and foremost that Hanratty was okay. If anything happened to him because Doyle was too busy, Doyle could never forgive himself. He left the room, ran down the stairs, and went out the front door.

Doyle ran across the driveway, onto the grass around the side of the house, then finally to the backyard where Hanratty was laying.

"Hanratty," said Doyle. "Hanratty, speak to me. Are you okay?"

Doyle didn't see any blood, which was a good sign. He hoped Hanratty's stringbean build had reduced the chances of a bullet hitting him. But that didn't mean he couldn't have suffered internal damage from the fall, thought Doyle.

He pressed two fingers against Hanratty's neck. He felt a strong pulse, which filled Doyle with a wave of relief.

Doyle slapped Hanratty across the face. Hard.

"Ahh, fuck! What was that for?" said Hanratty, his bloodshot eyes snapping open, then closing again as the sunlight reached them.

"I don't know, I just thought you might be dead or something."

"Am I?" asked Hanratty.

"No, I don't think so. You're pretty talkative for a dead guy. But your breath, on the other hand . . ."

"I'll be honest with you, Doyle. I've had a few drinks. Chances are, I was going to fall off that ladder, bullet or no. Speaking of which, I'm not hit am I? I can't really feel much."

"No, I don't think you're hit. Can you get up? We need to find out if anything's broken. Try standing up."

Hanratty cautiously lifted his upper body off the ground, but it came up with little difficulty. No shattered spine there. When he attempted standing, his legs were as wobbly as a caffeinated octogenarian's. Hanratty stumbled until Doyle grabbed him by the shoulders, holding Hanratty up until he could steady himself.

"Okay, Hanratty—are you hurt or just drunk?"

"I think . . . both."

"Do you need an ambulance?" Doyle pulled out his cell phone.

"No, don't worry about me. I'll be fine. I'd be more concerned with the car that just started."

Doyle realized that Hanratty was right. Someone had just fired up a car in the garage. If Brookes had gotten up . . .

Doyle ran around the house again, only to see a silver Cadillac peeling out of the garage as the gates opened. For a second, and it was just a second, Doyle thought he saw a face in the rear window of the vehicle.

"Oh, shit," thought Doyle, as he sprinted for his own confiscated vehicle, only to notice that the tires had been slashed.

So, Brookes probably has a knife and a hostage, thought Doyle. *This day isn't getting any better.*

Carefully considering his options, Doyle ran to the backyard.

"Hanratty," yelled Doyle. "Where's your bike?"

Hanratty was laying on the ground again. "Over there," he said, opening his eyes from an apparent nap. "Behind the tree."

"I'm gonna borrow it," said Doyle.

"Like you did with that car? Yeah, I guess I'll say good-bye to my bike."

"Go back to sleep," said Doyle, as he sprinted towards the bike.

Doyle hadn't ridden a bicycle in some years, but he grabbed Hanratty's wheels, ran towards the driveway with it, and then hopped on and pedaled out of the gates. He took out his cell phone and dialed William.

William answered immediately. "Doyle, is that you? Are you okay?"

"I'm fine. But Brookes is on the loose, and I think he has a hostage with him. I'm not sure—but I think it might be Chapman.

"Bloody hell," said William, gravely. "Okay, Doyle, where do you think he's headed?"

"I don't know," said Doyle. "He's got to be scared right now. He knows he's exposed—we know who he is, who his father is. We know he murdered two people and more and or less caused a third death. If we catch him, he'll be going to prison for a long, long time. If you're in that sort of desperate situation, where would you go? And don't say 'the YMCA,' William—I'm not in the mood."

Doyle heard nothing but silence on the line.

"William, are you still there? Where are you?"

"I'm still here, Doyle. I was just thinking. And to answer your question, I'm pulling into the driveway right now."

"What are you doing there?"

"Isn't that where you are?"

"No, I'm on a bike," responded Doyle.

"A bicycle?"

"Yes, that's another word for it."

"Why are you on a bicycle? Isn't he in a car?"

"Yeah, but he slashed my tires, and Hanratty had his bike here, so . . ."

"Well, where are you now, Doyle?"

"About two blocks away from the south side of the house, from the looks of it," said Doyle.

"Just stay there, Doyle—I'll be with you in just a moment," said William.

"But we're losing him!" said Doyle.

"And you'll lose him even faster if you continue to pedal that ridiculous bicycle. Look, I'm right beside you now. Don't you feel a little bit foolish?"

Doyle turned his head and gave William the finger. And then he stopped pedaling.

William rolled down the window. "It's good to see you, too!" he shouted.

"Yeah, yeah," said Doyle, laying the bike down on the immaculately green lawn belonging to another clearly wealthy person. "Sorry, William—but I've just been involved in more action in twenty-four hours than I've had in the past ten years of law enforcement. I'm a little riled up, if you can't tell." Doyle climbed in the passenger-side of William's car.

William smiled. "Don't worry, Doyle—you're handling yourself very well. You're still alive, for one. And we know who the killer is. Now it's just a matter of tracking him down."

"Did you forget the fact that he kidnapped perhaps the most well-known actor of our time? Something which I should have prevented by—oh, I don't know—killing the bad guy?"

"Inconsequential," responded William. "We'll find Brookes, save Chapman, take the bad guy into custody, then our job here is done. I'll have earned my pay, and you'll become some sort of Minnesotan hero, I'm sure. It'll all work out."

"How can you be so sure?" asked Doyle.

"Because we're both good at what we do," said William.

"Oh," said Doyle. He had never thought of his job in those terms before.

"William?" asked Doyle. "Can I talk to you about something? It's about your pay . . ."

Here it is, thought Doyle. *I had to tell him sooner or later. Might as well just get it over with. Rip the band-aid off. Besides, I'm sick of this being on my chest.*

"Not now, Doyle."

"But really, it's important. Please?"

"Not now—clearly we're very busy. We can discuss payment later. For now, just concentrate on what we're doing."

Doyle nodded submissively. "Where are we going?"

"Brookes, obviously," said William.

"I know—but where?" asked Doyle.

"If you had Timothy Chapman hostage, who would you call to make some quick bucks before you make a getaway?"

"His Jewish attorney?" asked Doyle.

"Think harder, Doyle."

Then, it suddenly seemed obvious.

"Kimberly," said Doyle.

"It's what I'd do," said William.

"But how do you know he's after money? What if he just wants to kill him?"

"He won't—I assure you. If he just wanted to kill him, he would have already killed him. He wouldn't have taken him."

"Yeah, that makes sense. But what if he's crazy?"

"Crazy or not, he's logical. As far as I can tell, everything he's done thus far has been with purpose. He wants money, and he'll do whatever he has to do to get it."

"Do you think he's at Kimberly's place?"

"Either he'll be there, or he'll be calling from an outside location. It really depends on if he has a secure holding place or not."

"This was done completely without forethought," said Doyle, "so he probably doesn't have a secure location set up, which means he'll go directly to where she lives."

"Very good, Doyle. I suspect you're right. Now, to find where she lives," said William.

"Let me make a call," said Doyle.

Doyle didn't know how badly his reputation at the department had been tarnished, but he had to take a chance. For the first time ever, Doyle was contacting Superintendent McDonald about something that was actually relevant to an investigation.

Doyle waited for McDonald to pick up.

"McDonald," she said as she picked up the line, her voice as smoky and assertive as ever.

"Superintendent?"

"Yes . . ."

"This is Detective Malloy."

"Ahh, Doyle. I was wondering if you'd be calling. Certain allegations are traveling around, as I'm sure you're aware."

"Yes, I know."

"Are they true?"

Doyle sighed. "No, they're not true. I swear."

"You weren't arrested in your underwear causing a ruckus outside the apartment of Kyle Gordon at the approximate time he was being murdered?"

"Well, okay, that part is true."

"Were you at all involved with the murder?"

"No, I wasn't," said Doyle.

"Can you fully explain everything that took place without causing any further embarrassment to this department?"

"Yes, actually I can."

"Very well, then. I believe you. Now, Doyle, what is it I can help you with."

"Two things. First, I need an address for Kimberly Chapman. She's of semi-celebrity status, so it won't just be in the phone book."

"I can do that," responded McDonald.

"Secondly," Doyle paused just briefly for dramatic effect, "do not let Burnside out of your sight."

"What?" asked McDonald. "I know he's your boss, but . . ."

"No, I mean it," said Doyle. "Full surveillance—monitor his calls, where he goes, everything. Trust me, it's important."

"Is this going to be bad, Doyle? Do I have to start writing the press release?"

"Soon.

"Okay. Doyle—do you know who committed the crimes? If so, please tell me—we can send out squads . . ."

"No . . . I mean, yes, I know, but I can't tell you yet—I just need a little more time," said Doyle.

"Doyle?" asked McDonald.

"Yes?"

"Please don't let me down," she said. "I'd hate to write two press releases, if you get my meaning."

"Do you usually write press releases when a detective gets promoted?" asked Doyle.

"Not usually," she said. "What I mean to say is, 'Don't fuck up.'"

"Ay ay, Superintendent," said Doyle. "Bye."

William took a left turn.

"You didn't tell her it was Brookes," said William. "Why is that?"

"Because I told her to watch Burnside. If Burnside and his son make any contact, which I'm sure they will—she'll be able to figure it out for herself. Then it won't matter what I say, or what mistakes I've made—the evidence will be there."

Again, William smiled.

Doyle's phone rang. He answered it.

"This is Doyle."

"I have your address," said McDonald. "And, Doyle?"

"Yeah?"

"Burnside just left the building."

"Stay on him," said Doyle.

33

DOYLE AND WILLIAM HADN'T EVEN HAD a chance to park when a frazzled, frantic Kimberly Chapman scrambled out of her dorm hall and ran for her car, nearly stumbling every step she took.

"Kimberly!" yelled Doyle.

Her head turned, her eyes darting in every direction, trying to find the source of the voice.

"Over here, quick!"

She recognized his face, and quickly (or as quick as she could go with her impractical high-heels) made her way to William's vehicle.

"Someone kidnapped my dad!" she nearly screamed. "I have to go to the bank. I need money. The man gave me directions. I have to go because if I'm late he'll kill my dad and I don't want him to do that and I really have to pee but I don't have time and . . ."

"I know," said Doyle. "Just get in the car."

Kimberly starting crying. "Okay."

She climbed in the back seat. William drove out of the lot.

"Now tell me very specifically what Brookes told you," said Doyle.

"Brookes? The butler? Are you kidding me?" said Kimberly. "That's who kidnapped my Dad? The butler did it? That doesn't really happen in real life, does it?"

"Yeah, it does sometimes," responded Doyle. "What did he say?"

"He told me to get fifty-thousand dollars cash and bring it to the Lagoon theater near Hennepin. Let's see here . . . uhh. . . " she sniffed, "uhh, he told me to buy a ticket to *Wedding Crashers 2*, and sit in the back row, fourth seat to the left."

"Okay, then what?" asked Doyle.

"Then he said he'd give me the keys to the car that holds my dad," she said, as the tears started pouring again. "He put him in the trunk."

"Don't worry, Kimberly—I'm sure he's okay," said Doyle comfortingly.

Kimberly wiped tears with her arm, smearing her makeup.

"What do I do?" asked Kimberly.

Doyle looked at William for advice, but William looked right back at him.

"What do you recommend, Doyle?"

Doyle thought about it. This was important. This could lead to a man of great notoriety either living or dying. All depended on what Doyle decided, right now, right in this moment.

"We play it out," said Doyle.

"Why is that?" asked William.

"Two reasons—if we play it out, he won't suspect anything out of the ordinary, so he won't do anything stupid,"—Kimberly gasped as he said this—"and, most important, if Brookes is giving the keys to Kimberly, that means he has another ride. I have a good idea who might be providing said ride. We need to get them both."

"Brilliant," said William.

"Are you a detective in training?" Kimberly asked Doyle.

"A detective is constantly learning new things," said Doyle. "Don't worry—I've handled many cases just as difficult as this one. More difficult, in fact."

"Okay," she said, not sounding so sure.

"Have you heard about the Keanu Reeves' dog-napping?"

"Yeah," she said.

"Well, I'm still working on that one. It's not easy, I'll tell you that much."

"It was probably Dimitri Prutkov," she said.

"Oh?" said Doyle.

"Prutkov," she responded. "Dog trainer of the celebrities. Although he doesn't get much work now that he's attempted stealing some pretty important dogs."

Kimberly blew her nose.

Doyle scribbled down a note. "That's exactly who I thought it might be, right before I was pulled off the case."

"He tried joining Pause for Paws, but I had done some asking around," she said. "Stop the car! There's my bank."

She jumped out of the car before William had fully stopped the car. She toppled a little, but regained her composure.

Doyle looked down at the name on his notepad.

"William, how much of detective work is pure, dumb luck?"

"For you, quite a bit of it apparently."

34

OYLE AND WILLIAM ANXIOUSLY awaited Kimberly to come out of the bank with the ransom money.

"Will it really be that easy for her to just walk in there and ask for a bag of cash?" asked Doyle.

"I wouldn't be surprised," said William. "I think celebrities can get away with just about anything."

"You sound like someone who's spent a lot of time in Hollywood," said Doyle.

"Oh, please. Plenty of celebrities reside in London. Hugh Grant, for example. He's certainly gotten away with a lot," said William. "Don't get me wrong, I like the bloke."

"But I think he got away with that whole scandal specifically because he's British, don't you think?" said Doyle. "I mean, it was like he just said, 'Oh, dear me. What a silly chap I've been. Carry on, now.' And that was that."

"Perhaps," said William.

Kimberly came out with a canvas bag that had "FIRST NATIONAL" printed on the side. She climbed into the backseat, and William stepped on the pedal.

Doyle turned his head and stretched towards the back so he could peek inside the bag. "Cripes in a handbasket, that's a lot of hundos," he said.

"I know, if that—" and Kimberly paused here, carefully selecting her words, "—asshole, gets away with this money *and* my father, I'm going to be pissed."

"Don't worry—you'll have your father and the money back in no time," Doyle said. "You know, as long as everything goes okay."

William coughed.

Wɪʟʟɪᴀᴍ ᴘᴜʟʟᴇᴅ ᴛʜᴇ ᴄᴀʀ ɪɴᴛᴏ ᴀɴ ᴀʟʟᴇʏ three blocks from the Lagoon theater. With reluctance, Kimberly got out of the car and headed towards the entrance, after much assurance and many inappropriate quips from Doyle.

As Doyle and William watched Kimberly walk down the sidewalk, a black, unmarked state vehicle approached from the opposite direction, and Doyle had no doubt who was inside it. He wasn't terribly concerned, in fact he was excited that everything was falling into place; Brookes would get the money, exit the theater and get into Burnside's car, and then if McDonald's people were watching, as he hoped they were, both Brookes and Burnside would be going down.

"Two fucking birds, and I'm one big fucking stone," mumbled Doyle.

"Pardon?" asked William.

"This might work out," said Doyle.

"Mmm," agreed William. Both were intently watching Kimberly as she entered the theater. Burnside pulled half onto the curb, also waiting.

Doyle and William lowered themselves in their seats, as to not be seen by Burnside. Doyle dialed McDonald.

"Doyle?" she answered.

"Do you know where he is?"

"In front of the theater—don't worry, we're on him. I have two undercovers watching as we speak, and they're in direct contact with me."

"As soon as a man gets in the car—he'll look really fancy, though a bit beaten about the face—have the undercovers go in for the arrest."

"Doyle—who's the man? Why are we going to arrest him? And what about Burnside? I need some answers here before I can authorize any of this."

"Fair enough. The fancy man—Darren Brookes is his current name, although he was formerly Darren *Burnside*, hint, hint—is holding Timothy Chapman hostage for fifty-thousand dollars ransom. Right as we speak, Kimberly Chapman is giving Brookes said fifty-thousand in exchange for the keys to the trunk of the car where Chapman being held. I have no doubt that, after they make the exchange, Brookes will be getting into the car with Burnside, who is likely to bring Brookes someplace safe and hidden. Burnside likely has no idea that we know about his relation to Brookes, and the other cover-ups he's done in the past."

"Doyle—will you be able to back up all these allegations you're making?"

"Absolutely," responded Doyle.

"Very well, Doyle. Don't let me down on this."

"I won't. Just be sure your people are there to arrest Brookes and Burnside."

Doyle hung up.

And then came the long, hard part. Waiting.

THE EVENTS THAT FOLLOWED TOOK PLACE so quickly that Doyle later had trouble reconciling it as reality rather than a dream.

Doyle initially felt relief as the figure of Kimberly Chapman emerged from the Lagoon, but this feeling was quickly replaced by fear and a surge of adrenaline when he saw the gun to her temple, held tightly by a white gloved hand. Doyle thought he saw a smile on Brookes's face as he pushed Kimberly forward, her feet stumbling clumsily along the sidewalk.

Doyle found himself reaching for his own gun, only to realize he didn't have it on him anymore. He imagined his was likely the gun Brookes was holding, as Brookes could have easily picked it up after the confrontation in Chapman's house. Then Doyle distinctly remembered removing the magazine. Had Brookes been wise enough to replace it? Had he dug it out of the drawer that quickly before he ran out of the room?

Doyle had but seconds to contemplate this as the black car being driven by Burnside came forward two blocks, bypassing Kimberly and Brookes, and parked sideways directly in front of William's car. Burnside burst out of his car with his gun drawn and his badge held high.

"STEP OUT OF THE VEHICLE, YOU ARE UNDER ARREST!" yelled Burnside, sweating profusely, his eyes bloodshot and strained, his face doing a full-on cuttlefish.

"DOYLE!" Kimberly screamed, as Brookes pushed her along in the opposite direction.

Doyle hadn't foreseen this scenario playing out.

"What do we do, William?" whispered Doyle, his heart ready to burst.

"You have a gun pointed directly at you. I suggest we get out of the car," said William.

"Okay." They both opened their doors and got out of the vehicle.

"You—put your hands on the top of the car and don't move. Malloy," Burnside got really close to Doyle's ear, he whispered, "I gave you plenty of chances to do things right, Doyle. You're out of chances."

"What you don't understand is that there's a difference between doing things right and doing the right thing. As far as I can tell, I'm the only one here trying to do the right thing. Well, me and my partner over here," said Doyle, nodding to William.

"You two will have plenty of time playing partners in prison. Now get your hands behind your back, Doyle. Don't make me club you."

As Burnside approached Doyle, a familiar voice yelled "FREEZE!"

Doyle could see Brookes, who had neared the vehicle he had taken from Chapman's residence, look around nervously for the location of the voice.

Doyle was also curious, although it seemed that Burnside recognized the voice immediately. Burnside turned a deeper shade of red than Doyle had never seen before.

Across the street, Officer McNulty was positioned behind a Chevy Celebrity, his gun pointed directly at Chief Burnside.

"McNul—" Burnside began to croak, but McNulty yelled again.

"FREEZE! I'M TALKING TO YOU, BURNSIDE. DON'T MAKE ONE MORE FUCKING MOVE."

The sudden realization of the situation he was in seemed to dawn on Burnside almost slowly, though it was only parts of a second. Doyle later thought that Burnside had seen all of the criminals—the drug dealers, murderers, rapists—that he had put away, and saw himself in that same position.

Burnside looked down at his gun as though he had never seen it before.

He raised his arm and fired. Twice.

McNulty fired once. He made direct contact. Burnside's right femur, to be exact.

Burnside screamed. He fell backwards, knocking against the front of his car, and then rolled sideways and dropped to the ground, writhing in pain. His gun clattered to the ground when it escaped his hand.

"DAD!" yelled Brookes, as he was shoving Kimberly into the backseat.

With lightning reflexes, Doyle also dropped to the ground and picked up the gun, and then he ran.

He ran full-force, full-determination, with no thought whatsoever of anything else.

He ran at Darren Brookes, who was holding a gun, pointed directly back at Doyle.

The gun that may or may not have been loaded. Doyle took his chances.

Brookes' eyes widened with the knowledge that Doyle was not going to stop, take a defensive position, use the usual tactics.

So Brookes squeezed the trigger. Repeatedly.

Doyle thought he had been lucky and that there were no bullets, because he was still running directly at Brookes. Then he felt the ripping, tearing pain in his left shoulder and a sort of wet throbbing on his right cheek.

Doyle was about to raise his gun and fire right back, but he had somewhat misjudged the time required to do so, as he was only a few yards away from Brookes. Instead, he just kept running and braced himself for the impact.

Doyle lowered his head, closed his eyes, and smashed into Darren Brookes with a wet, hard thump.

During that single moment of impact, Doyle heard a few things: a popping, a crunching, and a thudding. He contemplated briefly that it would be interesting to dissect what specifically caused each of those sounds. He thought maybe he'd ask William what he thought, but as he opened his mouth to ask said series of interesting questions, he tasted the blood, and then he found everything going quite dark, so he thought he'd lie down for a little nap.

35

DOYLE ROUSED IN THE MIDDLE OF A CONVERSATION. ". . . so I said to him, 'I don't care if my absence cost the studio hundreds of thousands of dollars—I just spent the last twenty-four hours in a tiny linen closet and the rusty trunk of a car.' Mr. Weinstein ate his words, obviously."

"Is he waking up?"

"I think I saw his eyes move."

Doyle's eyes flickered as he let in the bright light of the hospital room. Everything came into focus, and he was startled by the number of people staring at him. Although he was relieved to see so many friendly faces, he fixed on the one not-so-friendly face.

"What are you doing here?" croaked Doyle.

"Just showing some respect, I guess."

"But I thought you hated me."

McNulty smiled, but even his smile didn't seem all that terribly warm. "I never hated you—I just don't like traitors. Things have been weird around the department, and I thought you'd been playing everyone. After all, you, umm . . ." and McNulty paused to choose the right word, "typically don't work too hard. But I was wrong—Burnside was playing everyone. I should have seen that sooner. I'm sorry."

"It's okay," said Doyle. "At least you shot him."

This time McNulty's smile was genuine. "Yeah, I did do that."

"Well, take it easy, Doyle," McNulty said and left the room.

Amanda approached Doyle next.

"I'm impressed," she said. "It turns out you really knew what you were doing. I guess even I should have a little more faith in you."

"Well, it would have been nice," said Doyle.

Amanda looked down.

"But, I forgive you," said Doyle. "In fact, as soon as I'm out of here, let me take you out. Wherever you want, whatever you want to do. I just want to spend time with you."

"I'd like that," said Amanda, smiling warmly.

"You didn't actually consider going out with McNulty, did you?" he asked. "I mean, do you actually like him?"

"I like that he shot Burnside," said Amanda. "But that's as far as it goes."

Doyle laughed, then grimaced in pain.

"But to answer your question, yes, I'd love for us to go on our date," said Amanda, reaching her hand towards his.

Doyle took her hand and held it.

"So, what happened exactly?" Doyle asked to no one in particular. "I mean, in the end?"

Superintendent Beth McDonald answered. "Well, Doyle—your heroic, albeit not terribly thought out move, that being head-butting Darren Brookes directly in the face like an ornery goat, worked out quite well. You both hit the ground, my other undercover, Officer Hannesen, handcuffed Mr. Brookes—who, by the way, lost about half his teeth from that little move," McDonald beamed at Doyle, "and Burnside, meanwhile, was also arrested by Officer McNulty. Burnside put up quite a fight."

"I wish I could have seen it," said Doyle.

"Oh, you definitely can. It's all over Youtube. Everyone within a three block radius was recording with their video cell phones."

"Sweet," said Doyle. "What's going to happen to him?"

"He's already lost his job. We've booked him as an accomplice to kidnapping and misuse of police authority. We'll be bringing up charges based on his past cover-ups for his son, as soon as we gather all the evidence."

Doyle nodded.

"Oh, Doyle, before I forget," continued McDonald, her voice lowering so no one else could fully hear. "There's a little matter of a Mr. Palmer, whom you had a confrontation with, I believe."

"Who?" asked Doyle. Do I know a Mr. Palmer?

"I understand he's from an agency called Gaff and Gafferty."

"Oh, God," said Doyle. "Listen, I can explain everything."

"No need," said McDonald. "Mr. Palmer had a long list of outstanding warrants. We've reached an agreement. You don't have anything to worry about."

"Oh, thank God," said Doyle.

McDonald resumed her normal speaking voice. "Really, Doyle— you did an incredible job today. I understand that Burnside had been dangling the possibility of a senior position above your head. Well, that can still be arranged, if you're interested." McDonald smiled.

"Of course, there are other things to consider," said William.

McDonald turned to William. "Such as?"

"I'm just saying, Doyle is a very gifted detective. He has options."

"Listen, Sherlock, if you think you'll be taking away my star detective . . ."

"I'm not saying anything of the sort. Doyle can do whatever he wishes," stated William.

McDonald glared at William.

"No more fighting, please" said Kimberly Chapman, running over to Doyle's side. She kissed the one cheek not covered in bandages. Amanda gave her an unpleasant look.

"You were great," Kimberly said.

"Absolutely," added Timothy Chapman, approaching Doyle's other side. "Young man, you single-handedly saved my life and more importantly, my daughter's life. I only wish there was something more that I could do for you."

"I think you've already done plenty, Mr. Chapman. Wasn't it you that bailed me out of jail that night?"

"Ahh, how did you find out?" Chapman grinned.

"Frankly, I don't know many people who could afford to do something like that."

"One of the benefits of being successful is the ability to help out others in tough situations, something I was glad to do for you. When your girlfriend here . . ."

Amanda smiled at Doyle.

"That is to say, she *is* your girlfriend, correct, Detective Malloy?" asked Chapman.

"Yes, of course," said Doyle, giving her a "thumbs up." He then realized how terribly corny that gesture was in such a situation. Fortunately, Amanda raised her thumb as well.

"Besides," continued Chapman, "I had a feeling you'd be playing a pivotal role in solving the murders. I was disappointed that Chad would do something as heinous as murdering Marta."

Kimberly looked down and studied her hands.

"Yes, but to be fair, your mentally unstable butler orchestrated everything. Chad made a horrible, rash decision, but I think Brookes would have carefully planned the death of anyone who stood in his way."

"And all of it over nothing," said Chapman.

"Which begs the question," said William, "What was the purpose of the empty safe?"

Chapman looked contemplative. "Trusting anyone, especially when you're successful, can be difficult. Even in our friendly state."

"Which means?"

"A couple years ago, I got the idea for the safe, just as a matter of finding out who I could or could not trust. I figured I would only tell a select few people in my employ and see if anyone would attempt to break in.

"It was my mistake, as I can see now, to use my daughter as a device in this plan. Kimberly didn't know it was empty, but I told her about it regardless because I didn't trust her boyfriend. I see now that I was right to not trust him, but I feel horrible using my daughter in such a way. Kimberly, will you forgive your old man?"

"Yes, of course, Daddy," Kimberly said as she went around to the other side of the bed to hug her father.

"You see, Doyle, William—I knew I couldn't trust everyone, but I had no idea that it could lead to murder . . . three murders, no less."

McDonald spoke up. "We understand your position, Mr. Chapman. But next time, you may want to invest in an employee-screeing service. Leave the questions of who cannot be trusted to the professionals."

"Fair enough, madam," said Chapman.

Chapman turned to leave with his daughter's hand in his, but he stopped himself before exiting. "Oh, I almost forgot."

Chapman put his hand into his coat pocket.

"Doyle, I know you cannot be well compensated for the work you do," said Chapman, "and I've heard from Ms. McDonald here that you've had to hire outside help at your own expense."

"Which the department is going to fully cover," added McDonald.

Doyle was so ecstatic, he could have kissed McDonald on the lips. But then he thought better of it.

"So I want to make sure you are well taken care of," said Chapman, removing his checkbook from his coat pocket.

"I'm sorry, Mr. Chapman," said McDonald, "but you cannot give any money. That can be considered a bribe and put the department at considerable risk. I'm sorry."

"Oh, I see," said Chapman, starting to put his checkbook away.

"I can't take money," said Doyle, "but if you would like, Mr. Chapman, you can certainly invest in my new business."

"Oh? What would that be, Doyle?"

"William Wright and I are about to open our own private detective agency."

William's mouth dropped, but then he nodded enthusiastically.

"Malloy and Wright, detectives to the stars," suggested Doyle.

"Wright and Malloy, more likely. It's already my bloody business, we'd just be adding your name on," mumbled William.

"You'll be hearing a lot of that if you stop into our agency," said Doyle happily.

"I'll be happy to invest in your business, as long as I can continue to call you Doily, as I find that just so endlessly amusing."

"You have a deal," said Doyle.

"Doyle, does this mean you . . ." began McDonald.

"Yes, I'm afraid it does. I'm quitting the force."

McDonald looked disappointed. Hurt, even.

"If you ever need any assistance, just let me know," she said. "And if you ever want to come back, the door is always open."

"Thanks, I appreciate that," said Doyle. "But I think we'll be okay."

A crotchety old nurse came into the room.

"Visiting time is over. All of you need to scram."

McDonald stood and went to Doyle. She offered her hand. Doyle shook it.

"It's been a pleasure, Doyle. You're a good cop. A good detective. Not easy to come by. Your father would be proud."

"Thanks," he said.

"Call me, as soon as you're out," said Amanda.

"I will," responded Doyle.

Amanda left along with McDonald.

"If I have any trouble, I'll be calling the two of you immediately, you have my promise," said Chapman, leaving a check upside down on Doyle's chest. "Take care, Doily."

Kimberly simply waved and smiled.

As they left the room, William picked up the check and said, "Oh, bugger me."

"Good?" asked Doyle. He too wanted to know the value of the check.

"We can buy a new sign, I can assure you of that," said William.

"How about a new office—the dentist office seems a little odd doesn't it?"

"We're keeping the dentist office," said William.

"But we—"

"Keeping it," repeated William.

"You know, I believe you're still technically my employee," said Doyle.

"No, I don't think so," laughed William. "My obligations have been fulfilled, our initial contract is now completed."

"Partners, then?"

"Bloody well right," said William, patting Doyle on the arm, inadvertently giving him a jolt of pain. "Oh, right—gunshot to the shoulder. Sorry about that."

"Don't mention it," said Doyle.

"Well, I'll let you get some rest, then," said William. He turned to leave, pocketing the check as he did so.

"William?" Doyle asked.

"Yes?"

"When you come next, will you bring me some tabloids?"

"Sure, why?" asked William.

"We need to find some celebrities in trouble," said Doyle.

"In this town," said William, "that's not going to be difficult."

Epilogue

Room for More

DOYLE ENTERED MURRAY'S RESTAURANT in downtown Minneapolis wearing a brown trench coat that William had given him as a special present for becoming a real detective. Doyle wore it with pride, though he knew it looked a bit ridiculous. And way too English. It didn't help that his arm was in a cast, and he wore an Indiana Jones-inspired Fedora to cover a great deal of scar tissue that remained on his forehead.

Yup, he thought to himself. A class act all the way.

As the waitress directed him towards the table where Amanda was waiting patiently, it occurred to Doyle that he hadn't considered that she would be wearing anything other than a police uniform. It was logical that she wouldn't be, but he'd rarely seen her in anything else, except when they'd gone out for coffee or a movie after work.

What she was wearing was definitely not approved police work attire. Clad in a gorgeous lace dress that seemed to boost up her already plentiful bosom, Amanda looked far different than in her typically unflattering blue.

Doyle felt his eyes were going to bug out of his skull like in those classic Looney Tunes shorts. He worked at pulling them back into their sockets.

"Doyle," she said.

"Yeah," Doyle responded.

"Why don't you sit down—you're just kind of, um, staring right now."

Doyle, becoming conscious of himself, realized she was quite right. A few restaurant patrons near them looked curiously at the mangled weirdo in the trench coat. Doyle waved at them with his good arm, then sat down.

"Sorry about that," said Doyle. "I just wasn't expecting you to look so . . . so . . ."

"Beautiful? Elegant? Sexy?" she suggested.

Doyle looked again at her bosom. "Big," he answered.

Amanda shook her head. "Well, I guess I'll take that as a compliment. It's something, anyway."

"Don't mention it," said Doyle. "But really, I've never been the romantic type. Then again, I haven't had much chance to. Most girls I date tend to split or switch teams."

"Well, maybe it's time to give romance another chance," she said.

"Maybe," he said. "And yes, you are beautiful."

Amanda smiled. "Thanks."

Doyle noticed Amanda examining his battered body. "Are you feeling okay?" she asked.

"I think so," he responded. "Still pretty sore."

"That was one heck of a thump you gave Burnside's freaky son," she said. "And gave yourself, for that matter."

"It wasn't the smartest plan," Doyle admitted. "But it worked, for whatever that's worth."

"Worth quite a bit, I'd say," she said. "You saved the life of a very wealthy celebrity. William told me he gave you quite a down payment on your new P.I. business. Is that true?"

Doyle smiled and nodded.

"I hope you don't forget about me when you start taking on all these exciting cases," she said.

"Well, I was kind of hoping you'd be sticking around for a while," he said. "I can certainly use a connection with the police, since my employment has essentially ended."

"Of course I can help," she said. "As long as you give me all the juicy details of your cases."

"That might be a possibility," said Doyle.

Doyle and Amanda shared a comfortable moment of silence.

"Did you make it to the funeral?" she asked.

"Who, Marta's? No, I wasn't in any shape for that. Besides, I'm not so good in those sorts of situations. But William was there. He said it went really well."

"Was Timothy Chapman there?" she asked.

"Yeah, apparently he gave Marta's family a hefty check, not all that dissimilar from the one he gave me. He said it was to cover the cost of their flight from Colombia, although I've never seen a flight that cost that much."

"Well, that's really sweet of him. And probably a smart legal move as well."

"No doubt about it, he's a smart man. After all, he trusted me, right?" Doyle smiled.

"'Smart' may not be the best word to describe that, but certainly 'courageous,'" Amanda responded.

Doyle reached out with his available arm and touched the top of her hand. It seemed to catch her by surprise, but she soon responded by taking his fingers into hers.

Doyle's heart raced.

"Good evening, lovely people!" the waiter nearly yelled, scaring the bejesus out of Doyle, taking him out of an exquisite moment.

"Hi," said Amanda, glowing with satisfaction.

"Would ze couple like some fine wine with zere meal tonight?" asked the waiter, with the most sickeningly put-on French accent Doyle had ever heard.

"Sure, red's fine," said Doyle. He looked at Amanda, seeking approval.

"Oh, sure—that's fine," she responded.

"Red, very well, sir, but what kind of wine? We have many varieties and vintages available. Would you like me to show you ze menu?"

Doyle looked at Amanda again. She shrugged.

"Ya know, how about a beer. Do you have beer?" asked Doyle.

"I'll take one, too," said Amanda eagerly.

The waiter grimaced as though he had sucked on a sour lemon. "Right away, sir and madam."

After he left, Amanda said, "Good choice."

"Thanks," said Doyle. "I've never much cared for wine. Again, not a lot of experience in the ol' dating field."

"That's fine," she said. "I've always been more of a beer girl myself."

"Listen, I hope you don't mind that we skipped the movie today. It's just that I got awful busy with William, and you know how he can be sometimes."

"Sure, of course. What have you guys been up to? You don't have a case yet, do you?"

"Well, not exactly," said Doyle. "I mean, not an official one at any rate. We're just sort of, um, researching a bit, and uh . . ."

"Really, what are you doing?"

"We're stalking his ex-wife," said Doyle.

Amanda nodded. "Any particular reason?"

"It's something he's been working on for some time now, and he asked for a helping hand. Being his partner and all, I thought it would be nice to offer my services. Is that okay? You're not going to leave are you?"

Amanda appeared to think about it.

"Nah, I won't leave. I may be turning into a lesbian though."

"Very funny," said Doyle.

"Just be careful about getting between spouses," she said. "That can get really ugly."

"I know. He hasn't spoken with her in well over a year, and she's somewhere here in Minneapolis, at least according to his most recent sources. She's an actress, so she may very well have a stage name that she goes by now."

"Can I help?" she asked.

Doyle felt caught off guard. "What? Didn't you just try to warn me about getting in between spouses? And now you want to do it?"

"I just want to investigate," she said. "I don't care if it's a touchy situation. I just want to do something that doesn't require me to sit behind a desk and answer a phone all day."

"Can I think about it?" asked Doyle.

"I don't know," responded Amanda. "Can I think about whether or not I want to see the inside of your apartment tonight?"

Doyle was in the process of understanding her implication when his cell phone vibrated quietly in his pocket.

"Son of a bitch," said Doyle.

"What?" asked Amanda. "Fine, I don't need to see your apartment then. But in case you didn't know, I was offering sex. Idiot."

"No, no, not that," said Doyle. "My phone just rang."

"Oh," she said. "Sorry."

"It's William," he said, looking at his phone. "Let me see what's going on."

"Uh huh," said Doyle on the phone. "Yup, okay. Got it. Really? I don't believe it. Well, okay, I believe it. Yup. Uh huh. I'll be right there."

"I have to go," he told Amanda. "I'm really sorry—it's a case. A real case, not just stalking former spouses. I gotta run."

Amanda looked intently at the table, seemingly registering everything Doyle had just said.

"Really, I'm sorry I have to go. I loved being here with you, and spending this evening with you. But I have to do this. This is big. Really big."

"Well," she said slowly. "Can we meet up when you're done? Maybe later tonight, at the Rabbit Hole?"

"I can't," said Doyle. "I'm going far tonight. All the way up to Brainerd."

"Really?" she asked. "Why?"

"There was an accident on a film set, possibly a murder. I don't know, but it sounds pretty ugly. I doubt this story will stay out of the news."

"How long could this take?"

"I don't know—I really don't. I've never been involved with something like this before," he said.

"You were just on a murder investigation," she said.

"This is different. Trust me."

Amanda nodded. "Okay, then. Take me with you."

"Come again?" he asked.

"Take me with you. I can help. I just got out of training, so everything's fresh in my memory. Three minds are better than two, right? Plus I've seen tons of *CSI*, so I can come up with some weird scenarios that could crack the case wide open. Come on, Doyle—what's the worst that could happen?"

"I'm not so sure—William might not like it."

"Who cares? I'll do it for free. I just want to be along for the ride. Maybe spend a little more time with you. You know?" Again, Amanda reached out her hand, took Doyle's hand in hers.

Doyle looked in her eyes. They were pleading with him.

"Okay," he said. "But you better not hinder the investigation."

"Oh, please," said Amanda. "I'll have the case solved before you and William even locate the hotel bathroom."

Hotel? thought Doyle.

Amanda smiled at him. "You might just get lucky yet, Malloy."

About the Author

Brian Landon is a graduate of the University of Minnesota, a member of the Loft Literary Center, Sisters in Crime, and The Midwest Heartless Murderers, a group of mystery writers formed under the guidance of mystery author Ellen Hart. His humorous essays have appeared in several regional publications including the *Minnesota Daily*, the *Wake*, and the *Wayfarer*. He lives with his wife, Jaclyn, in Blaine, Minnesota, where he is working hard on the second Doyle Malloy mystery.

This is his first book.

Acknowledgements

Like any first book, this wouldn't have been possible without a tremendous amount of support, advice, and suggestions from others. I'd be a horrible, horrible person if I didn't give credit to a few certain individuals who truly deserve recognition. First and foremost, the incomparable Ellen Hart, who offered continuous advice and helped shape the book into what it is today. I also need to recognize the other two members of the Minnesota Crime Wave, Carl Brookins and William Kent Krueger, who taught me how to navigate the wild world of publishing.

This book wouldn't exist at all if it weren't for the consistent motivation from my incredibly talented writing group "The Midwest Heartless Murderers." They are: T.J. Roth, Kirstin Thomas, Jessie Chandler, and Joan Murphy Pride. Seriously, I couldn't have done it without you guys.

And finally, my phenomenal wife, Jaclyn, who promised to love me even if I became an utter failure.

That, my friends, is true love.

Doyle Malloy
will return in
The Case of the Unnecessary Sequel
Coming March 1, 2010